welcome to chaos HIGH

Tommy McNally

contents

CHAPTER 1

Grrr! How could he do this to me! My uncle had enrolled me in one of those private schools where girls compete to wear the shortest skirts! Freedom College... Even the name didn't sound good. I guess by "freedom," they meant the freedom of our legs here.

Okay, as a Muslim girl, I might have recently taken my piety to the next level by spending my days and nights at the mosque. Or maybe a few levels up... And yes, I might have told some young couples making out in public to continue their activities at home and annoyed them by sitting next to them and praying loudly when they didn't listen. I suppose I had overstepped my bounds. Unfortunately, those youths knew my uncle, and my actions reached his ears. I had a big blow-up! But still, I didn't deserve to be taken from my beloved Islamic high school and sent to this private school that resembled St. Peter's Basilica as punishment.

According to him, my uncle would end this exile after a year and take me back to my old school, but I didn't know how I would endure this school, which resembled the Private Adultery College, for a year... I wish he had given me a room confinement or thrown a slipper at my butt like any other parent. But my folks were cunning. They knew if they gave me room confinement, I would read the Quran all day. As for the other punishment, my bumper was sturdy and slipper-proof. So those wouldn't work either.

If my parents were alive, I'm sure my fate wouldn't be like this. But after their death, my uncle took care of me, and since he was far from religion, my effort to live Islam to the fullest bothered him, and he didn't like it at all. We were like night and day in religious matters. I was sure he wanted me to say "Hallelujah, hurrah," instead of "Salam Alaikum."

On the first day of my punishment, I had to go to my new school. As I walked down the corridor to my class, I looked up at the ceiling. All the lights were intact and shining brightly. You could easily tell you were in a private school by looking up. In my old school, some of the fluorescent lights had passed on to eternity, and some flirted with us by blinking on and off.

I reluctantly dragged my feet to the door of my new class, almost doing a Michael Jackson moonwalk to avoid going in. Before entering, I sighed and tugged at the grey school skirt that came to my knees, but the laws of physics didn't allow the fabric to stretch and cover my legs. My uncle had bought this short skirt as a punishment, and there was nothing I could do. I already missed my old school skirt that reached my ankles.

According to the freedom-far rules of Freedom College, head-scarves were not allowed here. I had also removed my headscarf as per the school regulations. Although I had only recently started wearing a headscarf, removing it had saddened me greatly. Because, according to Islam, it is a clear command from Allah -the almighty God- for women to wear the headscarf and cover their bodies to preserve their modesty from the gaze of men. Being used to modest clothing, I felt like a fish out of water now.

After cursing my new school shirt, which was pale pink and so thin that it revealed my bra, I opened the door to my class. I entered.

When all the heads in my approximately twenty-person class turned to me, my furrowed brows and narrowed eyes targeted their gazes. Since the class had started about ten minutes ago, our bearded, bespectacled, stout, intellectual teacher had turned his head to me from his podium.

Suddenly, dozens of different voices rang in my ears. Dozens of different emotions invaded my heart and mind. Why? Because I was a telepath. Yes, you heard it right. I can hear what people are thinking without them having to say it. I can feel everything they feel as if I am feeling it myself. Although this sounds like a great superpower, believe me, it is not. Because when you learn people's true thoughts about you, you often wish you didn't know.

One of the other reasons my uncle enrolled me in this school was because, according to him, many students in this class had superpowers like mine. Who knows what kind of special powers my new friends had. I would learn in time. And because of this, my uncle thought I would adapt better to this school than my old one. And here I was.

As soon as I entered, the thoughts of a classroom full of students targeted me like arrows, and my head hurt so badly that I thought I was having a brain hemorrhage. I could feel all the thoughts about me, and most of them were unpleasant. I leaned against the door for support and closed my eyes. I had to be strong. After pausing for a few seconds, I managed to clear my mind a bit. I took a deep breath and opened my eyes again.

Despite my sulky mood, greeting everyone was a cornerstone of our religion, so I greeted everyone:

"Salam Alaikum."

Giggles echoed in the class. Had I said something funny? Wouldn't a single soul respond with "Alaikum Salam"? It was as if my beautiful city Istanbul, where my school was located, had never been conquered by my glorious Sultan Fatih. Or maybe the Crusaders had taken it back without me noticing.

Finally, a girl sitting in the middle rows with her hair carefully braided and a short skirt paused her gum chewing and responded, "Hello, dear."

I rolled my eyes as I stood at the door. Well, whatever... I would leave her to God. I doubted she believed in God, but since our religion encourages having positive preconceptions, I should hope she was a Muslim.

Entering with my right foot, I started reciting Surah Al-Ikhlas. It was a beautiful action that brought blessings.

Towards the end of my prayer, I heard another girl's voice:

"I came without an umbrella. If you're praying for rain, please stop."

When my prayer ended, I sighed. Maybe it wasn't rain but a flood that was needed. I couldn't help but think that a flood might bring these mockers to their senses...

At that moment, our teacher with a smoker's voice at the podium said, "Welcome. You must be the girl who transferred from the Imam Hatip school. Your name is Ece, right?"

"Yes, teacher."

"I am your English teacher. My name is Mesut. Please, take a seat."

Mesut, huh... 'I am not happy at all,' I wanted to say, but I restrained myself and swallowed my words. I looked around briefly.

Then I sat in the empty seat next to the boy with long red hair slicked back like a llama licking it, in the front row by the door.

Oh, this new skirt of mine... When it rode up a bit as I sat down, I frowned and tugged it down. Seeing it wouldn't work, I lifted my bag and placed it over my bare legs. I wasn't used to wearing clothes that exposed my skin.

The red-haired boy next to me subtly glanced at me. Hearing his thoughts with my telepathic ability, my face wrinkled. In moral terms, I could say that my body had caught his interest, especially my feet. Ugh!

Just as the long-haired boy next to me was about to introduce himself, I turned to him angrily and raised my finger threateningly, "Don't even think about it!"

The boy recoiled and pulled back. "Okay, don't be mad!" he said, but at the same time, I read his mind thinking, "Tough and dominant... This girl is just my type." I sighed in frustration.

I turned back with patience. I was sitting and listening to the lesson when minutes later, I felt a tap on my shoulder from behind and turned around. The person who poked me was a pretty girl with slightly sunburnt skin on her tiny nose. This beauty queen girl must have spent her summer stocking up on vitamin D in the south. When was the last time I had gone on vacation? It must have been a long time since I had been using vitamin D drops for two or three years.

The drowsy-eyed, button-nosed girl behind me spoke:

"Silky, coconut-scented hair, sea-green eyes; plump, pouty lips that beg to be kissed, and a baby-faced visage... Apparently, even among the veiled girls, there can be beauties," she said, scrutinizing my face carefully. With my telepathic ability, I could sense her sincerity and that she genuinely found me beautiful. "So, you'll be sitting in front of me, Ece. I hope, just like you unveiled to enter this school, you'll also unveil your exam paper and give me a copy."

When I lowered my eyes to look at the notebook on her desk, I saw the name "Derin Demirhan" on the label.

"Derin," I murmured, repeating the name I had just learned. "My headscarf is my concern, but my friends know me for my generosity when it comes to my exam paper, don't worry," I replied quietly so the teacher wouldn't hear.

The girl with the beautiful eyes smirked, "I thought you spider-brains considered cheating a sin, but I guess I was wrong. I'm glad."

I clenched my teeth. "If it's a sin, it's not a big one because I won't be helping you steal another student's rightful place," I explained, trying to remain calm. "Also, the spider you disdain is a blessed creature that saved our prophet's life. If I'm spider-brained, then so be it. Besides, if it were a bad creature, would Spider-Man movies be watched by millions?"

After mimicking me, the girl hissed like a snake, "Don't watch too many movies, sweetheart. Watching movies on the internet should be a sin for you, right?"

Watching movies on pirate sites was indeed a sin and an infringement of rights because the original creator sells their work for a fee, and we were obtaining it from the pirate, watching without paying. But that aside, this girl was driving me crazy with her taunts. Still, I didn't want to cause a scene on my first day at school. I could cause one tomorrow...

Since my faith was being mocked at this seat, I decided to sit somewhere else in the class... Ah, the wanderer at just 18 years old...

Grabbing my bag, I got up from my chair and started walking around the classroom. I was trying to choose a new place to sit where I'd be less ostracized in this posh school... Perhaps the window sill? Though there was a risk of falling there.

Just then, I saw a boy at a distance, sitting at the second-last row by the window, raise his hand. I turned my face towards him. A brown-haired, clean-faced boy, who seemed to understand my situation, was beckoning me. I accepted his invitation and went to sit beside him.

"Fatih," said the slightly taller boy, extending his hand to me. Then he withdrew it, embarrassed. He probably thought I didn't want to touch a boy's hand due to my former school. It was true that this was a sin.

"I'm Ece. Nice to meet you. Tell me, Fatih, didn't you conquer Istanbul from the infidels, or am I remembering wrong, my sultan?" I said with a playful expression, glancing at the students who didn't look like Ottoman descendants. "If Istanbul is still the Ottomans', where are these Ottomans? If you haven't conquered Istanbul yet, I'm ready to go on a jihad with you, my sultan, let's go for the conquest!"

Fatih, understanding my point, smiled slightly and sadly. "We must have fallen into some Byzantine trick. I'm afraid this isn't the Istanbul I conquered."

CHAPTER 2

My seatmate Fatih seemed like a good guy, but since I preferred to be friends with girls, I went to the school cafeteria alone during lunch break.

When I saw that the large, spacious cafeteria on the bottom floor was a buffet, my longing for my old school subsided momentarily from the excitement. After putting some salad, a bit of rice, and a nice-smelling lentil soup on my tray, I stood in front of the meats at the buffet, lost in thought. I was hesitant. I could accept even seagull meat to some extent, but if this meat was pork, I would sidestep away like a crab. Because in Islam, eating pork was forbidden. (Plus a very unhealty diet anyway.) Finally, I decided to bother the cook.

"Um...what kind of meat is this?"

"Beef."

"It doesn't contain pork, right?" I asked cautiously, making a cute face while mimicking a pig sound, "Oink oink."

"No, it doesn't."

"Are you sure?"

"Of course."

"Swear it!"

The bespectacled man paused briefly after starting to say "Swear it!", then slightly frowned. "Girl, what kind of question is this, like a judgment day inquiry! I said it's beef, eat it! It's good for you. You look pale. It will build your blood."

"Well, it's on your conscience... Anyway, I'll take some."

If he gave me pork, may Peppa Pig chase this man in the afterlife, and when she catches him, may she force him to swim in a mud pool. Amen...

I sat at one of the 8-10 person white dining tables in the large dining hall. Just as I was about to fork my salad, I was startled by a familiar voice from right beside me, "Hello Ece. Enjoy your meal."

When I turned my head, I saw Derin standing with her tray. The girl who annoyed me in class... How did she appear beside me so suddenly? I hadn't even seen her coming. This girl was as sneaky as a snake. In class, when arguing with me, she even made a hissing sound similar to a snake's.

With her kohl-rimmed hazel eyes, confident demeanor, and wavy hair highlighted in places, cascading down to her chest, she must have been the prettiest girl in class. Though at that moment, I was reading Derin's mind, and oddly, she was thinking similarly about me.

"Peace be upon you," I responded using an Islamic greeting, which made Derin curl her lips in displeasure. "And enjoy your meal too."

When I glanced at Derin's tray, I saw she had only taken meat products. What else could be expected from a snake girl...

As Derin continued to hold her tray with one hand, she directed her other hand into her black, leather bag slung over her shoulder. As I watched her place a few DVDs on my tray, on top of my fork and spoon, I looked at her in confusion.

Reading the rhyme and somewhat obscene title on one of the DVDs and looking at the cover photo, I realized the film was about... how to put it... a young girl and boy who wanted to strengthen their neighborly relations. Neighborliness was important, of course, but judging by their exaggerated intimacy in the photo, it seemed long past time for them to combine their homes and crown this with a ring. Perhaps it had even been as long as having a baby.

"W-what are you doing, Derin?" I squealed, looking away from the DVD case that risked ruining my ablution.

"Oh, it's a welcome gift, Ece! Watch it at home when you're bored with homework, it might come in handy."

"I won't need it!" I squealed.

Winking, Derin said, "There's a first time for everything, beauty," and turned around, sashaying away. I watched her with my mouth agape as she sat down a few tables away with her friends. Oh my God, what kind of sex school had I ended up in!?

As I sighed heavily, a girl settled in front of me at the table. She put her tray down. When I turned to look at her face, she stammered, "H-hi E-Ece."

"Hello," I said politely. "Enjoy your meal." I was trying to shake off the shock of the recent event.

The pretty-faced girl added, "I-I-I'm in y-your c-cl-cl-"

"Same class, yes," I completed her sentence. But I immediately regretted it, as if urging or rushing a stuttering girl. Our religion says if you cover someone's fault, Allah will cover one of your sins in the afterlife. "Sorry, I interrupted you."

The brunette girl smiled. "My name is Si-si-sin..."

Sin-Sinyorita? She had a bit of a Spanish look... or Sin-Sinderella? With her cloud-blue eyes, delicate physique, and Barbie-doll nose, she was pretty in that sense.

"My name is Sinem," she said, extending her hand.

I shook her hand gently. "I'm Ece. Nice to meet you."

When Sinem's blue eyes fell on the obscene DVDs on my tray, she giggled.

"Um..." I stammered, thinking of how to explain. "It's Derin's doing. Since I'm new at school, I suppose it's expected to be bullied."

Hearing this, Sinem's face fell. But then, trying to cheer me up, she made a joke about the DVDs on my tray: "F-for after dinner, as dessert?"

I smiled. "If I watch these, I might eat oleander fruit in the afterlife, roasted and poisonous. I'll pass."

Sinem's lips curved upwards. "If you want, I can take them," she said, gesturing at the DVDs with her eyes. She sensed I wanted to get rid of them. "Don't let them go to waste. They are a blessing," she stammered.

"I'd appreciate it if you did, Sinem. But, um, actually, it's not right to joke about blessings," I gently warned her. "It's not religiously acceptable. Especially to call sexual objects blessings..."

"You're probably right," Sinem murmured, rolling her eyes upwards, "God forbid," she said quietly. Sinem seemed like a sweet girl. After taking the DVDs from my tray, she put them into her small handbag.

As we ate, we talked about this and that. Then Sinem brought up her stuttering:

"I've seen many doctors, psychologists," she said, struggling with her words again. "But they couldn't fix my speech."

I shrugged. "I think your speech doesn't sound bad at all, it's quite nice," I said sincerely. And I truly thought so. "I think you're worrying over nothing. And those who don't like it can go away, let them mind their own business!"

"Thank you for the morale boost," Sinem stammered with a forced smile. "But I can't help but worry. I won't stop until I find a good doctor."

"Hmmm... Maybe you're approaching it the wrong way, Sinem."

"What do you mean?"

"I mean... Ask Allah for it too, while you're going from door to door. After all, the one who can cure you is Allah."

Sinem scrunched up her face. "I don't think this is something prayer can fix. Is a miracle going to happen and I'll start speaking fluently?"

"Believe me, you will," I said, reaching forward and gently patting her arm over her white shirt, trying to encourage her. "If you believe Allah created you, think about it... Is creating a human difficult for Allah, or is fixing a minor issue like your stuttering difficult?"

"Doesn't Allah have anything better to do in this vast universe than deal with my problems?" Sinem said, her words stumbling over some bumps again.

"Of course He'll deal with you. Your parents care for you, don't they? Allah's mercy is much greater than theirs, so why wouldn't He care for you? You should ask Allah for everything. Our prophet said to ask Allah for everything, even for a shoe lace. But ask with belief."

Sinem thought for a moment. "Alright then. I'll try."

I decided to make a vow to Allah. If Sinem's speech improved, I would bind my tongue in her place. Meaning, I wouldn't say bad words to my uncles or grumble about them taking me out of my school.

Feeling that I might have overwhelmed her with this conversation, I changed the topic: "Anyway, never mind that now, Sinem. Tell me, who in the class should I watch out for? So I can steer clear of them since I'm new and don't know anyone." As someone who tried to avoid every sin, I struggled to avoid gossip.

Sinem looked around, then leaned in and whispered, "For example, Derin, who sat in front of you when you first entered the class, is a total wh-wh-wh-wh-who-whor."

I reached out and stopped her, "I think I get what you're saying, dear. No need to complete that word and sin, Sinem." My deep feelings about Derin seemed to be right. "Are there any other weird types in the class?" I continued to spoon my soup.

Sinem suddenly said, "Our English teacher from this morning is gay," which shocked me so much that I started choking on my soup. "Are you okay, Ece?"

Sinem got up and walked behind me, patting my back a few times to help me stop choking.

"Thank you, Sinem. I'm fine."

As I wiped my mouth with a napkin, Sinem returned to her seat.

It would not be so surprising if Sinem turned out to be a lesbian aswell. I jokingly asked her:

"Sinem, I hope you're not a lesbian. Please say no. I can't handle more shocks in one day."

"I'm not."

"You're not bisexual either, right?"

Sinem chuckled. "Nope. I'm not asexual, metrosexual, or anything like that," she stammered sweetly. "I thought I'd tell you before you asked."

"Thank God."

"But I'm in love with our teacher."

"What?!"

"Just kidding, girl. It was a joke."

I narrowed my eyes and made a mock biting gesture towards her. "You almost gave me a heart attack!" In the religion of Allah, the act of homosexuality was forbidden, as indeed our holy book spoke of a tribe destroyed by Allah due to their homosexuality.

CHAPTER 3

2 days later...

During the break before the last class, I had stopped by the restroom. When I entered the girls' bathroom, no one was inside. The marble floor was obviously freshly washed, still wet. The toilets were so hygienic, as if my mother, who poured bleach three times a day, had touched them. I mean, this school could be a den of immorality, but its packaging and presentation were good, for God's sake. Isn't that how the devil always works anyway? If sins weren't dressed up in fancy packages, who would go through fire for them...

After using the last of the five stalls lined up, I unlocked the door and stepped out. I tidied myself up a bit. Meanwhile, I heard sounds coming from somewhere near the exit door of the girls' restroom. The sounds of lovebirds making out...

"Do you love me, Kerem?" asked a familiar-sounding girl's voice. This girl was none other than Derin.

"Yes."

"Liar?"

"Girl, if I didn't love you, would I be making out with you in the girls' restroom?"

I frowned as I listened to the love chatter of the lovebirds. I wasn't going to stand here and wait for them to finish their fooling around. I decided to go over and tell them not to do this in a public space.

I started walking towards them with firm and swift steps. Derin and her boyfriend, entwined while standing at a corner, turned to face me, pausing their lovemaking like they were on a break from a matchmaking show. I stopped and washed my hands in the sink.

Kerem, whose name I had just heard, had most of his shirt buttons undone. If I hadn't intervened in time, Derin probably would have unzipped his pants too. Kerem was about 10 centimeters taller than me, and judging by his built body, he was interested in sports or bodybuilding besides fooling around in the restroom. Derin, with her languid hazel eyes, small upturned nose, slim figure, and long messy hair, was actually a pretty girl. They looked good together. Like in that Netflix series, Elite... Which was about students making out like there is no tomorrow.

After flipping my long hair back, I stood in front of them, placing my hands on my hips. Glaring at them as if I was about to bite, I scolded them in a harsh voice, "What do you think you're doing here!"

"Making love," Kerem said in a husky voice, running his fingers through his dark brown, chin-length hair. "What are you doing, beautiful?" I felt uncomfortable as he eyed me up and down.

"I think she was doing poo poo," Derin interjected, answering for me. I couldn't deny, she guessed correctly... And this made my face flush with embarrassment. The couple laughed. "I hope you didn't forget to flush, Ece," Derin added. "Freedom College isn't like the school you came from. We live civilized here, my dear spider." Her voice was quite mocking and annoying.

"I noticed, your civilized life is obvious," I said, pointing at them with my hand. "But I think you're overly civilized. Mating in the girls' restroom, really?"

"If you're uncomfortable, you can leave," Derin said nonchalantly. "Kerem and I will stay a bit longer. Because once you leave the restroom, we need to spray perfume to freshen the place, you know..."

At that moment, a blonde girl with a complexion like a Russian, but shorter, giggled as she touched up her makeup near the exit door. "Spraying perfume won't save this place after Ece leaves, Derin," she said. "We should go straight for demolition. That's the only way."

I was thinking what a terrible elementary school-level joke that was when Derin responded, "You're right, Alya," to the urban renewal enthusiast. They must have been friends. Alya's face was familiar. After a bit of thought, I remembered she was the girl who sat right behind me in class. Although we didn't have any conversations.

When I realized I was outnumbered three to one, I thought it was time for a tactical retreat. I sighed in frustration and started walking. "Do whatever you want!" As I headed toward the exit, I tripped over a boot extended in front of me, falling face-first onto the marble floor. Alya had tripped me!

A few groans slipped out between my lips. I was in a lot of pain and remained collapsed where I had fallen.

I cursed Alya. I was going to keep swearing, but my voice cracked from the pain, so I stopped. I had no intention of crying and giving them more satisfaction.

At that moment, Kerem came over. He bent down and extended his hand to me.

"Leave me alone, don't lift me!" I said angrily. "You're already standing in front of me like a Biscolata commercial model with your chest exposed. For heaven's sake."

Kerem, taking my criticism somewhat into consideration, buttoned the lower button of his shirt and stood up. "I just wanted to help."

"I can get up by myself," I said as I slowly stood up. Since the bathroom floor had just been washed, my hands, knees, and everything else were wet. My shirt was the most soiled since I fell directly on my chest.

As Alya looked at me mockingly, she murmured, "The floor is slippery, dear. Be careful!"

"Slippery, huh... I'll show you slipping, Alya!"

As soon as I finished my sentence, I grabbed Alya's hair with one hand and wiped my other dirty hand on her face. But then something very strange happened. I felt something cold and slippery wrapping around my right ankle and climbing up my leg like a vine. In that shock, I let go of Alya.

When I looked down, I saw it. A giant anaconda! When our eyes met, it hissed at me. I felt like my heart would stop from fear. In the blink of an eye, the terrifying snake continued to climb up my leg, inside my skirt, moving upwards. It was approaching my groin area. I had always been afraid of snakes, and now, paralyzed with fear, I couldn't move or scream for help. My whole body was trembling.

Alya said, "Don't move, or it will bite."

"B-bite?" I stammered in fear.

"I'm saying it's Derin, it will bite," Alya explained. "The snake wrapped around your leg is Derin. My dear friend can turn into a snake, Ece."

My eyes fell on the heap of clothes right next to the giant snake. These were Derin's school clothes. Alya must have been right. As Derin turned into a snake, her clothes had fallen to the ground. I had suspected from her hissing in class and her general demeanor, but still, learning that Derin was indeed a snake girl was a shock to me. My uncle had said that there were children with special powers like me in my new class, and he was evidently right.

While Derin was crawling on my leg, I was helpless. When I read her thoughts with my telepathic ability, I realized she was thinking about how my shoes were out of fashion. And as she climbed my legs, she was thinking about the Turkish folk song "Uzun İnce Bir Yoldayım" ("I'm on a long, narrow road"). It was like a joke... Although I could take her thinking my legs were long and slim as a compliment.

I was scared, but learning that the snake was actually Derin calmed my fear a bit. I mean, it was better than it being a real snake, right? It being my classmate, I thought, wouldn't bite me. H opefully... With these thoughts, as I regained my courage, I found the strength to speak: "Derin, what you're doing is harassment. Okay, it was a good prank, but that's enough. Please turn back into a human now."

After hissing one last time, Derin quickly descended from my leg. She slithered towards her clothes on the floor. When she turned back into a human, I saw her completely naked. She was a beautiful girl, I must admit, both in face and body. She had the right amount of curves in the right places, and her skin glowed smoothly... After a second or two of staring, I quickly looked away. In my religion, it was as forbidden to look at a naked woman as it was to look at a naked man.

From the rustling sounds, it seemed Derin was putting on her clothes.

"I had to turn into a snake to separate you from Alya," Derin said. "Don't let me see you fighting again, or I'll bite." She hissed through her teeth as she finished her sentence.

"I fear lies more than snakes," I wanted to say, but to be honest, I feared both.

Once Derin and her two minions left the girls' restroom, I was alone.

I didn't know what to do about my wet shirt. Moreover, during the scuffle, a few buttons had popped off my shirt, and my chest was more exposed than it should be. I couldn't leave the restroom like this. I decided to ask a friend for help. Since I had only one contact saved in my phone at this school, my choice was easy. My friend answered the phone on the second ring.

"What's up, Ece?" my classmate I sat next to asked.

"Don't ask, Fatih. I had a fight with a girl, Alya, and my clothes are not suitable for public appearance right now. I need your help."

"W-what!? You fought? Where are you, Ece?"

"In the girls' restroom."

The phone call ended. A minute later, I heard his voice from outside:

"I can't stand that annoying girl either. Did you beat her hope-fully?"

I smiled. While hiding behind the slightly ajar bathroom door, I called out to Fatih, "I look a bit disheveled, but if you saw Alya she is in worse condition..."

"Good job, Ece."

"Yeah, but my shirt is kind of torn and wet. I called you hoping you might have a spare outfit in your locker."

"Hmm..." Fatih murmured. I heard rustling sounds. Seconds later, the girls' bathroom door, behind which I was hiding, opened a bit more and I saw Fatih.

He had taken off his own shirt and was holding it out to me. He was only wearing a sleeveless undershirt that clung to his broad shoulders and triangular torso. Embarrassed as my mind wandered to silly places, I averted my eyes.

"I don't have a spare shirt, but it's not a big deal," Fatih said.

"Thank you," I muttered, trying to cover my chest with my arm. "But what will you do? I mean, without a shirt..." I took his shirt from his hand and closed the door. After taking off my clothes inside, I began to put on Fatih's shirt. This shirt could fit two girls like me! It was big, but better than nothing.

"What will I do? I'll manage. Now get dressed, Ece. I should head back to class. If I stand outside the girls' bathroom in just my undershirt any longer, people might start spreading rumors about me being a pervert."

Chapter 4

Fatih, who had lent me his shirt, returned to class. After putting on his shirt, I also returned to my class for the last lesson. When I entered the classroom, my eyes found Fatih sitting by the window. He was wearing a navy blue zip-up hoodie. Thankfully, he had found something to wear. I felt a bit relieved that he wasn't left in just his undershirt because of me.

When I sat at my desk next to Fatih, I turned to him and joked, "I'm going to report you to your parents for not adhering to the school dress code. What's with this outfit, man?"

"Look who's talking... You're wearing a huge men's shirt that looks like a sleeping bag. I should be the one reporting you."

I smiled. "Let's call it even and not report each other." I rolled up the sleeves of the shirt I was wearing. No matter how I adjusted it, it was too big for me, and I looked like a ghost haunting a cursed mansion in this oversized garment.

There were ten minutes until the lesson started. As I looked out the window, I noticed a piece of paper on Fatih's bag on the windowsill. There was a drawing of a girl on it.

A drawing of a girl?!

Could she be his girlfriend?

As I examined the beautiful brunette girl that Fatih had drawn so skillfully, I asked, "Did you draw this?"

Fatih turned his head to look at the drawing. "Yes."

"You're talented," I murmured. "Mashallah."

"Thank you."

With my telepathic ability, I could have easily pulled the identity of this girl from his mind, but it felt like an invasion of privacy. So I decided not to delve into Fatih's mind.

I wanted to ask who this girl was, but I kept quiet to avoid seeming too curious. My curiosity must have shown on my face because a few seconds later, Fatih couldn't help but explain the drawing. "She was a friend. She's no longer alive."

"I'm sorry," I murmured, looking at the drawing. Then I aimed my eyes at Fatih's. Looking into his eyes, I could see that this girl was important to him. He was still grieving. Perhaps he wished he could change her tragic death but couldn't... I didn't need my telepathic ability to understand this. Fatih's emotions were sealed in his eyes, and likely in his heart as well.

At that moment, I saw Derin walking towards us with her long, flowing hair and all her swagger. You'd think she had two unicorns in her backyard singing songs for her, she was that cool. When she reached us, she stood by me and teased, "The shirt suits you, Ece. It's a bit big, but at least you can wear it next year. I assume it's Fatih's shirt."

I nodded, embarrassed.

Derin spoke with a smug smile, "Or did you and Fatih flirt in the bathroom while Kerem and I were out? I mean, you're wearing his shirt after all..."

"No! I- we..."

While I stammered in embarrassment and shame, Fatih thankfully intervened, "You know I'm not looking for a new relationship, Derin."

"I know, Fatih. I just enjoy teasing Ece and watching her face turn different shades of red. It's as sweet as profiteroles to me."

"Too many profiteroles can make you sick, Derin," I said, crossing my arms and turning my head to look out the window in exasperation. I was now sure. This annoying girl was my test in this worldly life. May God give me patience.

"Oh, look at those cheeks, blushing with embarrassment!" Derin said as she pinched my cheek, making me grimace and wipe my cheek with my hand.

"Derin, get your paws off me!"

Derin giggled. "I'm letting you go for today." After taking a break from teasing me, Derin's eyes landed on the drawing of the girl that Fatih had made.

Derin sighed wearily and muttered to herself, "It's December again, right. Same every year..." She looked at Fatih and his drawing, clearly implying something related to him. But I didn't understand what she meant. Did something happen every December? Was it related to Fatih? I couldn't figure it out.

Derin leaned against the empty desk next to ours, holding onto the desk with her hands, and comfortably crossed her legs, clad in black Gucci boots. "You're coming to my birthday party this weekend, right Fatih?" she asked. "I hope you could arrange your schedule."

"Yes, I sorted it out, Derin," Fatih replied. "I'm coming to your party."

"Good." Derin turned to me with a hesitant look and finally spoke to me, "The whole class is invited to the party at our villa,

Ece. You're also invited to my birthday. Of course, if celebrating birthdays isn't too much of a sin for you."

As always, after making a snide remark to me, she bit her lower lip to keep from laughing... I could skip her birthday party. If only I could find the nurse who delivered her, I had a few words to say to that woman!

I was going to politely decline Derin's invitation.

But then I couldn't help thinking... My uncle, who thought I was too caught up in religious matters, had enrolled me in this open-dressed Freedom College to punish me. And I had to stay here for a year. But if I started behaving normally like the other girls—or what my uncle considered normal—hanging out with boys, going to parties, he had promised to reduce my punishment and reward me by transferring me back to my old school at mid-year. So attending Derin's party could save me. This way, I could escape this cursed school before the year was up. And thinking about it, what harm could one day at a party do? At most, Derin and Alya would tease me a bit at the party, which wouldn't be anything new. Yes, I could attend the party...

"I'm against celebrating Santa Claus at the end of the year, my belief prohibits us to celebrate Christmas. But I can come to your birthday, Derin."

Derin raised an eyebrow, surprised by my acceptance. "Hmm... Nice. But if you come to my house and get between me and Kerem, I'll throw you into my pool. I'm serious, Ece. No standing over us like a family doctor offering birth control."

"I won't interfere with you there," I replied. "I only interfere with people splitting by meiosis in public." They were flirting even though they weren't married. What they were doing was adultery and a sin. But everyone's sin was their own. I had no right to interfere with them.

We exchanged phone numbers. Derin said goodbye and left us to settle in her seat on the other side of the classroom.

After the last lesson, Fatih and I left school and walked to the area where the school buses were waiting. Taking advantage of the 5-10 minutes before the bus left, Fatih lit a cigarette. We stood outside the bus, chatting.

Even a nasty habit like smoking looked good on him. The way Fatih held his cigarette, brought it to his lips, and exhaled the smoke seemed irrationally attractive to me. His angular face and intense, harsh gaze suited his cigarette.

Then again, glorifying something forbidden, like finding smoking attractive and expressing it, was haram in our religion. So I repented for admiring the way Fatih smoked.

During our conversation, Fatih occasionally fell into deep silences, looking at me with a worried expression. Was he worried that I would be bullied again at Derin's party? I was sure Fatih had something on his mind that he wasn't saying. In the end, I decided to use my telepathic ability to peek at what he was thinking.

Hmm, I was right. When I accessed his thoughts, I saw that he was worried about me. And it wasn't just about Derin's party. He was worried from another angle too. For some reason, he didn't want to get too close to me. He even wanted to distance himself. His mind was dark and sorrowful. It was so dark that I didn't want to wander around in it any longer... So I paused my telepathy.

I decided to ask normally why he was looking at me with concern:

"What?" I shrugged. "Why are you looking at me like that?"

"Are you sure it's a good idea, Ece?"

"You mean going to Derin's birthday party? Even if I'm religious, I have the right to have fun, Fatih. Plus, my presence will add a... celestial touch to the party. Right?"

Fatih's lips curled up. "Sure, joke about it... But Derin and her gang have been picking on you since you arrived. At the party, they'll likely subject you to psychological, physical, and maybe even chemical attacks."

"Let them tease me. I won't give in easily."

"It's up to you, Ece. But if you're thinking of attending the party in a headscarf or modest clothing, at least wear your swimsuit underneath and definitely bring your snorkel. Because Derin and her Islamophobic gang will definitely throw you in the pool then."

He wasn't wrong. If I went in modest attire, I'd provoke them even more. "True, but do I even have non-modest clothes in my wardrobe?"

"Pool water is cold in December," Fatih said, hinting.

"Don't say that!"

"I will."

"Do you think someone can learn to swim in three days, Fatih?"

Fatih's eyes widened as he looked into mine. "You don't know how to swim, Ece!?"

"I do, but a friend wants to learn to swim in three days. That's why I asked," I said, rolling my eyes. "Yes, I don't know how to swim! And yes, I'm a silly girl who hasn't learned to swim by the age of 18. Okay? Are you satisfied now?"

"Don't get angry. If we had the time, I would teach you. I'm on the school swim team. But unfortunately, we only have three days. Anyway, joking aside, we might not be able to solve your swimming problem, but at least we can prevent you from drawing too much attention by getting you some suitable outfits for the party. If you're free after school tomorrow, we can go shopping together. I know a thing or two about fashion."

"Okay, let's do that," I said, sighing.

Chapter 5

F riday, 6 PM...

As agreed yesterday, today after school, Fatih and I were heading out for some shopping. According to him, there were a few stores he knew of where we could find me an outfit for the party. The weather was a bit chilly, so I wore my navy blue jeans and gray sweater, topped with a long black puffer coat. Fatih, however, didn't seem to feel the cold; he was out in just black jeans and a black t-shirt. His high muscle mass must have been keeping him warm, I suppose. As we walked side by side, we chatted.

"Why did you transfer to Freedom College, Ece?" Fatih asked. "I mean, from what I know of you, you seem conservative. I'm just surprised you chose our modern, progressive school when there are so many others that might suit you better."

"I didn't choose it. My uncle forced me here."

"Your uncle?"

"Yes," I sighed. "It's a long story."

"I'd like to hear it."

After taking a deep breath, I began, "My parents are no longer alive. They died in a boating accident. After their death, my uncle took care of me. God bless him, he didn't leave me alone, and he met all my needs, but... well, our religious views clash a bit. During a period when I was overly devout, he enrolled me in your school temporarily to punish me and to mold me into the ideal girl he had in mind. He hoped that by distancing me from my old conservative school and enrolling me in a secular one, my excessive piety would diminish. And so, here I am, in the same class as you..."

"Did you wear a headscarf before transferring to our school?" Fatih asked.

"Yes. I had only recently started wearing it. But still, having to take it off when I joined your school made me feel sad. God willing, I'll wear it again when I return to my old school."

Fatih, listening intently, murmured, "I'm sorry for you. I know how distressing family pressure can be. I've experienced similar torment."

"Really?" I asked as we walked side by side on the sidewalks of Kadıköy's back streets. It was cold and the sun was setting, but the streets were still crowded. Young lovers walked hand in hand, arm in arm.

"You've probably heard, our class at Freedom College is re-served for students with special talents, or rather, powers."

"Yes, I know," I said. "My uncle warned me that I might have friends with super abilities."

"Until two years ago, I also had a special talent. It was something present in my father, grandfather, and even earlier generations. It was like a family seal. And my parents were proud that I possessed this power too. But one day, I lost it."

"What do you mean?" I asked, astonished. "Did it just vanish, poof?"

"Yes," Fatih continued. "Naturally, my family was very upset about losing this power that they held in such high regard, passed down through generations. They tried all sorts of methods to help me regain it. Some were quite unpleasant. And they still pressurize me a lot to 'get better,' almost ostracizing me. My classmates, too. They all have different special talents, and because I turned into an ordinary person, almost all of them look down on me. I feel the pressure every second. Just like your uncle's pressure on you, it wears me down."

"I understand," I said sadly. "It's very wrong for them to ostracize you. Just as it's wrong for my uncle to punish me for my faith, it's equally wrong for your family and friends to treat you this way. I don't judge people by their business cards, but by their hearts. Even if you were extremely untalented as a person, it wouldn't make me love you any less. I mean, as a person. As an individual..."

Fatih, evidently moved by my words, sidled closer to me as we walked and draped his arm over my shoulders. Gently caressing my shoulder, he said, "I'm glad you came to our school. And I'm glad I got to know you."

Normally, I wouldn't like a guy holding me like this and it would make me uncomfortable. It did make me a little uncomfortable now too, but not as much as I had expected.

"Thank you," I said quietly. To break the emotional moment and the embrace, I sidestepped like a crab, moving away from Fatih and making him remove his arm from my shoulder. Then I started a playful conversation to lighten the mood: "I'm not going to ask about the superpower you lost, but tell me about one of your talents. It doesnt have to be a superpower, but still an extraordinary talent. I don't want to hear clichés like 'I swim well' or 'I play the piano.' Surprise me, Fatih!"

Fatih thought for a moment. "I can eat three hamburgers and three chicken burgers in one sitting. With a soda, of course. Otherwise, it's tough."

"You eat very unhealthily," I replied.

"No, I eat a balanced diet."

"H- how is that a balance, Fatih?"

"I'm balancing red meat and white meat."

I chuckled. "You silly goose!"

"Do you have any extraordinary talent like mine, Ece?"

I didn't want to talk about my telepathic ability just yet. Hearing about it usually made friends distance themselves from me as if they'd seen a zombie. After all, no one wants every thought exposed... So, I brushed off Fatih's question: "I can touch my nose with my big toe."

"Hmm..." Fatih pursed his lips and nodded as if he found it interesting. "Flexible, huh?"

"Yes."

CHAPTER 6

After walking a bit further, we arrived at a boutique Fatih knew. It was quite crowded inside. After a brief look around and checking out the clothes, Fatih came up to me with a few tiny pieces of fabric in his hand.

"I found a few skirts that should fit you," he said, holding them up. "Try these on, Ece."

Damn, were these tiny pieces of fabric resembling dishcloths supposed to be skirts? Was I supposed to cover myself with these tiny things?

"If I sew these three so-called skirts together, if I'm lucky, it might barely turn into a normal-sized skirt!" I protested. "Do you really want me to try them on? Fit into such a skirt?"

"Getting into one of these skirts is better than being thrown into Derin's pool."

"Pufff!" I grumbled. "Okay, give them to me, let me try at least." I took the skirts from him and went to the dressing room.

Once inside, I took off my pants and started trying on the skirts one by one. The first skirt was so short that I couldn't even be sure if my backside was exposed or not. I didn't like the fabric of the second one. When I finally tried to squeeze into the last and tightest skirt, I barely managed to fit in. I struggled to zip it up at the back, pushing the limits of physics. There it was... I looked at myself in the mirror inside the dressing room. No, no... I wasn't a mini skirt girl, that was for sure. I would try a dress instead.

When I asked Fatih for help, he quickly brought me a dress and handed it to me through the gap in the door. It was a black, sleeveless evening gown. Glittery, ending just above the knees, a midi-length dress. Its round neckline didn't offer too much cleavage, fortunately. The side slit was quite deep though. While standing, it didn't reveal much of my leg, but when sitting down, it left my leg quite exposed. I figured I could avoid exposing my skin if I held it with my hand while sitting down. After putting on the dress, I stepped out of the dressing room.

I met Fatih's eyes. "How does it look?"

"Hmm... Could you turn around?"

I did a full turn and waited for Fatih's comment.

"I still think they might throw you in the pool, Ece."

"Why?" I said in surprise. "I was dressed appropriately for the occasion..."

"Yes, but this time the dress suits you too well. They might throw you in out of jealousy."

I chuckled. "Don't exaggerate! It's just a plain dress, I won't attract much attention with this outfit."

Just then, my phone beeped, indicating a WhatsApp message from my uncle: "How are you doing Ece."

I replied: "I'm good. I'm out shopping with my friend."

"From school, right?"

"Yes, uncle."

"From your new school, isn't it, Ece?"

"Yes."

"Okay, have fun."

My uncle wanted me to hang out with open-minded friends at Freedom College, so he was pleased with my reply. If I could prove to him that I had changed—or at least make him think so—I could return to my old school soon.

But wait a minute... What's this!? My uncle wanted to start a video call with me on WhatsApp! I guess he wanted to see Fatih after I mentioned him.

Actually, thinking about it, this was a good opportunity for me. While sitting on the nearby beige couch with Fatih, I called out to him, "Fatih, please sit here. My uncle wants to do a video call. If I strike some intimate poses with you during the call, he'll think I've changed and opened up. That's okay with you, right..."

"Don't even mention it," said Fatih, sitting beside me on the couch. I answered the video call and showed us both, talking:

"How are you, uncle?"

"I'm good, youngsters. How about you?"

Fatih jumped in, "We send our regards. We're going to a friend's party this weekend. We went shopping to get Ece some new clothes beforehand. Hope it's not a problem. By the way, what's your name, sir?"

"Selim, my boy."

"Nice to meet you, Mr. Selim."

Following my instructions to act friendly, Fatih started behaving more intimately. He put his arm around me, gently stroking my shoulder over the dress. Then I felt his fingers in my hair, gently weaving through it. I must admit, this situation had stirred up some excitement in me. Normally, if a guy touched me like this, I would say, "Don't touch me or I'll bite!" but right now, I was tied up in presenting a friendly image to my uncle. Literally, I had tied myself up.

I was waiting for my uncle to finish the conversation and relieve me from the obligation of posing intimately, when he deepened the conversation with Fatih:

"Which team do you support, handsome boy?"

"Trabzonspor, what about you, Mr. Selim?"

"Galatasaray. Congratulations, by the way. You were impressive this season."

"Thank you, sir. Wish you luck next season."

As the conversation continued, Fatih, following my instructions to pose intimately, now had his hand on my leg. The slit in my dress had left my leg quite exposed when I sat down. Fatih gently pulled the fabric to cover my exposed leg. Then he placed his hand on top of mine, which was resting on the arm of the couch. His fingers intertwined with mine.

This boy knew what he was doing. Not only did he fulfill my task of being intimate, but he also took on the role of a jealous lover. He was delivering an Oscar-worthy performance for Best Supporting Actor...

But... Damn it, I was getting too excited! Why was I feeling this way now? Especially when Fatih was just my friend... Was there a reason for me to feel embarrassed and blush just because he held my hand, a reason for my heart to pound wildly? Somehow, I had gotten excited. So much so that my fingers, held by Fatih's, were visibly tensed and rigid. While conversing with my uncle and trying to maintain a cool demeanor in this situation, I was inwardly struggling with my unexpected feelings.

CHAPTER 7

While Fatih was holding my hand, I had to do something to calm down, or my uncle might get suspicious. Hmm... I could imagine Fatih as a girl and quell my excitement. He was too handsome for a girl, though, with such sharp features that could cut bread... Anyway, let's pretend he was a girl. He's a girl, girl, girl, girl, girl...

"Are you going to the party together?" my uncle asked.

"Girl- Ouch! Pardon?"

"Yes," Fatih came to my rescue. "We would like to go together, Mr. Selim, if that's okay."

"Okay? Go have fun. Live your lives, young ones, live your love."

God forbid... The only thing left was for my uncle to tell us to make out wildly at the party... How broad-minded was he!

"My battery is low, uncle. I have to go," I said and ended the call.

I quickly pulled my hand out from under Fatih's and placed it on my thigh.

"Fatih, you took it too far! I wanted you to be sincere, but you entwined like an ivy."

"I did it because you asked, Ece. Otherwise, you're not my type."

"Not your type?"

"You're not."

"Not his type... What kind of type interests you, sir?" I asked sarcastically.

"Athletic, with high muscle mass, Ece."

"Muscle mass... Like a cow? Cows have huge muscle mass, you know. There's one I know on the farm, Sarıkız. I'll get her for you. You can benefit from her meat and milk."

"When I said muscular, I meant human muscular."

Squinting my eyes, I said, "I'll show you muscle," and punched him on the shoulder with all my might. Oh my! Did I miss Fatih's shoulder and hit the door or something? My hand really hurt! His shoulder was so firm.

"If you're done brushing off the dandruff from my shoulder, now give me a real punch," Fatih said, trying not to smile.

"Jerk... By the way, just so you know, you're not my type either, Fatih."

"And what's your type then? Men who aren't handsome?"

"No, Mr. Arrogant. I like... as a type... Actually, I don't have a type. But even if I did, it wouldn't be you." I hadn't even dated anyone in my life. Flirting didn't suit my religion, so it didn't suit me either. My type was the man I would marry. "Anyway, let me take off this dress. It wasn't bad, but we might try a few more."

As I started walking towards the fitting rooms, I stepped on something and lost my balance, finding myself on the ground in an instant. Judging by the ripping sound I heard, a part of my dress might have torn slightly when I fell. "Ah!" I groaned. "Which thoughtless customer left these shoes on the floor after trying them on? One should either pick them up or put them aside."

"See, you got struck by God for insulting a sugar-pie-hearted guy like me. Are you okay, Ece?"

"Other than my charisma, nothing else got hurt, sugar-pie.... By the way, that's my favorite dessert, did you know!"

"Hmm... I prefer strawberry magnolia." Fatih gently helped me up, and as I dusted off the dress that got dirty from my fall, i said: "I heard a ripping sound from the dress. Since I caused this, I'm now obligated to buy it. Returning it secretly would be unfair."

"At least you won't need to try on more outfits. It was clear from your face that you didn't like shopping for dresses, Ece."

"You hit the nail on the head."

"And you hit the shoe on the floor and fell, clumsy sparrow."

I rolled my eyes. "Are you related to Alya, Fatih? Both of your jokes are equally cold, that's why I ask." Spotting the high-heeled, black shoes that had tripped me, I muttered, "Hmm, these might actually match the dress." I turned one of the heels over and checked. "Size 39, good."

"Try them on then."

I sat back down on the sofa where we had been sitting and put on the shoes. Then I stood up and walked. "For a heel, it's comfortable. I might buy these too. After all, they say... what doesn't break your foot matches your dress."

"Did Kim Kardashian say that?"

"No. I did," I muttered.

"Ece, by the way, the curly-haired girl with a big chin standing to our right has been staring at you for about ten minutes. You might not have an ideal type, Ece, but maybe you are her type... Otherwise, she wouldn't be staring so intently."

"God forbid!" I grumbled. "Did she see something inappropriate?" I slowly turned my head to the right out of curiosity. No way! The girl Fatih was talking about was Betül. My friend from my old school... She was wearing a hijab.

Betül was the last person I wanted to see right now. Just like me, Betül was a very religious Muslim and she knew I had transferred to Freedom College -a non religious school- and here I was, sitting in a revealing evening dress with a boy next to me. She was definitely judging me.

Now that I had made eye contact with Betül, I couldn't pretend not to see her. Reluctantly, I waved at her. Betül didn't wave back but focused her piercing gaze on me and started walking towards us. She stopped right in front of us.

"How are you, Ece?" Betül asked in a cold tone.

"I'm fine, Betül. How are you? It's been a while, hasn't it?"

"Yeah, yeah... You seem to have adapted to your new school. Judging by your body-revealing dress and your boyfriend..."

I shook my head. "Actually, it's not like that, Betül. I... something happened-"

"Did a flying school registration form land on your desk and you accidentally filled it out, ending up at Sex College, I mean Freedom College?" Betül said mockingly. "Look at that. And then, while walking in the boutique, you must have bumped into a mannequin and the evening dress on it jumped onto you. The boy next to you is probably here to help you take it off. Did I get it right?"

Grinding my teeth, I said, "First my new school and my uncle, then Derin and Alya, and now the party I never wanted to attend, also Fatih's endless chatter, and now I have to deal with you too, Betül! I can't stand you right now!" I sprang to my feet, eyes blazing. "Don't come any closer, or I'll bite!"

Fatih muttered, "Look... She even had a dig at me, didn't she?"

As I started walking towards Betül, Fatih grabbed my arm, saying, "Easy girl, slow down!" trying to calm me.

"She's gone mad!" Betül said, stepping back. "I was going to wish you a long and happy marriage, but Ece, you might suffocate your boyfriend with a pillow while he's asleep."

"Go away, Betül! Or I'll bite, and then you'll need tetanus shots and God knows how many rabies shots."

Betül seemed to have a fear of needles because she quickly walked away and disappeared...

Once I was alone with Fatih, after a moment to calm down, he asked, "Was she a friend from your old school?"

"Yes. But we weren't very close."

"Don't let it get to you," Fatih said. "In time, you'll make friends at our school too."

"Hopefully. Sinem seems like a nice girl, for example."

"She is. Did you know her father is a singer? Sinem also has a beautiful voice. Or had, I should say. After the earthquake, when she started stuttering... you know the situation."

"God's tests are ironic, aren't they? The atheist uncle's religious niece, me; the super-powered family's non-super-powered son, you; the singer father's stuttering daughter, Sinem..."

"I guess we're being tested at our most sensitive points."

"Otherwise, it wouldn't be a test," I said. "If you're taking a math test, no matter how good you are in science, those math questions you can't solve will come up. There's no escape."

CHAPTER 8

After our shopping trip, Fatih, being the gentleman he is, had kindly accompanied me home. When we reached the front of my apartment building, I said goodbye to him outside. Then, I walked through the garden alone and headed towards the entrance door of the apartment. Just as I was about to open the door, I heard a voice from behind, coming from the street. A little girl was pleading, "Can someone help me? Please!"

Curious, I turned around. Standing on the sidewalk where I had just said goodbye to Fatih was a delicate girl around 8-9 years old with long brown hair. But the strange part was, she was wearing Fatih's clothes: his black jeans and black t-shirt.

Actually, saying she was wearing those clothes is a bit misleading. It would be more accurate to say that the little girl was practically swimming in Fatih's clothes, given his 6-foot stature and large build. The jeans, far too big for her, had slid down and bunched around her ankles, while the t-shirt looked like a black dress on her.

When we made eye contact, she called out to me, "Hello, where am I? I don't remember anything." Her voice was trembling with fear.

I hurried over to her. "Don't be scared, sweetie. I'll help you." I crouched down in front of her, holding her tiny hands, and asked, "Do you remember your name?"

"Ce-Ceren."

"I'm Ece. Nice to meet you."

"Nice to meet you too, sister. Um, I'm a bit cold."

"We're right in front of my house," I murmured as I took off my coat and draped it over Ceren's shoulders. "If you'd like, we can go inside. I can find you some suitable clothes, and I'll make a few phone calls to try to reach your family. What do you think?"

After a moment's hesitation, she nodded. "Okay. Thank you."

"Come on, Ceren," I said, standing up. I picked up Fatih's fallen phone, jeans, and boxers, then took Ceren's hand and led her into the apartment building. We took the elevator to the fourth floor. Knowing my uncle and aunt were out of town on business and would be back the next morning, I opened the door with my key.

Once inside, I took Ceren to my room.

"Your room is beautiful," she said, looking at the dozens of plush toys arranged on the wall-mounted shelves.

"Thank you. By the way, you can take any of them you like, Ceren."

"Really?"

"Of course."

Seeing her reach for my Minnie Mouse toy with pink bows and a red polka-dotted dress, which was on a shelf too high for her to reach, I took it down and handed it to her. A joyful smile spread across her face, and I was glad to see some of her fear dissipate.

"You're lucky because I kept some of my childhood clothes as mementos and didn't throw them away," I said. "I have something in my closet that should fit you." I pulled out a cute pink and white tracksuit with a kitten design from my wardrobe and handed it to Ceren. "How about this? I hope you like it."

"I like it," she said with a sweet, dimpled smile as she looked over the clothes.

"Then go ahead and change, Ceren. I'll try to reach your family."

After leaving the room and closing the door behind me, I went to the living room and called my friend Sinem.

"How are you, Sinem?"

"I'm good, Ece. What's up with you?"

"You won't believe it! I was with Fatih today and—"

"Ooh, what did you two do?" Sinem teased.

"Nothing, we just went shopping. Get your mind out of the gutter! But the real issue is that Fatih... suddenly disappeared! And a little girl appeared in his place. Fatih had told me about a special ability he used to have but lost. Could that ability be shape-shifting? Do you know anything about it?"

"You're spot on, Ece. Fatih's ability was shape-shifting. He could turn into any person he wanted. Wow! Girl, you fixed him!" Sinem laughed. "Congratulations."

"Fixed? What did I do?"

"Ece, the guy lost his shape-shifting ability three years ago. You've been his desk mate, you hung out, probably flirted a bit, and within a week, Fatih's ability reactivated. I think you had something to do with it."

Annoyed, I closed my eyes. "We weren't flirting!" I snapped. "Besides, it's not like he's fully regained his ability. If anything, I've broken him because he shifted randomly and doesn't even remember who he is."

"Even so, it's still a significant improvement, Ece."

"You think so..."

"Yes, I do. His family has tried everything for three years without any sign of his ability returning. Maybe if you keep spending time together, especially if you become more than friends, Fatih will fully regain his powers."

I groaned in exasperation. "You're obsessed with the idea of us dating!"

"With his athletic build and your model-like physique... You must be taller than 5'7". You two would make a great couple."

"Your mouth could use some tape, Sinem. Every other word from you is about setting me up. Never mind that; do you have Fatih's parents' phone number?"

"Ooh, trying to get close to the boyfriend's parents, huh? Go for it, Ece!"

"I'm going to come after you! Sinem, I want to call Fatih's parents to have them pick him up—or rather, Ceren. Do you have their number?"

"Unfortunately, no. But I do know his sister's number. One sec... Okay, found it! I'll send it to you on WhatsApp."

"Thanks."

My annoying friend Sinem sent Fatih's sister's number and then added an F, a heart emoji, and then an E. Rolling my eyes, I sent her a skull emoji, followed by two poop emojis to vent my frustration.

As I was saying goodbye to Sinem on the phone, Ceren came into the living room, holding my Minnie Mouse plush and wearing the tracksuit. She sat next to me on the long couch.

"It looks great on you, sweetie," I said, fixing the collar of her tracksuit. As I took my hair tie off my wrist and put Ceren's messy hair into a bun, she looked at me with her bright hazel eyes. "It looks even better now that your hair is done."

"Thank you so much, Ece."

"You're welcome, sweetie," I said, gently pinching her cheek. "I reached your sister. I'll call her now, and hopefully, they'll come to pick you up."

Ceren nodded.

While Ceren went to the bathroom, I called the number Sinem had given me. I spoke to Fatih's sister, Zeynep, explaining the situation. She was shocked and excited.

"That's the situation, Zeynep," I said. "If you want, you can come to pick up Fatih, or rather Ceren. Either you or your parents, whoever is available. Don't worry; she's in safe hands until then."

After a moment of silence, Zeynep asked, "Ece, you're Fatih's new desk mate, right?"

"Yes."

"Do you see him outside of class as well?"

"Sort of. We talk during breaks, after school, and we went shopping together today."

"In that case, could Ceren stay with you tonight?" Zeynep asked.

"I don't mind, but won't Ceren feel uncomfortable staying at a stranger's house? If you don't have time to come, I can bring her to you instead."

"It's not that. I'll be honest with you, Ece," Zeynep said, taking a deep breath. "I believe you're good for Fatih. His ability, which has been locked away for three years, reactivated after you entered his life. It seems he didn't fully control the transformation today, but it's still a significant step. If Fatih stays with you tonight, he might gain better control over his ability."

First Sinem, and now Zeynep. Both seemed to think I had magically fixed Fatih. Even though I didn't share their belief, I didn't want to dash their hopes, so I could host Ceren for the night. She was a sweet girl, after all.

"Alright, Zeynep. Ceren can stay with me."

Just then, Ceren returned from the bathroom and came over to me. I handed her the phone to talk to her sister. Zeynep explained that she couldn't pick her up tonight and that Ceren should stay with me. After the call, we ended our conversation.

CHAPTER 9

While having dinner with Ceren in the kitchen, I decided to put on a cartoon for her to help distract her and make her forget about what happened.

"What would you like to watch, Ceren? Do you have a favorite cartoon?"

"Hmm... Maybe King Julien."

"Let me see if I can find it," I muttered, opening Netflix and typing the name into the search bar. Recently, I'd been considering canceling my subscription in protest—a small response to their latest offensive move. Netflix was removing films produced in Palestine, standing in support of Israel, a nation responsible for the deaths of thousands of innocent children and infants. I typed the name of the cartoon Ceren had mentioned into the search bar. "Here it is! This is the one, isn't it?"

"Yes, Ece sister," said Ceren as she ate the chicken wings I had ordered for her. I had also given her some fruit juice. It had been a while since i drank Coca Cola, because as i already mentioned before, i didnt want to support İsrael: a country that kills innocent kids and babies. As of this moment, the number of innocent children killed by Israel exceeded 17,000 and was rising day by day.

Not so fun fact: Did you know, friends, that during Israel's ongoing genocide against Palestine, it is not only Muslims who are suffering? In the sacred land of Palestine, the birthplace of Prophet Jesus (peace be upon him), Israel has, within the past year alone, demolished three churches to rubble and claimed the lives of many Christians as well. İsrail is killing some of the oldest Christian communities in the world and erasing their heritage sites.

I had ordered some burger for myself as well. Since I was helping a girl in distress, I deserved a little treat. It was a bit spicy, and if I overdid it, it sometimes upset my stomach, but they made it so well that I indulged from time to time.

We sat together and watched King Julien for almost an hour. I hadn't laughed this much in a long time. "It's supposed to be a children's cartoon, but I have to admit, I enjoy it too, Ceren."

"I figured you would like it, Ece sister."

"The main character, the Madagascar lemur king, is incredibly selfish, incompetent, and a rather unusual protagonist. He spends half his day dancing and shaking his butt. The other half, he spends kicking his assistant's butt..."

Ceren giggled. "Exactly. But my favorite character is Clover. She's a female lemur warrior who's loyal to the king and an excellent fighter."

"Oh yes, I really liked her too," I said. "If I were a monkey, I'd probably resemble her."

"You'd be as beautiful as she is, Ece sister."

"Do you think Clover is beautiful?"

"For a monkey, she's very beautiful, Ece sister. She even wears a wedding dress in one of the later episodes. It looks great on her, I think."

"Hmmm. I'd be happy to watch all the episodes with you, Ceren. I really like this series."

"Yes, let's watch them all together!" Ceren leaned over and hugged me from her seat. I think she had grown fond of me. I had already found her very sweet. I put my arm around her shoulders, gently patted her, and gave her a kiss on the hair.

We talked about various topics for a long time. One thing led to another, and before I knew it, it was bedtime. Since I knew my uncle and aunt wouldn't be home tonight, I comfortably put Ceren to bed in their room.

The Frog Prince... I chose this story as a bedtime tale for Ceren. Considering she had undergone a transformation like the hero in the story, it seemed fitting. Sitting at the edge of the bed, I read her the tale, and by the end, she had fallen asleep. I covered her up and went to my room. I undressed, leaving only my underwear on, and lay down on my bed. After such a tiring day, I quickly fell asleep.

"Ece sister?"

"Hmm?"

"Are you sleeping?"

"Mmm."

"I'm a little scared. Can I sleep with you?"

"Mmm hmm," I murmured, half-asleep.

In the middle of the night, Ceren had come into my room, and we had this conversation, but I was too groggy to remember it clearly. She took my affirmative answer and climbed into my bed, snuggling up behind me. Since we were both petite, we fit into the single bed without much trouble. I didn't even realize she had joined me and fell back asleep. She slept cuddled up to me.

"Oof! Hey, easy!" I grumbled as my sleep was interrupted while lying in bed. My eyes were still closed, and I wasn't fully awake. It felt like something—or rather, someone—was pressing down on me, and it was uncomfortable. It seemed like they were lying on my back as I lay face down.

Dimly remembering that Ceren had come to my bed in the night, I asked, "Ceren, could you please move over a bit? You're squishing me."

Why was she so heavy? She had her arm draped over my waist. She was lying on my back, and I felt most of her weight on my bottom.

When Ceren didn't respond, I repeated, "Sweetie, you're squishing me. Could you please move over?" Finally, I managed to open my eyes a little. I lazily rubbed my eye with one hand and tried to pull my body out from under Ceren, but I couldn't muster the strength.

Wait a second... This arm wrapped around my waist was too hairy to be Ceren's.

The leg pinning me down was also unexpectedly thick and hairy.

My eyes snapped open. "Fa-Fatih?"

"Hmmm?" Fatih's sleepy voice grumbled.

He had returned to his own body! So I was under Fatih right now, and I was only in my underwear!

Oh my goodness!

CHAPTER 10

In a panic, I thrashed around violently on the bed, trying to get up quickly from underneath Fatih, and in the process, I lost my balance and fell off the bed.

"Ah!"

I had hit my head on the floor. I squeezed my eyes shut and pressed my palm against the throbbing spot. While I lay sprawled on the ground, Fatih woke up and sat up in bed. "Ece?" he said. "Are you okay?"

When the pain in my head subsided a bit, I opened my eyes slightly and looked at him from where I lay on the carpet. Damn it, he was naked! I quickly averted my eyes. Apparently, when he reverted to his true form again last night, the clothes I had put on Ceren had naturally become too tight for Fatih, and feeling uncomfortable, he had taken them off and continued his sleep naked.

"Please put something on, Fatih! When I look at you like this, it's a sin, I'm committing a visual sin because of you."

Thankfully, I had brought his clothes from yesterday to my room. I picked up the clothes piled on the floor and handed them to him. Fatih quickly started to dress.

Trying not to look at him, I felt around the carpet with my eyes closed, searching for my own clothes. Thankfully, I found a piece of fabric. As I stood up and hastily tried to pull my clothes over my legs, I lost my balance again because the sweatpants were too tight on me, and I fell to the floor once more.

"Ouch!"

The reason my sweatpants were too tight was because I was mistakenly trying to wear the smaller pair I had given to Ceren. Ugh! I was as clumsy as King Julien from the cartoon we watched!

"Ece, you keep falling. You're going to kill yourself. Be careful!"

"You don't get to talk, Fatih, it's all your fault anyway!"

Because I fell repeatedly, I must have made a wrong move, and a cramp-like pain shot through my left thigh, about a span above my knee. It hurt so badly that I bit my lower lip and writhed on the floor, rubbing the aching spot with my hand. "Oh, this cramp is killing me! I hope it goes away soon."

"Don't worry, I'll take care of it now," said Fatih after he put on his T-shirt and jeans. "I'm an athlete, I know how to deal with cramps."

He got off the bed, picked me up, and laid me back on the bed. Today, I couldn't seem to escape from Fatih!

He laid me on my back on the bed, then sat between my legs. He started massaging the aching part of my thigh with his hands.

"There was no need, really, Fatih," I said, embarrassed. My cheeks were burning. "It'll pass soon."

"A few minutes of massage will seriously reduce your pain," insisted Fatih. "If I don't do this, the pain will last for days."

"I'm really fine. Don't bother." I pulled the bedspread over my chest and between my legs, leaving only my legs exposed.

"It's no bother," said Fatih.

It was sinful for an unmarried man to touch an unmarried woman's leg, and normally if he tried to do this, he'd get a kick to the face from me. Like the fighter lemur girl Clover, I would normally take him down. But since this was a treatment method and he seemed to know what he was doing, I was behaving more peacefully and without kicks or punches.

What he did helped my pain significantly, but a few seconds later, my fear of God outweighed my pain, and to avoid sinning, I decided to tell Fatih to stop.

"That's enough. Thanks," I said, sitting up in bed.

"By the way," murmured Fatih. "I don't know if we drank too much, but for some reason, I can't remember how I got to your house or what we did together. Did we... do anything, Ece, if you don't mind me asking?"

"Nothing happened between us, Fatih," I explained. "After saying just yesterday that I'm not your type, you couldn't have slept with me in less than a day, could you?"

"You never know with these things."

CHAPTER 11

Repenting for letting Fatih touch me briefly earlier, I decided to get out of bed.

"Fatih, close your eyes so I can get dressed," I said, keeping the blanket wrapped around me.

Fatih grinned mischievously. "I've already seen plenty of you, do I still need to close my eyes, clumsy sparrow?"

I narrowed my eyes and shot him a deadly glare. "Yes, you do, Mr. Sugarpie." If he teased me by calling me a clumsy sparrow, I would tease him by calling him a sugarpie. After all, he used that term for himself yesterday.

"Alright, alright," Fatih said, covering his eyes with his hands.

I got up, went to my wardrobe, and put on a white T-shirt and black shorts. "Okay, I'm ready."

Fatih opened his eyes and stood up. He walked to the window. "Would you mind if I opened the window and smoked a cigarette?"

I pursed my lips. "Does it suit you, Fatih? You're a swimmer, you shouldn't smoke."

"Cigarettes and I have a deep love, Ece."

"Really? What kind of love is that?"

"I die for cigarettes, and they burn for me."

I giggled. "That's a nice saying. But you won't get off the hook so easily with me, Fatih. Cigarettes cause various diseases, from cancer to COPD, cardiovascular diseases to diabetes."

Fatih looked at me with indifferent blue eyes. He didn't seem scared by the diseases I listed. But I knew how to get his attention.

"Also," I continued, "they cause sexual dysfunction and bad breath."

Fatih raised an eyebrow. "You should be a doctor."

"I'm considering it. It's beneficial for the afterlife too. If I get a patient to quit alcohol and cigarettes, which are sins, I get rewarded in the afterlife for every cigarette and drink they don't consume."

"Hmm... Is smoking a sin?" Fatih asked, twirling a cigarette pack in his hand.

"Smoking is not a sin but a reprehensible act close to being forbidden. Moreover, it involves the rights of others because the smoke threatens the health of those who breathe it in. According to the religious authority, if the smoke of your cigarette affects a non-smoker, you need to seek their forgiveness. So, it would be great if you quit smoking..."

Fatih looked at the cigarette pack in his hand. "I don't know..." he murmured. "I've been thinking about quitting for a while, but who knows when I'll succeed. We'll see. It is up to fate."

I grabbed my scissors from the bedside table. "Yes, as you said, it's up to fate. And fate has decided today is the day you quit smoking," I said, reaching for the cigarette pack in Fatih's hand. I intended to cut it. But with a swift move, he pulled the pack away.

I reached out again to grab it, but he raised it above his head. They say the third time's the charm, and I managed to snatch the pack on my third attempt! But as I tried to move away to cut it, he grabbed me by the waist.

"It's not that easy, Ece."

"Tell your cigarette to say its last prayer."

He wrapped his arm around my waist, pulling me close to prevent me from escaping. As he reached for the cigarette pack, I kept it away, struggling to break free from his hold at the same time.

"You can't escape!" he said confidently.

"That's what you think. I'll win!"

Even though I freed myself from his hold for a moment, he caught me again within seconds. As I lost my balance during the struggle, I fell face-first to the ground, taking Fatih down with me. He landed right on top of me.

"Ah!"

This boy was heavy! And how many times today had he pinned me down? If my biology knowledge weren't sound, I'd worry I might get pregnant from being pinned down so often, but fortunately, I knew that wouldn't happen.

"Are you okay, Ece?" Fatih asked, worried. He stood up and gallantly extended his hand to me. I took advantage of his distraction to cut his cigarettes with my scissors.

"You're so cruel, Ece."

"I told you I'd win." I stood up, flexing my arm muscles in triumph. "I wrestled a crocodile. I tangled with a whale. Just last week, I killed a rock and injured a stone. I even sent a brick to the hospital. Yes, I'm so cruel that I can make medicine sick."

Fatih smiled as he looked at the remnants of his cigarettes. Even though it was a bitter smile... "You're no less than Muhammad Ali. Credit where credit is due."

"Muslim power, my dear," I said with a wink. "Maybe if you weren't smoking, you wouldn't have run out of breath and lost to a girl who's 15 centimeters shorter and weighs half as much as you."

Fatih looked at me incredulously. "Even though I don't think that's why I lost, I'll stay silent to not undermine your victory. Since I lost, I'm quitting smoking right now."

"Yes!" I did a victory dance. "That's enough celebration," I said, sitting on my bed. I opened my hands. "I need to say my daily Sinem prayer, give me a minute, Fatih."

"Sinem prayer? I don't know much about Islam, Ece. What's the Sinem prayer?" Fatih sat next to me on the bed.

"Oh, how do you not know the Sinem prayer? It's my favorite prayer after the Dilara and Betül prayers." Seeing Fatih's confused look, I added, "I'm kidding, silly. There's no such thing as a Sinem prayer. Or a Dilara and Betül prayer. What I mean is, I pray for my friend Sinem every day. I read the Fatiha prayer three times for her, hoping her stutter will improve."

Realizing I had just made light of prayers, I asked God for forgiveness and repented. It wasn't right to take religious matters lightly, even as a joke.

"I like Sinem too. I hope your prayer is accepted, Ece, and her speech improves."

"Join me in reciting the Fatiha, so we can increase the chances of it being accepted."

"I don't know..." Fatih said hesitantly.

"Why not?"

Fatih grimaced. "I've forgotten it a bit. I used to know the Fatiha, but I guess I've grown rusty."

"A Fatih who doesn't know the Fatiha... That's unacceptable."

I sat and taught him the Fatiha. It took just 4-5 minutes for him to memorize it well. Then we both prayed for my friend Sinem.

Suddenly, there was a knock on the door...

"Damn, it must be my uncle and aunt!" I said, covering my face with my hands. I jumped up in panic. "They said they'd return around this time on Saturday morning. Which is right now... I got so caught up hanging out with you that I forgot. If they see you here... You need to hide somewhere!"

Contrary to me, Fatih stood up calmly. "Relax, Ece. I have a better plan."

"W-What plan?"

"You go answer the door, Ece, leave the rest to me."

"Okay." I started walking toward the door, curious about his plan. So, I decided to use my telepathic ability to sneak into Fatih's mind like a sly thief.

Hmm... So this was his plan: Instead of hiding, Fatih planned to pretend to be my boyfriend, thinking my uncle would be pleased to see me with a boy rather than getting angry. And he wasn't entirely wrong. If my uncle saw me opening up and hanging out with boys, i would have my ticket to go back to my old school.

While exploring Fatih's mind, I came across another strange thought. He found me unusual, sweet, and even a bit attractive. Because of this, he hesitated to get close to me and thought he should distance himself.

What kind of logic was that? Why would someone with positive feelings for a girl want to distance himself from her?

Although I felt like focusing on this issue, I had a more pressing problem right now. My uncle and aunt... I needed to focus on them. And maybe, the best solution was to do as Fatih suggested and turn the problem into an opportunity by pretending to be a couple.

CHAPTER 12

I went to check the door. When I opened it, there stood my uncle, his short, curly, light brown hair contrasting with his thick glasses.

"How are you, my dear Ece?" he asked as he and my aunt entered. They removed their shoes.

My aunt Sema, with her wavy, long hair and carefully applied makeup, looked as elegant as ever, not showing her 45 years at all.

It was equally hard to believe my uncle was 52. He went to the gym once a week. Keeping up with such a charming wife wasn't easy, of course.

"I'm fine, how are you?" I asked, standing at the door and taking their coats to hang in the wardrobe. "How was your journey?"

"Oh, long trips always make my feet swell," said my aunt Esma.

Fatih joined us casually, greeting my uncle and aunt with a warm "Welcome."

"Thank you, son," my uncle replied. "Welcome to you too. Your name is Fatih, if I remember correctly? How are you, dear?"

It seemed Fatih's plan had worked. My uncle and aunt had no problem with me having a boy over while they were away.

"Thank you, Uncle Selim. I came over after school yesterday. I spent some time with Ece. I hope that's okay with you."

Fatih moved closer and gently wrapped his arm around my waist. Focused on his role as my boyfriend, he was softly caressing my belly under my shirt.

If I didn't have to put on a show for my uncle and aunt, I'd break Fatih's hand. Then, I'd bite the hand of the doctor who put it in a cast, but anyway... I'd just have to grit my teeth a bit.

"No worries," my uncle said. "This is practically your home now, Fatih. You can come whenever you like. Our Ece is under your care."

Using my telepathic power, I glanced into my uncle's mind. His thoughts didn't surprise me: "I hope Ece has gotten close with this boy."

Oh, great! Why didn't I have conservative parents who'd say, "If you're not home by 10 PM, I'll break your legs"? Okay, maybe they wouldn't have to actually break my legs, a bit of roughing up and a slight bone fracture would do.

Fatih's hand was still under my shirt, and I didn't like it. To avoid a hormonal surge from his fingers gently moving across my bare skin, I tried to escape by saying, "We were just about to leave. Right, Fatih?"

"Yes, my dear Ece," he said, kissing my cheek. He was perfect at playing the boyfriend role.

"You put on your shoes," I told Fatih. "I'll go change into my jeans and be right back."

I quickly headed to my room. I took off my leggings and put on my navy jeans from the wardrobe. I was ready. Just as I was about to leave my room, my aunt Esma appeared at the door.

"Ece dear, can we talk for a couple of minutes before you go?"

"Of course."

When my aunt gestured towards my bed, I sat down. She joined me, sitting beside me.

Yes! I thought she was going to scold me. Please, let her scold me! I wanted a classic, strict, heavy-handed Turkish aunt. Was that too much to ask?

"It seems you've been spending time with Fatih lately," Aunt Esma began.

"Yes."

I gave a short answer. If I exaggerated, saying Fatih and I were dating, that I was in love with him, holding hands, cuddling, I could get my ticket back to my beloved old school. My uncle and aunt had promised that if I moved away from my conservative ways, I could return to my old school. But I wouldn't exaggerate. That would be a lie.

And our Prophet has a saying: "My community might commit adultery, gamble, then repent; but never ever lie." Even if someone commits other sins, it is hoped that Allah will forgive if they repent and make a U-turn. But lying is never allowed. Truthfulness is a Muslim's signature, their red line.

"Your uncle had a chance to talk with Fatih on the phone yesterday. And based on his impressions, Fatih seems like a good boy," my aunt said. "But while it's still early, I'd like to give you some advice, dear Ece."

Was she going to say, "Don't spend too much time with boys?"

Did I not take a liking to that boy?

Or was he going to guard honor by saying, "My eye is on you"?

While I waited eagerly, Aunt Esma took a deep breath and continued, "Always use a condom when you engage in a relationship. Although it's not one hundred percent protective, it's at a sufficiently high level. You wouldn't want to become a mother before even finishing high school, Ece."

Was this it then? Closing my eyes in disappointment, I murmured, "Thank you for the warning, Aunt Esma," in a faint voice.

Ugh! My uncle and aunt were both the same. Thankfully, I listened to Islam's recommendations regarding moral matters, not theirs. And when the time came, I wouldn't be with anyone other than my future husband.

CHAPTER 13

S aturday, 5:15 PM...

I was about to leave home to go to my classmate Derin's birthday party. I had put on the black, strappy evening dress that Fatih and I had picked out yesterday. It was a glittery, knee-length, midi dress. The neckline wasn't very deep, but the slit on the side of the skirt was quite daring.

"Aunt Esma, isn't this much makeup enough?" I grumbled. "I'm just going to my friend Derin's birthday party. You're not giving me away as a bride, so why did you have to put half a kilo of makeup on my face, dear aunt?"

"A party is a party. In any case, Fatih will come to pick you up soon, and you'll be going out with him," said my aunt. "Wouldn't it be nice to look even more beautiful for him?"

We were in the bathroom, and since my aunt knew I had no interest in makeup, she was doing it herself. She had put on bright red lipstick and eye makeup that made my green eyes stand out more. And let's not even mention how she had dragged me to the hairdresser to get my hair blow-dried and styled into a waterfall braid. On top of that, she had made me wear a bra that accentuated my breasts and had even insisted on a thong.

Normally, I wouldn't allow any of this and would prefer to go to the party in a modest dress and with my headscarf, but there was a promise from my aunt and uncle to re-enroll me in my old school as a reward. So, I would endure it.

Endure... I suppose I would have to endure not only emotionally but also phsically. I could almost hear my breasts and buttocks cry because the underwear she had made me wear was very uncomfortable. I had just learned what kind of torture normal girls went through to look beautiful for boys.

"Auntie, didn't you always say I was naturally beautiful? Why did you suddenly feel the need to put me through a full-service beauty treatment?"

"Ece, yes, you're beautiful, but there's a difference between being 'Hmm...' beautiful that raises one eyebrow and being 'Wow!' beautiful that leaves jaws dropping. Our goal is the second kind."

"Invisibility isn't an option, I guess?"

"No, Ece," my aunt said as she skillfully applied my nail polish. "And... You know that empty apartment we haven't found a tenant for yet, the one three streets away?"

"I know. So what?"

"I might accidentally leave the key to it on the kitchen table soon," she said. "I'm very forgetful these days. If someone took that key and went to that empty apartment, spent the night there, and didn't spend it alone, say, with someone whose name starts with F, I wouldn't notice. I'm very forgetful and careless, you know."

I rolled my eyes at her matchmaking attempt. "Auntie, you should take B12 vitamins and iron supplements. They're good for forgetfulness." My only reason for going to that empty apartment would be to get away from my crazy aunt and uncle to have some peace and quiet.

"Our beautiful family doctor speaks," my aunt said with a suggestive tone. She pressed her lips to my hair and left a kiss. "It's just a suggestion, no insistence," she added about the apartment.

When my aunt finished painting my nails, I looked at my fingers. "From donkey hooves to Barbie doll fingers... It's alive! Aunt Sema, you work miracles with your hands."

"Oh, Ece, you just keep frowning at me. You don't know how lucky you are to have an amazing aunt like me."

In fact, I did love them. My little dumplings! Okay, we had different views on some things, but after my parents' death, they had taken care of me as best as they could, according to their traditions and beliefs.

Besides, our Prophet (PBUH) had maintained his respect even to his oppressive uncle Abu Lahab until the end, so I couldn't disrespect my uncle and aunt for the school issues, which were insignificant compared to that oppression.

"I love you, auntie!" I said emotionally, kissing her on the cheek.

"I love you too, Ece," she smiled.

When the doorbell rang, "It's probably him," Aunt Esma said. "Go on, answer the door. If he has a heart attack from seeing your beauty, you can perform CPR, future doctor."

I giggled. "I'll see about that. If Fatih doesn't look very handsome tonight, I might skip the CPR and recite the Fatiha for him instead."

"God forbid, girl. Don't say such things. Go on, answer the door, don't keep him waiting!"

Aunt Esma gave me a light slap on the butt to shoo me away, and I followed the hallway out of the bathroom. When I reached the door, I paused and pressed the buzzer to open the building's main entrance and waited a bit.

A minute later, Fatih emerged from the elevator. His sharp, all-black suit suited him well. With his triangular physique, his hair falling over his eyebrows, and his intense gaze, he wasn't bad at all as a fake boyfriend. If he had a heart attack, I wouldn't recite the Fatiha; I would perform CPR. After all, I owed him a massage after the cramp massage he had given me.

At that moment, Aunt Esma also came to the door to see us off.

As I prepared to leave, I picked up my bag and phone from the shoe cabinet by the door. Meanwhile, I greeted Fatih, "Welcome, Fatih! How are you?" He didn't respond. Since he had gotten out of the elevator, he had been silently standing at the door. To break the silence, I spoke:

"Aren't you going to say anything, Fatih?" Then, leaning closer to his ear, I added, "You better say something, Fatih, because my aunt put a lot of effort into dressing me up like this."

Fatih broke his silence: "Oh, coal-eyed beauty that shames the night. My silence is out of fear of tarnishing your delicate petals with my words. If I praised you until dawn, the night would end, but my words wouldn't, my Ece."

W-what! I was stunned by Fatih's breathtaking words. Aunt Esma was wrong. If anyone was going to have a heart attack from excitement, it was me. Not used to such romantic atmospheres, I made a joke of it:

"Since I'm a black rose because of my black dress... I guess you'll trim me nicely, handsome gardener."

Where had trimming come from! I was babbling out of excitement.

We said our goodbyes to Aunt Esma. Just as I was about to leave the house with Fatih, I remembered something and said, "Wait a second, Fatih," before returning to my room. I grabbed a few pieces of my childhood clothes and stuffed them into my bag. If

Fatih lost control outside and turned into Ceren again, I needed to be prepared. I left my room and returned to the door. As I put on my black, jeweled, high-heeled shoes, my uncle called out to us from the living room:

"Be back before 11, kids!"

God is great! Was my uncle actually getting a spiritual awakening? Did he really want me to come back early?

"11?" I asked with wide eyes.

"Yes. Tomorrow morning at 11... Or noon at the latest. You have homework, Ece, remember. You need to set aside time for it on Sunday."

I pouted. So, no spiritual awakening for my uncle. Oh well. "Okay, uncle. See you."

When Fatih took my hand gently at the door, I was momentarily surprised. But I quickly adapted and held his hand too. After all, it worked in my favor to appear like a couple in front of my aunt.

We took the elevator down to the ground floor. After exiting the apartment building, we walked towards the black Range Rover parked in front of the garden. Fatih continued to hold my hand. When we reached the SUV, Fatih stood by the passenger door and opened it chivalrously for me. Before getting in, I looked up at the apartment. Aunt Esma was looking at me from the window. When I waved to her, she waved back similarly. I got into the car. Fatih walked around the front of the vehicle and got into the driver's seat, and we drove off.

CHAPTER 14

We were heading to the Derins' house. As Fatih drove, he explained, "Their house isn't too far. We'll be there in 15 minutes."

"Let's hope so. God willing, we'll get there safely."

"God willing, of course," Fatih replied.

I turned to him from the passenger seat and asked, "Am I annoying you with my religious talk?"

He smiled. "No, Ece. I actually like it. Your words are pleasant, and I end up learning something about religion because of you."

"I'm glad to hear that. Then I'll keep 'annoying' you," I added as we stopped at a red light. "By the way, your SUV is nice. Your family must be doing well."

"My father is a contractor," Fatih said. "Although business is a bit slow these days, overall, it's good."

When the light turned green, we continued moving. "Are your construction sites around here?"

"Yes, mostly on the Anatolian side. Our older projects were in Trabzon city. We're originally from the Black Sea region. But since we moved to Istanbul five years ago, we've been working on projects here."

"Are you interested in your father's profession?"

"I'm not sure..." Fatih said thoughtfully. "It's a bit stressful, but then again which job isn't? My father encourages me to follow in his footsteps. He often calls me to work with him so I can learn. That's how it is... What about your family, Ece? What do they do?"

"They don't do construction like you family. They do the opposite. Try to demolish my life..." I sighed. "They haven't really let go of me yet... But, seriously, they're in the tourism sector. They run a hotel in Çeşme and travel back and forth between Istanbul and Çeşme for work."

We chatted throughout the drive, and finally, we slowed down as we approached a two-story villa. There was a large pool in the garden. Fatih parked by the side and confirmed, "We're here."

As we stepped out of the car, the sun was gently setting. It was unexpectedly warm for December, a leftover day from summer.

Walking towards the villa through the garden gate with Fatih, he spoke up, "I saw Halit from our class, sitting by the pool. I'll hang out with him. You might find Sinem inside, Ece. Have fun."

When I slowed down and stopped, Fatih did the same. Focusing my puzzled gaze on his eyes, I murmured, "So we're splitting up?"

Fatih shrugged. "Yes."

"Hmm... Okay," I said, trying not to show my disappointment. "If that's what you want..." I averted my now cloudy eyes.

"Ece? Are you okay?"

"I'm fine!" I said, gritting my teeth. "In fact, I'm very fine! Why wouldn't I be?"

"Look, Ece... If you want, I can join you at the party—"

"There's no need," I interrupted him. "I-I'll go find Sinem. She should be inside. You go join your friend. You must have missed him."

Leaving Fatih behind, I began walking towards the villa with angry steps. Fortunately, I saw Sinem at the door. She looked nice in her black mini skirt and beige blouse. She had on pink lipstick, and her long, blonde hair flowed over her shoulders in waves. We greeted each other, and I went inside with her. It was quite crowded inside. Many of Derin's friends from school and more had attended.

Sinem and I moved to a secluded living room. The luxurious furniture in brown tones and the massive chandelier stood out in this spacious room. A foreign pop song I didn't recognize was playing softly. On the large wooden coffee table in the middle of the sofa set, there were several cactus plants. These red, green, and purple cacti of various sizes, in three different pots, even appealed to someone like me who wasn't a plant enthusiast. I suddenly found myself wondering if the cacti on the coffee table could prevent the free-spirited students of Freedom College from fantasizing about making out on the table.

As I settled into the comfortable three-seater sofa, Sinem joined me.

"You look upset, Ece. Is something wrong?" Sinem asked hesitantly.

"Never mind," I sighed. "I don't want to ruin your mood with my trivial issues at such a nice party."

"I love parties and drinks, Ece. But do you know what I love even more?"

"What?"

"Gossip. So spill it, Ece, and cheer me up a bit."

Taking a deep breath, I explained. "Alright then... I'm a bit upset with Fatih."

"What happened?"

"We were supposed to come to the party together. I dressed up, put on makeup and everything. But when we got to the villa, Fatih just said 'everyone goes their own way now' and left me to hang out with his friend!"

"Oh, poor you!" Sinem said sympathetically and hugged me tightly for comfort. "My baby wanted to hang out romantically with Fatih, huh?"

"No, it's not that, Sinem! I don't know..."

"It is, it is."

"It's not!"

"Maybe?"

"Perhaps."

"I'm sure, Ece."

"Probably..."

"But Fatih even wrote a poem for me today," I murmured in sorrow. "In his words, I was a beautiful black rose. Holding my hand, opening the car door for me so gallantly... It was all just a show, wasn't it? Only to act like my boyfriend in front of my uncles, to help me out."

Sinem laid my head on her shoulder, gently stroking my hair in comfort. "How could he hurt my dear Ece like this, that blockhead Fatih! Ece, do you know the similarity between men and logs?"

"You should chop them all with an axe?"

"I was thinking of a less violent answer," Sinem said, stuttering slightly. "Both can warm you up, for instance. And both burn out quickly. It's not worth being upset over such fleeting things, sweetheart."

"I suppose you're right." I had never dated anyone until I turned 18, and I hadn't felt a significant void either.

"I'm going to get a drink, Ece," Sinem said as she stood up. "Want one?"

"No, I don't drink alcohol, Sinem. Thanks."

"I should've guessed. You say it's forbidden, of course. Not even for one night?"

"Most sins, even in small amounts, are still sins. Thank you, dear. Go ahead and get one for yourself if you like."

"Alright," Sinem said, getting up. "I'll be right back, sweetie."

Seconds after Sinem left the room, I saw a familiar face approaching. It was Kerem, Derin's boyfriend, whom I had met when I caught them making out in the bathroom recently. I didn't usually like long hair on men, but Kerem's hair, which reached his chin, suited him. His beige shirt partially unbuttoned, suggested he had been making out with Derin again. I had promised Derin I wouldn't give them moral lectures this time.

Kerem walked slowly to the couch where I was sitting. "May I sit down?"

"Of course, Kerem."

After sitting next to me, Kerem said, "I accidentally overheard your conversation about Fatih."

"Accidentally?"

"Okay, maybe I eavesdropped because the topic intrigued me," Kerem admitted. "I just want to say, you don't want to date Fatih, Ece. Trust me, Fatih is bad news."

"What do you mean by that?"

"Do you know how Fatih's last relationship and the one before that ended, Ece?"

"They broke up?"

"Yes. But permanently. Both of his girlfriends died."

"So?" I asked, looking at Kerem blankly. "Are you saying I shouldn't date Fatih because of that? People die, Kerem. Whether they're dating Fatih or not."

Kerem shook his head. "You're new at our school, darling. You don't know anything. Those girls didn't die naturally. After they started dating Fatih, accidents, misfortunes, and incredible bad luck befell them repeatedly until they couldn't escape fate and died."

"So you're saying girls who date Fatih are cursed. To death, no less... Is that it?" I laughed. "I don't believe in horror movie clichés like Friday the 13th. Fridays are blessed days for me and all the muslims."

"Go ahead and laugh. I'm just warning you..."

If I didn't date Fatih, it wouldn't be because of some silly urban legend. Fatih didn't want me anyway, so that would be the reason we wouldn't date.

Kerem, sitting close to me on the couch, draped his arm over my shoulder. "Ece, look," he said with a captivating tone. "You're a beautiful girl. Different. You shine among the girls in our class. You could easily have any guy you want, besides Fatih." His fingers trailed through my hair, tucking strands behind my ear as his gaze locked onto mine.

"Kerem, have you had too much to drink at the party? Despite dating Derin, it seems like you're hitting on me. I'd like to remind you that you have a girlfriend."

"Derin doesn't need to know."

"So you want to be with me. Is that it?"

"Yes," Kerem said, leaning in closer.

"Alright then, let's do this, Kerem... Find an empty, available room in Derin's house." I casually crossed my legs.

"Okay," Kerem said, his hand lowering to rest on my knee.

"When you go to that unoccupied room, you lie down on the bed there, will you?" I added.

When Kerem leaned in closer, nearly touching his lips to mine, he asked, "Okay, Ece. Then what?"

"Strip down in bed, Kerem."

"Alright, baby. And then, when I'm ready, should I call you?"

He was about to kiss me. "No," I said. "Don't call me. Just sleep."

"Sleep?"

"Yes, sleep. Because you'll only see me in your dreams, you hormonal Madagascar Lemur!" Would a girl like Clover even look at him? I lightly patted his cheek twice in jest and stood up, grabbing my purse. "If you'll excuse me now."

Kerem stood up behind me, grabbing my arm. "You'll regret not listening to me about Fatih!"

"Why? Is your superpower, making people regret things? Apparently, everyone in our class has a superpower."

CHAPTER 15

I shook my arm free, but Kerem wouldn't let go. "Would you please let me go?"

"Ece, look... Let's sit and talk for a bit."

"I don't want to talk to you!" I shrieked.

At that moment, Sinem entered the room with a drink in hand. Seeing us, she shouted, "Hey! Let go of her!"

Kerem snapped, "Stay out of this, Sinem."

Sinem, stammering slightly, replied, "I won't get involved, but my friends will." I didn't understand what she meant.

Suddenly, Kerem screamed in pain and began shaking his leg. I looked down in curiosity. To my astonishment, the tallest of the cacti standing on the coffee table had leaned over and pressed its spines into Kerem's leg. And it didn't stop there. The cactus pulled back and then struck his leg again with its spiny body.

The smaller cacti in the decorative pots on the table seemed to cheer their larger sibling on, swaying their bodies from side to side as if in a dance. The most charming of them all was a tiny purple cactus, no bigger than my thumb, with a red flower atop it resembling a little hat.

Kerem, in his agony, released his grip on my arm. Taking advantage of this, I stepped away from him, eyes wide as I continued to watch the cacti's attack. I wondered if I was dreaming and pinched my arm to check. The pain confirmed it was no dream.

After Kerem backed away from the table, he bent down and started to pluck the cactus spines from his leg one by one. "Sinem, tell your friends to stop attacking me. I've let Ece go, okay!"

Sinem raised her hand towards the three cacti on the table as if signaling 'enough'. She then approached the plants. "Thank you, Lora," she said to the largest cactus. That must have been its name.

Lora slowly straightened back to its original position.

Kerem grumbled as he left the room, while Sinem casually sat on the long couch.

"Can you talk to cacti?" I asked, standing by the table.

"Yes," Sinem replied. "Not just with them, but with all plants. I help them, and they help me. It's a gift I've had since birth."

"Wow... They said everyone in our class has a superpower. So this is yours, Sinem. It's quite impressive. You're like a real-life version of Ivy from the Batman movies!"

"Thank you, Ece. But I have one crucial difference from Ivy."

"What's that?"

"Ivy doesn't have a sweet friend like you," Sinem said, smiling at me.

"My dear!" I sat down next to Sinem and hugged her. "I'm so glad you're here." I held her tightly for a few seconds, squeezing the life out of her before letting go, to ensure she could breathe.

Truth be told, I was fascinated by Sinem's cacti. I stood up and leaned closer to examine the cactus family on the table. Since they had scared off Kerem, they hadn't moved. They stood there as if the earlier events had never happened. "Please thank Lora for me. She's my hero. But I especially love this little one with the red flower that looks like a hat," I said, pointing to the smallest cactus.

"Lina," Sinem called to the hatted cactus. "Ece really likes you."

To my amazement, Lina gently tilted her spines aside in a small section of her body.

"Is she waving at me?" I asked excitedly.

"No. She wants you to pet her."

"Oh, you sweet thing!" I hesitated a moment before slowly moving my hand towards Lina's de-spined area. I gently ran my index finger over the soft part of the tiny purple cactus, and she didn't budge. "If you keep being so adorable, giving me these cute poses, I might just have to take you home with me! I think I'll ask Derin if I can take this plant tonight."

Sinem smiled. "Lina says she would love that because she doesn't get enough sunlight here and there's too much cigarette smoke."

"Don't worry, sweetie, I'll take good care of you." When I finished petting her and withdrew my hand, Lina lifted her spines back up. "Good girl! Always protect yourself like this. That way, no nasty men can hurt you, like Fatih did to me... Oh God, forgive me for calling him nasty. But, dear God, you'd understand, he deserved it."

Just then, Derin walked into the room. She had chosen a purple, strappy, tight dress for the night. "How are you, girls? Enjoying yourselves?" As she came closer, I greeted her with a cheek kiss.

"Yes," Sinem said, taking a sip of her drink. "Your party is amazing, as always!" She picked up a wrapped gift from the couch, stood up, and handed it to Derin, exclaiming, "Happy birthday, darling!"

"Oh, you shouldn't have! Thank you." Derin took the gift from Sinem and unwrapped it. She held up the floral poplin blouse that came as gift and measured it against herself. "It's perfect. Thank you, dear friend." Derin planted a grateful kiss on Sinem's cheeks.

"You're welcome, Derin."

Derin then gave me a once-over, her eyes sparkling with mischief. "You know what, Ece," she said, "I was ready with a handful of teasing jokes, expecting you'd come to my party in a modest hijab. But you've surprised me by showing up like this, in this elegant dress, looking like a sultry mermaid. If I were a man, I'd-"

"Thank you, Derin," I cut her off, sensing that her compliment was veering into territory unfit for a general audience. Despite her sharp words, whenever I used my telepathic abilities to read her mind, I could tell she genuinely liked me. I had to admit, her slightly sunburned, peeling button nose had its own charm. However, the heavy floral and spicy perfume she was wearing today was overwhelming and unpleasant. "Here's my gift," I said, handing her a small package from my bag. "Happy birthday!"

Derin took the gift from my hand. "Thanks, Ece," she said, unwrapping it. She seemed pleased with the zircon-studded, pinwheel-design silver earrings inside. "Not a bad choice for someone with such poor taste as you," she jabbed as usual, her thumb caressing my cheek. "They'll do."

"I'm glad you like them. By the way, Derin..." I murmured, gesturing towards the cacti on the large coffee table. "Your cacti are lovely."

"Are they? My mother must have bought them. I actually hate cacti. I'm always afraid they'll prick me. If it were up to me, I'd toss them all out."

An urge to console Lina, my cactus, welled up inside me, but I restrained myself, not wanting Derin to think I was crazy.

"Could I take one? I really love the little one."

"I'd be happier if you took them all and rid me of them."

"Lina—uh, I mean, the purple one will do," I said.

"Fine. She's yours, Ece. Anyway, excuse me, girls. The house is quite crowded, and I need to greet my other guests."

"No problem," Sinem said.

"If you need anything, just give me a call. Bye!"

"Bye," I echoed as Derin left the room.

Sinem and I chatted for another five to ten minutes, then decided to get some fresh air in the garden. Naturally, I brought Lina along. When Sinem wanted to sit by the pool, I obliged, even though I had a deep aversion to large bodies of water. Not that I avoided bathing—cleanliness is from faith—but I meant pools and the like.

I had lost my parents in a tragic boating accident at sea. That fateful day, the coast guard had barely managed to save me from drowning. Since then, I'd harbored a phobia of the sea and pools, never learning to swim.

Derin's pool was quite splendid, about 30-40 square meters, with underwater lighting. The depth was clearly over my head. Water cascaded from swan-shaped fountains on either side, and the pool was encircled by vibrant red roses from a little beyond the loungers.

"I'm not a huge fan of pools," Sinem said, "but the magnificent red rose garden surrounding it... It's why I visit this spot every time I come to Derin's house."

"They are beautiful," I agreed. "But not as lovely as my Lina."

Sinem giggled. "I see you've grown fond of your new friend, Ece. You and Lina will probably sit around all day, cursing Fatih."

"That's the plan, indeed."

Sinem bent down to smell some of the roses, then walked towards the pool. I followed her. While I settled onto a lounger,

Sinem stood by the pool, enjoying the view. But the sound of a grating voice shattered the serene atmosphere:

"Sinem!" Alya, the witch, called out as she approached us. I despised this girl who had once tripped me in the school bathroom. "Why are you here at this party when you could be happily tending to your flowers at home?" Alya asked. She wore a white pleated skirt and a beige buttoned crop top, showing off her flat stomach. With her flawless features, she always reminded me of a Russian doll. Didn't she ever have a pimple or a mole? Unbelievable!

Sinem turned to look at Alya, who had just taunted her. Then, ignoring her, she resumed gazing at the pool.

Alya stepped closer to Sinem. "How's your stutter? Any improvement? Say 'swimming pool' for me, let's hear it."

Sinem sighed and began, "swim- swimming po-poo-poo-"

Hearing this, Alya burst into laughter. "Poo? You know where the bathroom is, Sinem, go take care of it!"

Alya and her typical cold jokes... This annoying girl never ceased to amaze me with her lack of progress in humor since our last encounter.

"Don't mock me!" Sinem snapped, clearly distressed.

"And what if I do?" Alya sneered. "Are you going to beat me up?" she mimicked Sinem's stutter. "If your punches are like your stuttering speech, I'd slap you three times before you even raised your hand, Sinem. Don't make me laugh!"

Seeing the situation escalate, I placed my cactus on the lounger and walked over to them. "Girls, please don't!" I intervened.

As I neared them, Alya suddenly turned her gaze to me. Her normally blue eyes had turned a menacing gray. A stormy, lightning-threatening gray, or perhaps the icy chill of an impending freeze...

"This is none of your business, Ece," Alya said.

Despite being unnerved by Alya's eerie eyes, I couldn't let her bully Sinem. "Leave her alone, Alya!" I insisted as I reached them.

"I said stay out of it!" Alya roared at me, making a sweeping motion with her hand. Suddenly, the marble beneath my feet became slippery. Somehow, the ground I was standing on had transformed into a sheet of ice. I found myself on a makeshift ice rink. Could this be Alya's special ability?

I didn't have much time to ponder. Losing my balance on the icy surface, I slid. And I ended up falling into the last place I wanted to be. Derin's pool...

CHAPTER 16

When I fell into the pool, Sinem and Alya were so engrossed in their fierce struggle, tangled in each other's hair, that they didn't even notice my distress. While they battled each other, I had already begun to thrash about in the water.

As I tried to call for help, I slipped under the water, swallowing a considerable amount. I couldn't swim, and the weight of my clothes and high heels only made it harder to stay afloat.

Through my frantic splashing, I caught a glimpse of someone sprinting towards me from the distant corners of the garden. It wasn't just running—it was a full-on charge, with such force that their shirt nearly tore off in the process—perhaps ripping off several buttons in the frenzy. It looked like Fatih. For a fleeting moment, I saw him dimly, and then I sank beneath the water again.

Minutes later...

I heard a girl crying...

"This wasn't supposed to happen! It's all my fault. Please, Fatih, save her!"

It was Sinem's voice.

Then I heard Fatih's voice. "You won't die! Not this time! I won't let you!"

Someone was applying force to my chest, with hands pressing down rhythmically. It felt as if they were about to break my ribs. The intense pressure on my chest made me wince in pain, and I let out a faint groan. Sensing the faint flicker of life returning, and hearing my weak cries, Fatih stopped performing CPR.

I coughed violently, having swallowed too much water. I was lying on my back on the grass, realizing that Fatih had saved me from drowning and then brought me back to life with chest compressions. I had joked with my aunt about giving Fatih a massage, but it turned out that fate had reversed our roles.

Fatih, his sky-blue eyes now damp, looked deeply into mine as he knelt beside me. "You scared us, Ece," he said, breathless. His trousers were soaked, and he was shirtless. His hair and entire body were wet. "Are you okay?" he murmured.

I coughed again. "I'm fine." As I tried to sit up from where I lay, Sinem helped me into a sitting position by taking my arm. Then she sat next to me, hugging me tightly. My tearful friend, Sinem, was still crying. "I'm fine, Sinem," I repeated, trying to calm her down.

"I'm so sorry, Ece," Sinem said sorrowfully. "You fell into the water because of me."

"It wasn't your fault." The real culprit was Alya, but I couldn't see her anywhere. Instead, a curious crowd had gathered around me. Most of them were Derin's friends, people I didn't know.

Fatih stood up and called out loudly to the group encircling us, "Can you all step back a bit? Give the girl some space to breathe!"

Upon hearing this, people slowly dispersed, leaving only Sinem and Fatih by my side. Derin, too, was standing a few meters away, covering her cheeks with her hands, looking at me with a sad expression.

I was shivering from the cold, my wet clothes making me tremble. Sinem continued to hold me, trying to warm me, but it wasn't very effective. Noticing my state, Fatih tried to drape his shirt, which he had just torn off earlier, over my shoulders.

Despite sitting there shivering on the grass, I rejected Fatih's offer, saying, "I don't want your shirt. Sinem is taking care of me. You can go back to your friends if you'd like. I wouldn't want to hold you back, Fatih."

A Turkish girl, even when freshly pulled from the clutches of death, must never compromise on her ability to give the cold shoulder to the boy she likes. It's our tradition, and we wear it proudly!

I didn't need Fatih. In fact, he needn't have rushed to my rescue when I fell into the water. I was just about to save myself. Almost there. Am I wrong?

"What happened?" Fatih asked with his usual obliviousness, completely unaware of how he had upset me this evening. "Are you angry with me, Ece?"

"I'm saying that after what happened in the school bathroom, I already owed you a shirt. If I take this one too, I'll owe you two. I'm telling you, don't give me more shirts," I said, my voice tinged with irritation. "Don't keep your friends waiting, Fatih. Why would you stay with me? Who am I, anyway?"

"Are you pushing me away, Ece?"

"Didn't you do the same?" I snapped.

As Fatih opened his mouth to defend himself, Sinem spoke up to diffuse the tension, "Fatih, Ece is going through an emotional moment right now. It would be better if you gave her some time and space, and talked later."

Fatih first looked at Sinem, then at me. He nodded as if to say "Okay," and said, "Alright, but before I go, I need to ask one question."

"The location of the pharmacy?" I said sarcastically. "Band-aids don't heal broken hearts. Don't bother."

"Ece, my question is this," Fatih said calmly, unfazed by my jab. "Did you fall by accident, or did Alya push you?"

I stared at Fatih, confused. "I fell, what does it matter?"

"It matters a lot, Ece. I need to know the answer, please."

I shrugged. "I think Alya did it. My feet suddenly felt like they were on ice. That must be her power."

Fatih closed his eyes calmly. A look of relief crossed his face. To understand what he was thinking, I closed my eyes and used my telepathic powers to peek into his mind: Yes, he was truly relieved, even pleased. He had been afraid that, like his previous girlfriends, I had been cursed and had fallen into the water due to bad luck. Because, as he believed, once curses started, they kept coming until the girl eventually died.

I was amazed that Fatih believed in the 'curse nonsense' that Kerem had told me about earlier today. The idea that Fatih's ex-girlfriends had all died one by one due to a chain of bad luck... It was utterly ridiculous! And even if such a thing existed and was real, I wasn't even dating Fatih, so why would this curse affect me?

"Well then, I'm leaving," Fatih said. "Sinem, please find Ece some dry clothes, okay?"

"I've got it covered," Sinem replied, standing up. She gazed at the blood-red roses around the pool. Raising her right hand confidently, she made a beckoning motion, and as if caught by a gust of wind, the petals of the roses in the garden detached from their stems and began to swirl in the air.

But the petals weren't just scattering randomly. Strangely enough, they all seemed to agree on where to go. Like a flock of migrating swallows, they formed clusters in the air.

"Ece, dear, can you stand up?" Sinem murmured, helping me to my feet as she took my arm. Then she directed Fatih to step back a few paces with her.

The rose petals were coming toward me. "Sinem?" I asked anxiously. "What's happening?"

"Trust me, Ece," she said, and I nodded.

Suddenly, the cloud of petals surrounded me. There were so many that I could see nothing else. My vision was completely obscured. For a while, they maintained a small distance, swirling around me. Right, left, up, down... It was as if they were dancing with me.

Then they began to move. The rose petals gently settled on my body, clinging to my clothes. I was mesmerized, watching them in awe. None of the petals touched my face or neck. They also avoided my arms and the area below my knees. But they covered the rest of me, layering themselves over and over until I was completely covered. Their flawless organization was astonishing.

I didn't know if it was because they absorbed the moisture from my water-soaked body or for some other reason, but the color of each red rose petal that touched me turned to black. A coal-black hue...

I was warm now. The rose petals, like a dress, were warming me.

Within seconds, the petals had enveloped me so completely that it was as if they had dressed me in a new gown over my soaked clothes. A gown of black roses. As Fatih had said in his poem about me today, I now truly resembled a black rose...

Remembering Fatih's beautiful poem softened my heart for a moment. The way he recited it to me, with that sincere expression and tender voice... The roses that covered me had also covered my anger towards him. At that moment, Fatih and I locked eyes.

"See, I told you, Ece," Fatih said, a hint of a smile forming on his lips. "You're a black rose, beautiful enough to make the darkest and deepest night envious... I'll be going now. See you later."

He turned and walked away slowly.

"The roses, like all plants, are my friends," Sinem explained as she watched me. She came closer. "These roses saw how you stood up for me during my argument with Alya. That's why they're shedding some of their petals to show their gratitude to you. They werc so upset by your near-drowning that they even turned black for you. I wish you could hear them as I do right now. Their cries and their thanks to you..."

"I must thank them," I whispered, my voice thick with emotion. "For clothing me. And in the most beautiful dress I've ever worn... They won't die, will they? These rose blossoms that have shed their petals."

"Don't worry, Ece," she reassured me gently. "What remains will be enough for them to live."

I was so moved that my eyes welled up with tears. Could a person really weep for flowers? I must be too tender-hearted

CHAPTER 17

No matter how much the rose petals tried to dry me off, it would be a stretch to say I was entirely dry when I was soaked down to my underwear. Thankfully, Derin, ever so thoughtful, offered to lend me some clothes.

We ascended to the second floor of the villa, entering her room. Derin's bedroom was so vast that, with a little effort, a family of four refugees could probably live there, managing as best they could. I dare say, if you included the walk-in closet at the far end, you could comfortably fit a family of eight or ten with plenty of room to spare. With the hundreds of garments in her closet to inspire them, perhaps one of the children might grow up to be a successful fashion designer, their life transformed.

As I casually surveyed the room, I heard a faint hissing sound. The sound of a snake, and it was coming from directly behind me.

"Derin?" I called out without turning around, my tone almost dismissive. "I've seen that snake transformation trick before, in the school bathroom. Don't waste your breath. You won't scare me a second time."

"Pardon?" Derin replied, coming closer and looking at me with puzzled eyes.

Wait a minute... Even with Derin by my side, the hissing hadn't stopped. It was still there, right behind me!

My eyes widened in terror. "De-Derin," I stammered, my voice betraying my fear. "If it's not you this time, then what's hissing behind me?"

"Tısssotti."

"Tısssotti?" I repeated, confused.

"Yes, my anaconda. I got him while I was on holiday in Italy."

"How delightful," I muttered sarcastically, frozen in place with fear. "Does he bite?"

"He doesn't bite."

"Well, that's a relief."

"He swallows, Ece. Whole. In one gulp, without a bite!"

"W-what!"

"Do you know what snakes love to eat most, Ece?"

"What?"

Derin placed a hand on my shoulder, leaning in close to my ear to whisper in a voice dripping with menace, "Spiders... Especially a big one like you. Simply irresistible."

The hissing grew louder, closer. Tısssotti was undoubtedly creeping up on me from behind.

"Look, I'm already scared enough as it is. Could you please not make this situation any more dramatic than it already is? And get Tısssotti away from me, pretty please?"

Derin gave a playful pinch to my cheek. "I don't know who else I'd tease if it weren't for you, Ece," she said with a grin. "Tısssotti! Back to your lair at once! How many times do I have to tell you not to snack on my guests!? Hmm?"

As Derin scolded Tısssotti, the hissing slowly faded away. It seemed the snake was obedient after all and slithered off. For the second time that day, I had narrowly escaped death... Perhaps I should have stayed home, peacefully praying eight to ten rak'ahs of Sunnah instead of attending this birthday party. Then none of this would have happened.

With Tısssotti's departure, Derin turned back to me, her voice light. "Now that's taken care of, where were we?"

"I was just about to recite the Shahada in fear," I replied, still trembling.

"That's not what I meant. I was going to lend you some clothes." Derin disappeared into her walk-in closet, emerging moments later with a selection of clothes and a pair of sneakers. "I don't have anything modest for you, my little spider. But I think these will fit you."

"Guests wear what they're given, not what they wish for. Thanks, Derin."

"You're welcome. Go ahead and change, Ece. I'm going to feed Tısssotti. He must be hungry if he was cozying up to you earlier."

"Alright. Just make sure to feed him well, so your guests can leave in one piece."

As soon as Derin left the room, I stripped off my damp clothes and donned the outfit she'd given me. Derin and I were of similar build, tall and slender, so the sleeveless, cropped, pale yellow top fit me perfectly. I paired it with the gray, elastic-waisted sports shorts she had chosen. After slipping into the sneakers, I was ready—though ready for what, I wasn't sure. With these skimpy clothes exposing me to the world, I was certainly ready for a multitude of wandering eyes. But it was just for one night. I could endure it.

Minutes later, Derin returned from feeding her snake. She eyed me with a playful grin. "Your butt looks amazing in those shorts," she commented. "I know you prefer dressing modestly, Ece, but isn't it a bit of a sin to hide all this beauty from the world?"

"Islam disagrees," I countered. "It's not appropriate to wear clothes that are short, see-through, or reveal your body shape."

"Short, see-through, and revealing? You just described my entire wardrobe, spider." Derin gestured to her own body-hugging, lilac dress. "I guess that means I'm destined for hell," she said with a laugh.

"Don't look at it that way. God rewards good deeds tenfold, while bad deeds are only counted as one sin. For example, by sharing your clothes with me in my time of need, you've earned ten times the reward. God wants the faithful to enter heaven, so He makes it easier for us. Ten to one, a great deal."

"Sounds good... But anyway, Ece," Derin said, shifting the topic, "I heard you and Fatih have been getting close."

"Where did you hear that?"

"The birds told me."

"Was the bird's name Kerem?" I asked, narrowing my eyes.

"Yes."

"Oh, that bird!" I grumbled. "Anyway... It's true that Fatih and I have been talking, but there's nothing between us."

"Probably for the best," Derin said, as she took a seat on the loveseat in front of the television, smoothing out her dress.

"Why do you say that?" I asked, sitting down beside her.

"Fatih hasn't been the same since his car accident. It's like he's stuck in the past. He's become really depressed. Especially around this time of year, in December, he completely withdraws."

"You've mentioned December before, Derin. What's so special about December?"

"December brings snow, cold winds... and makes spiders shiver, doesn't it, my little spider?" Derin teased with a mocking grin.

"Stop teasing and just tell me already! You're killing me with suspense!"

Derin pulled out her phone, scrolling through her photos. When she found the one she was looking for, she showed it to me.

The photo was of Fatih. He was lying in a hospital bed, looking utterly broken. His arm was hooked up to an IV, his face was bruised, and his leg was bandaged.

"This was Fatih after the car accident in December," Derin explained, swiping to another photo. This time, it was a picture of a girl. "And this... this is his late girlfriend. Eda."

"I've seen her before. Fatih was drawing her picture in class," I murmured.

Derin nodded. "Fatih and Eda were driving on the highway. Eda was behind the wheel. According to Fatih, the car suddenly veered to the right on its own. It crashed into the guardrail, broke through, and they plummeted down from quite a height. The car rolled over multiple times. Eda died on the spot. She took her last breath in less than a minute, right before Fatih's eyes. He survived, as you saw in that photo, but he was gravely injured. Since then, maybe from grief, he hasn't been able to use his special ability."

"How tragic," I whispered, my heart aching for the horror Derin had just recounted.

Then, Derin, who was sitting beside me, exclaimed, "Ece?" in a voice filled with astonishment. She pointed to my shirt. "What's going on here?"

"What?" I asked, confused. I looked down at my shirt, and to my shock, I saw it darkening before my eyes. The pale yellow was slowly turning black, until, within seconds, it was pitch black. Even my shorts had taken on a charcoal hue. "I have no idea how this is happening."

"So, this isn't your special ability?"

"No, it's not. I only have telepathy."

"Telepathy, huh... Well then, what am I thinking right now, spider brain?"

"I can answer that without using telepathy, Derin." I laughed. "You're looking at me with such an intense, almost hungry gaze that I don't need to be a mind reader to figure it out."

"You're assuming too much."

"Am I wrong?" I asked, surprised that I had misjudged her. "What were you thinking then?"

"Pill bugs in nature." Derin shrugged.

"Seriously?"

"Yeah."

"Oh, you got me good, Derin."

"Never trust anyone, Ece, especially not men."

Wise words, considering Derin's boyfriend had been hitting on me earlier tonight, and Fatih had been sending me romantic signals but had dismissed me from his side despite that.

Derin continued, "Let's talk about that little color-changing trick of yours. I found it quite fascinating, my little spider."

"I did too, Derin, but by the way, how much longer are you going to keep calling me a spider? It's starting to hurt my feelings."

"Hurt your feelings?" Derin raised an eyebrow, a sly grin playing on her lips. "Have you forgotten, Ece? I am a serpent. And serpents, well, they have a particular fondness for spiders. You could almost take it as a compliment."

"Is that so?"

"Of course not!" she laughed, her eyes glinting with mischief. "I just enjoy teasing you, my dear. You're so easy to rile up."

I rolled my eyes in exasperation.

"Now, where were we, my little spider? Ah yes, let's delve deeper into your fascinating ability to change colors..."

CHAPTER 18

"Now, here's what we're going to do," Derin began to explain, rising from the couch to stand before me. "Take off your shirt, Ece. Let's try another one and see if you can turn its color to black as well. I believe you can."

Sitting comfortably on the couch, I replied, "I wouldn't be surprised if it works as you say. After all, I turned the red rose petals that fell on me by the pool black today. So let's try, as you suggest."

Derin, standing directly in front of me, made a gesture with her hand, indicating I should hand over my shirt. "Turn around, girl!" I warned her.

"Turn around, girl," Derin mimicked me with mockery. "Ece, you're such a prude! It's just us girls here. Don't exaggerate, just take off your top already. We're conducting an experiment, for heaven's sake!"

Instead of bothering with turning her around, I figured it would be easier to just turn my own back to her. So I stood up, turned away, and began lifting my shirt from the hem, pulling it up and over my head. As I freed it from my neck, I extended the shirt behind me toward Derin, while using my other arm to cover my chest. Since I had removed my wet bra earlier, I was now bare-chested.

Derin took the shirt from me. "Let's take off your shorts too, and then I'll bring you some fresh clothes."

"But I'm not wearing any underwear!"

"Relax, girl, we're not going to eat you."

My cheeks flushed with embarrassment as I used a decorative pillow to cover my body, slipping out of my shorts and handing them to her. I sat back down, trying to cover my private areas with the pillow and my hands.

Derin called out toward the door, "Tisssotti, dinner is served! A plain Ece fillet, no spices. I've stripped her bare for you. Come and feast before she gets cold!"

"Derin! Stop making fun of me and give me some clothes!"

Laughing, Derin sashayed toward the wardrobe room. She returned with a white, asymmetrical, knee-length dress and clean underwear.

I took the dress and underwear from her. As I turned away to dress, I felt a sharp pinch on my shoulder. It was like a bite. This girl had actually bitten me!

"Derin!" I shrieked, "why did you bite my shoulder? Can you please behave?"

"Old habits die hard. Once a snake, always a snake. When nature calls, sometimes I just feel like biting."

Her explanation, bizarre as it was, made some sense to me.

Yet I was dressing under immense psychological pressure. Tisssotti, my nudity, the nibbling on my shoulder... Stress always upset my stomach. I just hoped this time it wouldn't.

When I was finally dressed in the outfit Derin had given me, we began to wait. We waited and waited... But the dress remained white. "It's still as white as if it's been washed with a decent laundry detergent," I murmured. "We must be doing something wrong."

"Or missing something... Ece, do you know what was common when you turned the roses by the pool black and when you turned your clothes black in my room?"

"What was it?"

"Fatih," Derin explained. "The missing element in the equation is Fatih. If we bring him into the mix, I'm sure that dress, which looks like it's been freshly washed, will turn pitch black, just like in the detergent commercials."

Derin pulled out her phone and began showing me pictures of Fatih from her album. Seeing his photos reminded me of how he left tonight, and my anger flared up again.

"It's working," Derin said, pointing to my dress, which had begun to turn black. "You react to Fatih like a bull seeing a red cape, my dear Spider-Girl."

"This is such a strange situation. I don't understand why I'm like this. Anyway, I've kept you long enough, Derin. You should tend to your guests. I'll go back to Sinem."

"Alright," Derin said.

"Thank you for the white dress. Or should I say, the black dress now?"

"You're welcome."

I left the room, descending the stairs in my newly blackened dress. My eyes scanned the crowd for Sinem. Thinking she might be in the room we first sat in when we arrived at the villa, I headed in that direction. Passing by a naughty couple kissing along the wall, I entered the room. But Sinem wasn't there. Instead, I found someone I wasn't looking for. Fatih...

Fatih was sitting on a long couch in front of the television, but his eyes weren't on the screen. He sat with his elbows on his knees, his head bowed, brooding alone like a sorrowful owl.

As Derin had said, he must be suffering from his December woes. At least, I thought, it's better to suffer from heartache for a month than to endure period pains every month. Or perhaps I was wrong. Maybe I shouldn't speak without knowing the extent of his pain.

And I could learn the extent of his pain—after all, what was the point of my telepathy if I didn't use it? My ability wasn't as flashy as shape-shifting, controlling plants, or turning into a cobra, like my friends, but it had its uses. And now was one of those times. Standing in the doorway, I closed my eyes and opened the door to Fatih's gloomy mind.

Blood, fire, and pain...These were the first sensations that greeted me as I began to read Fatih's thoughts.A car overturned, lying on its roof. The rear of the vehicle was ablaze.I could smell the burning in my nostrils, as if I were there.

Inside the overturned, crumpled car, a girl was trapped in the front seat. This fair-haired, beautiful girl was breathing rapidly. Something had pierced her chest—a metal rod that had broken off during the crash...She pressed a trembling hand to the wound on her chest, but the blood wouldn't stop. It didn't look like it would stop. It flowed in torrents.

Fatih was in the seat next to her. Though his arm had been broken in the crash, he tried to cover the wound with his other hand. But it was no use.Both Fatih and Eda knew it.Eda was breathing her last breaths.

Fatih was helpless. What could one do, what could one say, knowing their beloved, the love of their life, was going to die within seconds?The last tears that streamed down Eda's cheeks would stay with Fatih for the rest of his life. This was his curse. Eda's curse was taking her life, but Fatih's would rob him of the light in his soul. Forever...

Eda withdrew her hand from her wound and took Fatih's hand. "I love you," she whispered with trembling lips. "Don't forget me, Fatih."

"I love you," Fatih responded, struggling to speak through the knot in his throat. "Nothing can separate us. Not closed eyes, not the setting sun, nothing... You're going to be okay, baby. No one can hurt you anymore. When the sun rises, you and I, together, safe. When the music stops, just hold onto my words."

Eda, now too weak from blood loss, managed a faint smile. She closed her eyes for the last time... Finally freed from the curse that had haunted her for weeks, she found the peace she had been searching for, even if it was in death. She left, sealing Fatih's heart with deep sorrow.

I ended my journey through Fatih's mind and returned to reality. A tear slipped down my cheek. I wiped it away with the back of my hand. I was deeply moved.

I walked to the couch and sat down beside Fatih. Without hesitation, I wrapped my arms around him and rested my head on his shoulder.

"Thank you, Fatih."

"For what?"

"For saving my life."

"You scolded me when I saved your life, and now you're thanking me," Fatih said, placing his hand on my knee. "I believe they might one day solve the mystery of the pyramids, but the mystery of girls? Never."

"Spare me the sarcasm, Fatih," I said with a hint of irony in my voice. "Or do you want me to change my mind and scold you again?" I pulled away from him, sitting up straight beside him on the couch.

"Alright, I take it back, Eda."

"Good for you."

He had just called me Eda. He had confused me with his late girlfriend. But I hadn't corrected him. There were so many things I couldn't fix between us. His mistaking my name was probably the least of them.

I couldn't stop thinking about the car accident Fatih had experienced. When I had read his thoughts, I had lived through that moment as if it were my own, deeply shaken by it. My eyes were still misty from the experience.

Fatih lifted his hand from my knee and gently brought it to my face. He wiped away the tear with the edge of his index finger.

"What is it, black rose? Why is there dew on your delicate petal?"

I shrugged. "Well..." Of course, I couldn't tell him the real reason for my tears. I doubted he would appreciate a girl who secretly delved into his thoughts and wept over them. I could have concocted a lie to deflect Fatih's question, but lying is a grave sin, after all. "Life," I muttered, "is full of tragedies and painfully brief. Contemplation only deepens the sorrow. Sometimes, one must seize the moment."

For instance, you could stop brooding over Eda, and perhaps you and I could venture into that moment together? Wouldn't that be delightful? I couldn't help but entertain the thought.

My musings on living in the moment must not have sat well with Fatih, as he promptly shifted the conversation elsewhere: "Living in the moment? Is there someone you fancy in class, Ece?"

Oh, patience! God, grant me patience. A lot of it.

Here I was, all dolled up for him, having adorned myself with more makeup, blowouts, and polish than ever before in my life, wearing a dress that would surely catch his eye, walking hand in hand with him to the party, throwing a dozen lover's tantrums his way, even wrapping my arms around him and resting my head on his shoulder... And now he asks if there's someone I like? Either he was blind, or he chose not to see.

"Hmm..." I murmured. "You first, then I'll tell. Is there a girl you fancy?"

His icy blue eyes, locked onto mine, roamed across my face. They lingered on my lips for a fleeting second before returning to my gaze.

You, of course, Ece...

He didn't utter these words, but as I slyly tapped into his thoughts, I heard them loud and clear. Would it kill him to be honest and say it out loud?

"I'll grab a drink," he said instead of replying.

Drink hemlock, neat and without ice, I might have said, but I let it go...

"All right."

"Would you like anything, Ece?"

Truth and courage...

"No, thank you."

Fatih rose from beside me and left the room. I sat back, listening to the romantic melody that began to play. It was perfect for a slow dance, though of course, Fatih the brute wouldn't ask me for one...

Shortly after, someone else approached the couch where I was seated. The boy had long, reddish hair that he had slicked back, as if a llama had licked it, and a freckled face that I recognized. It was Sinan, the boy I had sat next to on my first day at school. That was before I'd read his mind and discovered his peculiar thoughts about my feet, which led me to move away and sit next to Fatih when Derin teased me from behind.

Now, here was that very Sinan, standing in front of me with one hand tucked into the pocket of his navy jeans, asking, "Would you like to dance, Ece?"

After a brief hesitation, I replied, "Sure." If Fatih intended to continue this game of concealing his feelings, perhaps dancing with Sinan might spark some jealousy in him and break his resolve. At least, that was my hope. Let's see...

CHAPTER 19

When Sinan extended his hand to me, I grasped it and pulled myself up. Yet, the sensation of holding his hand was far from pleasant. I knew that Fatih and I were not officially a couple, but it felt as though a chamber of my heart accused me of betraying him. As the rest of my heart argued that I was doing it for Fatih's sake, the judge delivered his verdict: I was sentenced to dance with Sinan for five minutes.

We walked hand in hand, weaving past the couple engaged in conversation, until we reached a secluded, dimly lit corner of the room.

"I love this song," Sinan remarked as his hand slipped around my waist. I rested my hands on his shoulders, and together we began to sway in harmony to the romantic tune filling the shadowed room.

"I'm not familiar with it."

"It's an old song by Michael Bolton. You look stunning tonight."

"Is that the name of the song?" I asked playfully.

"No, Ece, I'm talking about you. You are stunning."

"That's relative, I think."

If that weren't the case, Mr. Fatih wouldn't have brushed me off so easily...

As fate would have it, the subject of my thoughts appeared just then, entering the room with a full glass of drink in hand. Fatih's eyes found us without difficulty, and for a few seconds, he stood there, watching as Sinan and I danced.

When Fatih returned to his seat in front of the television, he sank into it, deep in his brooding thoughts once more. It seemed that my plan to make him jealous had not worked. At least, not yet.

In that moment, I felt Sinan's hands subtly slide down from my waist. His mischievous fingers now rested on my hips, gripping them as our dance continued.

I couldn't let him keep holding me like that. I had to warn him sternly:

"You're touching something forbidden, Sinan."

"What?"

"My forbidden zone."

"Your zone?"

"That is forbidden."

"What is forbidden?"

"The- Oh come on! My bottom, Sinan! You shouldn't be touching it."

"So where should I touch, Ece?"

"Must you touch me somewhere?"

"That's how this dance is."

As I engaged in this futile argument with Sinan, I noticed Fatih downing his drink in one go and rising from his seat. He was heading in our direction, his stormy blue eyes locking onto mine. As he drew near, I took Sinan's hands from my hips and guided them back up to my waist.

"This party is getting boring, Ece," Fatih said, his face an unreadable mask. "Shall we leave?"

Was he truly bored of the party, or was it because Sinan's hands had been squeezing my hips?

"Now?" I asked, feigning reluctance.

"Yes."

Sinan interjected, "But we were dancing..."

Fatih turned to Sinan, casting him a withering look before his gaze returned to me.

"Are you coming, Ece?" Fatih repeated, his tone firm and slightly insistent.

"Yes, I'm coming," I said.

Don't be mad, my fierce husband...

The master of the house always has the final say...

Leaving the party was a relief for me as well, since returning home early meant I could perform the evening prayer without missing it.

After saying our goodbyes to Sinem and Derin, we left the villa and got into Fatih's SUV. We hit the road, making small talk about various trivial matters along the way.

"Besides that, I also enjoy learning languages," I chattered on from the seat beside Fatih. "I have this app called Duolingo on my phone. It provides step-by-step language lessons in whatever language you want. It's quite fun, too. The scoring and league system adds excitement to it, making it a competition with other users. The more language practice you do, the more points you earn."

"I use it too," Fatih said as he drove. "Lately, I've been focused on German in Duolingo."

"Oh, that's great! I've been learning Arabic on Duolingo recently. I'm ashamed to admit that I don't know how to read the

Quran, and I'm hoping to learn Arabic through this app. But one downside of Duolingo is that you only get five chances to answer questions incorrectly. If you lose five hearts, you either have to wait for hours for them to refill or enter a practice session to earn more hearts. It slows me down a bit."

"I've got a subscription, Ece. So I have unlimited hearts. If you want, I can give you my login, and you won't have to worry about losing hearts."

"That would be wonderful!"

As our journey continued, I decided to broach a more serious subject. "The girl whose picture you drew in class—was she someone important to you?" I asked.

Fatih was silent for a moment, his eyes fixed on the road. "Eda," he finally said. "She was my girlfriend. I lost her three years ago."

"I've heard strange rumors about her death from some people in class. And about your previous girlfriend's death as well..."

"I wish they were only strange rumors," Fatih sighed. "But as someone who lived through those nightmare days with my girlfriends, I can tell you that neither of their deaths was natural. It was as if they were under some sort of curse or spell. For days, they were plagued by a series of accidents and misfortunes, one after another, until they finally took their last breaths."

"Do you believe there's someone behind their deaths?"

Fatih nodded, his expression solemn. "I would give anything to find out who's responsible."

"Perhaps if you have another girlfriend, the culprit might reveal themselves once more, and this time, you could catch them."

Fatih shook his head slowly. "There won't be a next time. I won't get close to another girl just to put her life at risk."

"But what if the girl is fully aware of the danger and still willingly accepts the risk?"

Fatih remained silent, his gaze fixed on the road ahead. When we stopped at a red light, he finally turned to me. "No girl would take that risk."

"Let's imagine she would." I shrugged.

"Then she must have a death wish."

"Or perhaps she simply knows what she wants," I countered.

"I'd say she's suicidal."

"Brave is another word for it."

"She'd be a fool, throwing her life away like that," Fatih murmured.

"That would be her problem, wouldn't it?"

As the light turned green, our verbal sparring came to an end, and Fatih pressed the accelerator, guiding the vehicle forward. We drove in silence for a few minutes, the quiet settling between us like an unspoken truce.

Yet, something seemed amiss as Fatih began to slow down. The road was clear, and there were no lights ahead. We were still far from my home, so his actions puzzled me.

Fatih gently pulled over to the side of the road and brought the car to a stop. He unfastened his seatbelt and leaned back, reaching into the space behind our seats to retrieve a long, slim black case from the back seat. Settling back into his seat, he opened the case, producing a pencil and a blank sheet of A4 paper.

"Could you turn a little more towards me, Ece?" he asked.

"Alright." I shifted my position, facing him more directly.

Fatih began to sketch something on the paper he had placed on his lap, his movements precise and deliberate. A moment passed before I realized what he was doing. "Are you drawing me?" I asked, a hint of surprise in my voice.

"Unless you have any objections, Miss."

"No objections here, Sir," I replied, matching his playful tone.

Realizing he was sketching me, I instinctively licked my lips, adding a subtle shine to them. I crossed one leg over the other and turned slightly to the side, striking a pose. If he was going to draw me, I might as well look my best. I ran my fingers through my hair, giving it a quick adjustment. "You must enjoy drawing."

"I do. But I prefer to draw not with a pencil, but with the heart... Drawing and swimming. My two passions. Oh, and let's not forget stuffed eggplant and rice," he added with a sly grin.

I laughed at his last comment. "That's one of my favorites too. Plenty of oil, with green peppers on the side, and if there's yogurt to go with it..."

"Watch out, or you'll ruin your pose if your mouth starts watering. By the way, let's adjust your posture like this..." As he spoke, Fatih reached out to gently reposition me, guiding my hands forward. He placed them delicately on my knee, arranging my pose to his liking.

I momentarily lowered my hand to tug at the hem of my dress, making sure it was properly in place before resting my hand back on my knee.

Fatih glanced at me now and then as he continued to draw, his gaze intense, as if his eyes were brushing against my skin. I could almost feel the touch of his blue eyes on me, so concentrated and meticulous was he in his work. He looked so incredibly captivating in that moment—the strands of hair falling into his eyes, the sharp features of his face highlighted by the moonlight, and the way he wielded the pencil as though it were an extension of himself.

At one point, he adjusted the strap of my dress slightly, giving the fabric the precise fall he desired. Then, without pause, he resumed his sketching. For nearly a minute, he did not stop.

When he finally paused again, Fatih leaned closer to me, his hand moving to brush my hair. He gently tucked a stray strand behind my ear, his fingers tracing the line of my cheek down to my chin, which he tilted ever so slightly, altering the angle of my face.

His touch sent a shiver of excitement through me. His four fingers rested lightly on my cheek, while his thumb softly pressed down on my lower lip, parting my lips just a little. His eyes were locked on my mouth, and I wondered if my heart would stop beating from the tension of the moment—if it didn't, I could say it was a heart made of steel.

His thumb then brushed along my upper lip, trailing to the side, leaving a tingling warmth in its wake. My eyes involuntarily drifted to his lips, which seemed dangerously close... His finger touched my lips one last time, delivering a final blow to my self-control. Was he going to kiss me? The fluttering sensation in my stomach was unlike anything I had felt before.

Just as I wondered how much longer I could endure this tension, a voice broke through the charged air from outside Fatih's open window:

"Brother, we're so hungry. For the love of God, spare us some charity!"

Two young beggar boys, dressed in worn-out clothes, stood by the car. Though their faces were dirty, the light in their eyes shone brightly, making them seem almost angelic in their innocence. One looked about five or six years old, while the other seemed around nine or ten.

Feeling as if we had been caught in a guilty act, I straightened in my seat, lowering my gaze and uncrossing my legs.

Fatih leaned out the window toward the boys, resting his arm on the window sill. "I have a better idea, kids. How about I treat you to a meal? The four of us can go eat together. What do you say?" He ruffled one of the boys' hair playfully.

Both boys beamed, their lips curling up into smiles. "Sure!" they said in unison, and the boy with a missing front tooth added, "You're the best, big brother!" in a slightly lisping, endearing voice.

"What do you think, Ece?" Fatih asked, turning to me.

"I think that's a great idea," I replied with a smile.

His response had impressed me deeply. Most men, in the midst of a romantic moment, would likely have chased away two beggars with harsh words—or at best, tossed a few coins and sent them on their way. But Fatih had responded with genuine compassion to their plea for food. I prayed that God would reward his generosity, showering him with blessings in both this world and the next.

I stepped out of the car. Fatih led us to a nearby restaurant. As the four of us crossed the street, Fatih took my hand in his. For a brief moment, it felt as though we were a family with two children. It was a heartwarming feeling...

Chapter 20

Wе had ventured to the small kebab shop across the road, a modest establishment devoid of any flair or pretense. It wasn't the kind of place one would choose for its ambiance, but at such a late hour, options were scarce. The interior was deserted, leaving us free to select our seats, and we chose a table by the window. I sat next to Fatih, with the children seated opposite us. After placing our orders, I found myself gazing out the window, lost in the sight of the deserted street and the moon, half-hidden behind a veil of clouds.

Fatih broke the silence, turning to the children with a warm smile. "What are your names, kids?"

The younger of the two, a curly-haired boy of about six with a missing front tooth, spoke up first. "I'm Hasan," he said, perched on his chair with an air of pride. "And my brother is Mert."

Mert, who seemed to be around ten, gave a nod of confirmation. His chin bore a deep, old scar, a harsh reminder that life on the streets must have been tough for children so young.

"And I'm Ece," I added with a playful grin, before gesturing to Fatih. "And this here is the younger version of Keanu Reeves."

Fatih, with his piercing gaze, sharp features, and chiseled jaw, did indeed bear a striking resemblance to the famous actor—if Keanu had blue eyes and slightly shorter hair.

Fatih turned to me with a smile, a glint of amusement in his eyes. "You know, Ece, you're not the first to say that."

"Who else thought you looked like Keanu Reeves?" I inquired, curious.

"Alya," he responded, with a nonchalance that belied the significance of the name.

I made a mental note: Keep the Ice Queen Alya away from Fatih!

And yes, it was true—I had a tendency to get jealous over the most ridiculous things.

Fatih turned back to the children, his tone softening. "By the way, my real name is Fatih. It's a pleasure to meet you, kids."

"The pleasure's ours, Fatih Abi," piped up little Hasan, before directing his innocent gaze at me. "But who's this Keanu Reeves, Abla?"

"He's a foreign actor," I explained. "He was in The Matrix and some other movies."

Soon, our kebabs arrived, accompanied by a selection of appetizers, and we began to eat. Judging by his pace, Mert was likely to finish his two Adana kebabs long before I could even get through one. During a brief pause to catch his breath, Mert suddenly asked, "So, how long have you two been dating, Ece Abla?"

I bit my lower lip in embarrassment. "Well, um, we're not dating."

At least, I didn't think so...

Mert wasn't deterred. "Okay, so how long have you been married?"

My eyes widened in shock. "We're not married either!"

"Oh, Fatih Abi!" Mert whispered conspiratorially. "Are you cheating on your wife with Ece Abla? Shame on you!"

Fatih chuckled, shaking his head. "I don't have a wife, so naturally, I'm not cheating on anyone. What kind of questions are these, my boy?"

Mert, with a puzzled expression, glanced from Fatih to me and back again. "So, you're not married, you're not dating, and you're not having an affair... Then what are you? Don't tell me you're just friends—I can see from the way you look at each other that you're more than that."

We were defeated, speechless...

The boy was right.

As if to prove a point, Fatih placed his hand gently on my knee, where my short dress left my skin exposed. Our eyes met, and I saw in his gaze an unspoken acknowledgment of Mert's observation. His thumb softly caressed my skin, sending a wave of warmth through me, a silent confirmation of the truth in Mert's words.

Though I relished his touch, I knew it was inappropriate, so I gently reminded him with a glance. But before I could say anything, Fatih removed his hand, sparing me the need for words.

Turning to Mert, who had proven himself far too nosy for his own good, I teased, "A man who speaks little and eats much is to be treasured. Now eat up, Mert, come on." Then, as if to further drive home the point, I took Fatih's kebab from his plate and held it up to his mouth. "You too, Fatih. Eat."

He took a large bite from the kebab.

A little sustenance for my future husband...

Mert, not missing a beat, asked, "Well, if you two aren't dating, Ece Abla, will you go out to dinner with me tomorrow? I could tell my friends I have a girlfriend."

I chuckled. "I'd love to, Mert, but it's better to be honest with your friends. Besides, I have homework to do tomorrow."

"Ah, you owe me one, Ece Abla!"

At that moment, Fatih stood up from the table. "I need to use the restroom."

As he walked away toward the back of the restaurant, where the restrooms were located, I continued chatting with the kids, occasionally glancing out the window at the empty street. The road stretched wide in front of us, and on the other side, where Fatih had parked his SUV, there were no buildings, only a stretch of trees and bushes extending into the distance. The restaurant we were in was the only structure in this open space. The street was eerily quiet, with only the occasional car passing by, and the sidewalks were devoid of any sign of life, save for a solitary black cat perched atop a garbage can, peering inside.

I was waiting for Fatih to return when, after several minutes, something outside caught my eye—a strange man, standing about 15 to 20 meters away, across the road, near a tree, watching us intently. He was tall and broad-shouldered, clad in a long black trench coat that reached past his knees. His face was obscured by a balaclava, heightening the air of menace that hung about him.

A sense of unease crept over me as I scrutinized the man's suspicious demeanor. My curiosity piqued, I decided to delve into his mind. What I discovered there left me stunned:

It was him...

The one who loomed over Fatih like a dark cloud, the source of curses that ended in death.

I could hardly believe he was real, standing right before me.

All he wanted was for Fatih to suffer.

As I probed deeper into his thoughts, I could almost taste his hatred for Fatih, it was so palpable.

He bore no grudge against me, but if need be, he wouldn't hesitate to trample me underfoot.

He was ready to crush anything that stood in his way.

And I was ready to stand in his path.

Bring it on! I'm a Turkish girl, with the spirit of Çanakkale—I'll take on bullets if I must...

Turning my head towards the far end of the restaurant where the restroom was located, I called out to Fatih, "Fatih! Hurry, come here!"

I needed to show him the man in the balaclava—perhaps he would know who it was.

But when I turned back to the window, the man had vanished. I rushed outside and looked around. There was no one in sight. When I returned to the table, Fatih had come out of the restroom and approached me.

"Is something wrong, Ece?"

If I told him about the man now, Fatih would worry that something might happen to me. He would distance himself to protect me from being cursed, and our already fragile romantic relationship would come to an abrupt end. Perhaps it was best to keep silent, at least for now.

"Well... I'm about to miss the evening prayer. If we leave now, I might just make it."

"Sure. I've finished my meal anyway."

We resumed our seats at the table, and when Hasan finished his kebab, we were ready to leave. Fatih paid the bill. After exchanging goodbyes with the children and receiving their heartfelt thanks, we stepped out of the restaurant. I scanned the surroundings for the masked man but saw no sign of him.

As we walked to the car, Fatih took my hand again. Did this gesture mean something special? Were we dating, or were we not? I still couldn't figure it out. Having never dated anyone before, I was inexperienced in these matters.

We drove off in the SUV, and after a short ride, we arrived in front of my apartment building. When Fatih insisted on accompanying me until I was safely inside, we took the elevator together to the fourth floor. I rang the bell, and my aunt quickly answered the door.

"Well, look who's here... How was your evening, kids?"

"It was nice, Esma Yenge. Thank you for letting me go out with Ece."

"Oh, don't mention it, my dear!"

"See you on Monday, Fatih," I said, bidding him farewell.

When I saw Fatih lean towards me, I prepared to give him a kiss on the cheek. But my expectations were quickly dashed. Fatih slipped his arm around my waist, closing the gap between us, and before I knew it, his lips were on mine.

Not even the fiercest beat of Derin's mythical serpent could quicken my heart as Fatih's kiss had done. The brief exchange of our lips left me utterly shattered, a mere shell of the person I had been moments before. My legs trembled, barely capable of sustaining my weight, as our gazes locked, his eyes unwavering, his demeanor as unyielding as forged steel.

In contrast to my disheveled state, Fatih stood resolute, an embodiment of poise. "Farewell, my dark rose," he uttered, before turning away to disappear into the waiting elevator.

I raised my hand to bid him goodbye, only to find it frozen mid-air, suspended in the aftermath of his departure.

"Ece."

"Ece?"

"Ece, child, to whom am I speaking!?"

"Huh? Yes, Aunt Esma?" Fatih's kiss had thoroughly unraveled what remained of my senses, leaving me barely able to register her voice.

"Are you coming inside, dear? You've been standing there at the door."

"Yes, yes, I'm coming."

I could only surmise that Fatih's reason for kissing me was to maintain the pretense of our relationship before Aunt Esma, to imply that we were more than we seemed. While it may have been merely a ruse for her benefit, it undeniably affected me. And though there was a small chance that he had kissed me out of genuine desire, I clung to that possibility, savoring it deeply.

CHAPTER 21

U pon entering the house, I took my dear little cactus, Lina, adorned with red flowers, to my room and gently placed her by the window.

"Welcome to your new home, my dear," I whispered to the plant with a mother's tenderness. "Don't worry, there's no cigarette smoke here like at Derin's place. Not many people come to my room anyway. Fatih visited recently, that's all. I've already convinced him to quit smoking, so even if he does come again, he won't bother you with any smoke. But if Fatih does come, turn your back and don't look, alright Lina?"

I didn't want my little Lina's innocence to be tainted. After all, Fatih, a son of the Black Sea, was unpredictable, capable of suddenly kissing me without warning. Must be that Laz gene, warm-blooded people, generally speaking.

I cleansed my makeup at the sink and swiftly performed ablution. Donning my one-piece, fuchsia prayer dress that hung behind the door, I offered my evening prayer. Thankfully, I managed just in time, with five minutes left before the night prayer. Once the time arrived, I performed the night prayer too. Returning to my room, I shed my clothes. The thong I was wearing was uncomfortable, so I replaced it with my usual cotton underwear.

With the last bit of energy left from an exhausting day, I collapsed onto the bed in my undergarments.

Dıtdırı dıtdırı dıtdırı!

Who was this impertinent caller interrupting my sleep?

Still half-asleep, I reached for my phone on the nightstand, picked it up without checking the caller's identity, and brought it to my ear.

"Hmm?" I mumbled groggily, still half asleep.

"Ece," Fatih's voice came through. "Were you sleeping?"

"I was sleeeeping, my baby," I murmured.

"What was that, Ece?"

Damn! Had I just called him "my baby" in my sleep-induced stupor?

Panic-stricken, I shot up in bed. "I said... I said... I was sleeping... sleeping like a baby! Yeah that's what I said! I was sleeping like a baby. Then woke up and answered the phone!"

Saved myself at the last second!

Ugh! By the time that infamous black-coated madman comes around, this boy would have already killed me from a heart atta ck...

"Sorry I woke you up, Ece."

"It's okay," I said, glancing at my phone's clock. It was a little past midnight. "What are you up to, Fatih?"

"Just lying in bed. Thought I'd give you a call, Ece."

"I was lying down too."

"Hmm... It's a bit chilly. If you sleep in just your underwear like last night, you'll catch a cold."

"Don't worry about me, I'm not cold, Fatih."

"Are you wearing a nightgown, then?"

"No."

"Pajamas?"

"No."

"So, what are you wearing?"

I did not want to say the truth, which was: "I'm in pink, lacy underwear that's barely there"... Instead i replied: "None of your business, Fatih!"

Ah, how romantic I am!

Well, if the gentleman insisted on calling me his rose, he'd have to deal with the thorns as well.

"Let me guess what you're wearing, then," said Fatih.

"You won't give up until you find out, will you?" I sighed. "Go on then, make your guess."

"My guess is you're in your usual classic underwear like last night."

"Fine, you got it." I rolled my eyes. "There's a hint of reproach in your voice, Fatih. What, is it a crime to sleep in underwear?"

"No, I think it's sexy."

"Is that so..." Suddenly, I felt my cheeks burn. Unless my aunt had cranked up the thermostat, it must have been from embarrassment. Sitting with my back against the headboard, I fanned myself with my hand. "It's comfortable to sleep in underwear."

"Is it white?" Fatih asked.

"Well... pink."

"Are you still lying down, or have you sat up?"

"Fatih, did you eat some aphrodisiac or something? What's with these questions?"

When Fatih asked such things in that husky, deep, masculine tone, it inevitably stirred something inside me. I didn't want to lose sleep over this in the middle of the night.

"If you answer that last question, I promise not to ask any more."

"Alright, if you insist..." I murmured. "I'm sitting up in bed with my back against the headboard. My knees are drawn up a bit. One hand is holding my phone, the other is resting on my knee. Is that detailed enough for you?"

"Could I get a bit more detail, like if you've removed your lipstick, or whether your hair is up?"

"Is this a diner, Fatih? 'A little more detail,' like you're asking for a bit more rice?"

"More please."

"Alright then. Let me tell you... I've cleaned off my makeup. My hair is down and messy. My nail polish is gone. My high heels pinched my feet a bit, but by morning it should be fine. My lipstick smudged a bit when you kissed me, and I wiped off the rest." As I described these things, I recalled kissing Fatih, how he gently stroked my knee at the diner... Remembering what he'd done, I found myself absentmindedly running my hand over my knee where it had rested. "I hope I've been detailed enough this time."

"Thank you, Ece. I can picture you in my mind now."

"Then it's my turn to ask a question," I said. "Why did you kiss me tonight?"

"Because I wouldn't have been able to sleep otherwise."

"Because you wanted to kiss me?"

"Yes," Fatih replied. "Did you want me to kiss you?"

"You promised not to ask any more questions, Fatih. No answer for you."

"Ah, come on!" Fatih protested.

"Nope... Now let me see if I've got this straight," I said. "You said you couldn't sleep unless you kissed me. But given that we're chatting on the phone in the middle of the night, it seems that even after doing it, sleep still eluded you."

I heard Fatih take a deep breath on the other end. "Yes, I did say you're my remedy, but perhaps there's a dosage issue or something, I don't know."

"Blame the doctor who prescribed me in the wrong dosage," I quipped playfully. "Not me."

"I swear, that doctor's diploma... I'd just—"

I laughed. "Don't curse, you'll sin!"

"Alright, alright. I'll let the doctor off the hook. He should thank you, Ece. By the way, did I manage to help you make it in time for the evening prayer?"

"Yes, I did. Thank you. Did you manage to pray, Fatih?" Although I doubted he performed prayers, I felt compelled to ask.

"I don't pray."

"But have you ever thought about starting?" I asked.

After a brief silence, Fatih replied, "Honestly, I haven't thought about it. Not yet, at least."

"Alright, how about a bet, Fatih?"

"On what?"

"About you praying... I bet that within a week, you'll start praying. Maybe not all five prayers, but at least one per day."

Fatih laughed dismissively. "I highly doubt that, my dear."

"Are you in?"

"What's the wager?"

"Hmm..." I thought for a moment. I could have said a watch, for instance. A nice, stylish watch would have been lovely. And not a fake one. I wouldn't want Fatih to strap a watch on me that he bought from some African immigrant in Taksim. But after some thought, I decided against asking for a watch. "Betting something in Islam counts as gambling. It's a major sin, you know. So, how about we make a wager without anything at stake? Just for the sake of it."

"Alright. I'm in," Fatih replied.

"Deal then," I said, smiling. I wouldn't have made the bet if I wasn't sure I'd win. Of course, I had a very good plan. Losing was impossible, with God's will.

CHAPTER 22

Monday morning...

The first lesson of the day had just begun, yet I stood frozen just outside the classroom door, drowning in my thoughts. What fate had befallen me this time? How could I possibly step into class like this?

It had happened again. Just like the roses in the depths of Derin's villa and the dress she wore; my clothes had once again, without warning, transformed into a deep, inky black. Normally, I wouldn't be so distressed by such an occurrence, but this time it was my school uniform that had undergone this sudden metamorphosis. The school dress code required girls to wear gray skirts and pink blouses. Black was utterly forbidden.

As if that wasn't enough, my current class was math, taught by none other than Ms. Fulya—the most fastidious and discipline-obsessed teacher in the school. I only hoped she wouldn't be too harsh. Despite her diminutive stature, she was a figure we all feared.

Taking a deep breath, I pushed open the door and entered the classroom. I walked a few steps toward the teacher before stopping in my tracks, bracing myself for her reaction.

The moment she noticed my inappropriate attire, Ms. Fulya furrowed her brows and tilted her head slightly to one side. Her piercing gaze, magnified by thick glasses, swept over me. "Ece?" she barked in that stern tone of hers. "What are you wearing, girl?"

Just as I was about to stammer out an explanation, Derin chimed in, her voice nonchalant, "Spiders are black, teacher. Ece's just embracing her natural color." She shrugged with casual indifference.

I exhaled sharply, blowing the strands of hair from my face. Ah, Derin, always there to add her own little jabs at the worst moments.

There was a time when I believed that Esma, my aunt who blasted loud music and twerked in front of me while I prayed in peaceful reverence, might one day embrace modesty. But never did I dare hope that Derin would stop teasing me for even a single morning. Fine, let my aunt sculpt her figure however she wished, but at least she could keep her antics from interfering with my prayers. I would have gladly accepted her doing Pilates instead—it would have been far less distracting.

I tried to offer my explanation to the teacher. "Um... it wasn't intentional, teacher. Lately, for some reason, everything I wear turns pitch black. I'm not entirely sure why, but I think it might be indirectly related to my special ability. I'll learn to control it as soon as I can."

Ms. Fulya rose from her chair at the podium, placing her hands on her hips. "I understand, my dear, but I can't let you stay in class dressed like this."

Just then, I saw Sinem rise from her seat. "Teacher," she began, "I have an objection, if you'll allow me. Isn't this a class for students with special abilities?"

My eyes widened, and a shiver ran down my spine.

But it wasn't because Sinem was standing up for me.

She hadn't stuttered...

Not a single stutter!

"Yes, it is, my dear," Ms. Fulya responded. "This is the class for special students."

Sinem, now speaking with the fluidity of a seasoned orator, continued, "If that's the case, shouldn't you be supporting these special students as they discover their abilities, develop their powers, and overcome the challenges they face? If we are special students in a special class, isn't it more fitting that we be treated with special rules rather than the standard ones? Clearly, Ece is struggling with her powers unintentionally. We expect you to help and support her in resolving this, not close the door in her face."

My eyes welled up with tears. I fought hard to keep them from falling. Sinem was singing like a nightingale! And she was singing for me. I wanted to shout, 'Keep going, girl, talk until the evening if you must!' But that would've only disrupted the class more. So, I kept quiet.

"Hmm..." Ms. Fulya mused, her expression thoughtful. "Very well. Ece, I'll grant you some flexibility with the rules. You may return to your seat. Let's continue with the lesson."

"Forgive me, teacher, but before I sit down, there's something I must do." I dashed over to Sinem's desk, where she stood by the window, and threw my arms around her in a tight hug. Damn it, would these tears ever stop?

"Ece, don't overdo it," Sinem said gently as she returned my embrace. "All I did was explain your situation for you. No need to get so emotional."

"You idiot, you're actually speaking!"

"What?" Sinem asked, her expression puzzled.

"You're not stuttering, you fool!"

"Oh my God, you're right! I'm actually speaking! Wait a minute, I'm speaking! Teacher, with your permission, I'd like to sing a song!"

Ms. Fulya looked at the two of us as if to say, 'What am I going to do with these girls today?' She sighed heavily and rubbed her face with her hand. "Step out into the corridor and sing there, dear, if you must. We can't seem to start the lesson because of the two of you!"

Sinem grabbed my hand, and together we bolted toward the door. We left the classroom, shutting the door behind us.

The corridor echoed with Sinem's voice as she belted out a song by Ebru Gündeş at full volume. Her voice was beautiful, reminiscent of the famed singer herself. If I closed my eyes, I might have mistaken her for Ebru. Okay, maybe I was exaggerating because she's my friend, but still, her voice was a gift. Compared to the torturous off-key singing of my uncle in the shower, Sinem's melody was pure bliss. It would've been a tragedy for the world of art if her stutter had remained. Thank God she was cured. Eurovision, here we come!

"Don't say a word, let your eyes do the talking," Sinem crooned.

"Don't be silent, Sinem," I said. "You've got plenty to say. Let your tongue, not your eyes, do the talking. You go, girl!"

Hand in hand, we spun in circles, laughing and jumping like wild things in the empty corridor.

"How do you think your stutter went away?" I asked.

"I have no idea, Ece. I just did what you said. I prayed to God a lot, that's all. Maybe when the teacher started pressuring you, I snapped, lost myself, and experienced a burst of energy to defend my best friend. Like a Big Bang explosion! And that's how I found my voice."

"Hmm, perhaps... I was praying for you, too, after all. It seems Allah couldn't resist our prayers from both sides—left and right—and granted our wish."

"Praise be to Allah," Sinem said with heartfelt gratitude before continuing her song: "Or am I mad? Am I truly mad, deranged?"

If someone were to see us leaping through the corridor like crazed lemurs, they would surely ask the same question. We really did look insane!

As we continued to let loose in our wild frenzy, Ms. Fulya opened the classroom door and stuck her head out, her expression one of exasperation. "Girls, what's all this racket? Take your madness to the courtyard, please. Have some decency!"

"Sorry, teacher!" we called out, rushing out to the courtyard where we picked up our songs right where we left off.

By noon...

When the lunch break came, while everyone else filed out of the classroom, Sinem and I remained behind, deep in conversation. I had perched myself on the teacher's desk, swinging my legs lazily, while Sinem stood before me, arms crossed.

"Do you think your power might actually be turning your clothes black, Ece?" Sinem asked suddenly.

I shook my head. "My power is telepathy."

Sinem frowned, pondering. "Hmm... Telepathy, you say? So, that's like thoughts and emotions flowing out from one person and reaching another, right?"

"Yeah, something like that."

"Picture a napkin," Sinem began, as if explaining a grand revelation. "When you press a napkin onto a spill, it soaks up the liquid, just like telepathy absorbs someone's thoughts. But now imagine a soaked napkin. If you place it on a dry surface, the liquid leaks out, slowly, steadily, saturating whatever it touches."

I tilted my head in confusion. "What are you getting at, Sinem?"

"My point is, as a telepath, you've always been used to absorbing others' emotions. You've always been a dry napkin, so to speak. You haven't had many feelings of your own to deal with. But maybe things have changed. Maybe now, you're carrying a lot of sorrow—too many unspoken emotions. And like water leaking from a soaked napkin, your emotions are seeping out, manifesting as this blackness, this darkness staining everything you wear."

"It's a far-fetched theory, but... it's not entirely impossible," I mused. "So if you're right, then the solution would be to... get happy, I suppose? If I could just be happy, maybe I'd stop turning everything black."

"Well," Sinem said with a mischievous grin, "if Fatih falls in love with you and you two start dating, I bet you'd feel better in no time. Give yourself to him, lose your virginity, let go of the darkness, and bring back the colors—let them return swiftly and vibrantly!" She delivered the final line like a melody, singing it with dramatic flair.

I groaned. "What kind of slogan is that? Are you seriously advertising some detergent with an 18+ commercial, with sex, colors, and all that nonsense?"

Sinem was just like the daughter my uncle had always wanted but never had. They thought the same way. My aunt, my uncle, Sinem... They were all in agreement, all pushing for me to give myself to Fatih!

Speak of the devil... At that exact moment, Fatih walked into the classroom.

"How are you doing, girls?" Fatih asked, striding toward us. "Didn't you go down for lunch?"

"We're fine," I answered quickly. "Sinem's on a diet, and I thought I'd keep her company. How about you, Fatih?"

"I'm good," he replied, making his way to the teacher's desk where I sat. He stood directly in front of me, and to my surprise, placed his palms on my knees, gently caressing them with deliberate, tantalizing strokes. "So, what were you girls chatting about?"

"About Ece painting every piece of clothing she touches like some clumsy apprentice painter," Sinem quipped. "And I think I might have found a solution to her problem."

I raised my eyebrows and shot her a look that screamed, 'Do not say it!' Sinem shouldn't have mentioned that her theory was that I'd be cured if Fatih and I got together. I wanted him to come to me naturally, not out of some pity or an attempt to save me from my strange affliction.

Meanwhile, Fatih's hands continued their slow exploration of my knees, his touch sending sparks through my skin. There was no mistaking it—he was interested in me. And if things progressed between us, and if Sinem's theory held any truth, maybe I really could break free from this curse of turning everything black.

"Let go, let the darkness go, let the colors return... swiftly, vibrantly," I hummed to myself, echoing Sinem's ridiculous little tune.

Damn it, now her silly song was stuck in my head!

CHAPTER 23

Fatih's tantalizing touch was certainly pleasant, but engaging in such flirtatious behavior in front of Sinem? Unthinkable! Especially when the area between the knee and the navel was forbidden. There was a religious dimension to this too, after all. With that thought in mind, I slid forward in my seat and lowered myself from the podium. Every step taken away from sin was a profit.

As Fatih leaned closer, enclosing me between himself and the podium, he asked, "So, what solution has Sinem found, Ece?"

"We're still in the project phase. It's far too early to talk about any concrete solutions."

Fatih took hold of my hands. "Is there anything I could help with on your project?"

In truth, there was. According to Sinem, Fatih needed to fall in love with me. But that was not something I could ever tell him. In my mind, I had named this romance-themed project: Lay me upon the hill, scratch me, caress me.

"If you really want to help, Fatih, you could start by taking a step back," I murmured, for the distance between us had vanished entirely, and I was pinned between the podium and him. "Such intimate closeness is not appropriate. It's a sin."

"Don't worry, you won't be struck by lightning, Ece," he said with a casual tone, gently stroking my hands in his palms. "I'm taller than you; I'll act as a lightning rod and draw the bolts toward myself."

"Oh, great, now we have Alya the second!" I said, rolling my eyes. "Sitting in front of Alya in class all day has infected you with her awful sense of humor. And not only is it cold, but it's also religiously inappropriate. Joking about Islamic matters, taking our faith lightly, is sinful."

"Hmm, I didn't know that. I'll be more mindful of religious jokes from now on."

Fatih continued to keep me trapped between his body and the podium. I warned him once again, "Listen, my dear little contractor, let me put it in construction terms so you understand. I'm asking you to place the pillar a bit further back; it's inappropriate and sinful. Where did this craving for a 'warm snack' come from, right in the middle of the classroom, with Sinem around?"

"I think my blood began to boil when I saw you, Ece."

"Boiling, you say, Fatih?" I raised an eyebrow. Reaching behind me, I grabbed Sinem's small water bottle from the podium. It was half full. With the cap already open, I raised it high and poured the water over Fatih's head. As the cool liquid cascaded down, soaking him through, I couldn't help but laugh. "I hope this quenches your boil."

Fatih didn't flinch as I poured the water, his eyes merely watching mine with a sideways grin. Oh my goodness! I'd drenched the guy, yet he must have liked me because he took it all in stride, not uttering a word of complaint.

When the bottle finally emptied, I swung it in the air a few times, sending the last few drops his way.

"Does it suit a pious, devout girl to waste water, the most precious of blessings?" Fatih asked with a teasing voice.

And just like that—score, one for Fatih.

"You're right," I admitted.

Though he said it in jest, he was correct, and I felt a pang of regret for what I'd just done. Seeing my face fall, Fatih sought to cheer me up. "You've earned your punishment," he said as he whipped off his soaked shirt and, using it like a towel, playfully slapped my behind with it. Fatih's exposed torso revealed abs so finely sculpted that even the most renowned baklava shops would have been envious. A sight to behold...though once, I had lain beside him unknowingly.

"What are you doing?" I exclaimed in shock.

"You can run, but you can't hide!"

"I can run, and I can escape too, you mountain boy!"

I turned to flee, but within seconds, he snapped his shirt behind me again. "Hey, take it easy!"

As our playful chase continued, the flicks of his shirt somehow stirred a hormonal reaction in me. Earlier that day, I had decided not to fast at the last minute. Had I fasted, this flirtation would surely have ruined my reward.

Sinem called out to us, "If you two peacocks are going to continue your mating dance, I'll step outside."

"You're right to go," Fatih replied. "This dance isn't quite suitable for a general audience."

"Fatih, cut it out! Sinem, wait, don't go—we'll stop the... the playing around." I turned to Fatih, raising my hands as if to say "ceasefire."

At that moment, the classroom door creaked open, and Alya entered. She glanced coldly at me but cast a more interested look toward Fatih, then without another word, walked to the window to gaze outside.

"Put something on, Fatih," I urged.

"Why?"

"You'll catch a cold without your shirt."

"It's not exactly cold in here, Ece."

"People are coming in," I added. "You shouldn't just walk around half-naked."

Fatih came closer and whispered in my ear, "You didn't mind when Sinem was here, but now that Alya's entered, you've suddenly changed your tune."

I pursed my lips. "That's not true at all."

"It very much is."

I narrowed my eyes and locked gazes with Fatih. "Alya's here, which means other students will be arriving soon. That's all," I whispered, hoping Alya wouldn't hear.

Fatih draped an arm around my back, softly caressing my shoulder. "Is that so?"

"Yes, that's so!"

With his free hand, Fatih pointed toward Alya, still gazing out the window, looking like a flawless Russian doll, her beauty cold and distant. "So, you're not jealous of her at all, is that it, Ece?"

My mouth dropped open. "Me? Jealous? Of her? Absolutely not! Why would I be?"

"Maybe because, like you, Alya also thinks I resemble that handsome actor, Keanu Reeves?"

Of course, the answer was yes.

"Of course not!"

"Alright, fair enough. I have no idea how that thought even crossed my mind," said Fatih with a chuckle. "Anyway, I should at least go say hi to Alya, or it'd be rude."

"Why would it be rude? She's just standing there, watching the garden."

"I'll chat with her for a couple of minutes, then I'll grab my spare t-shirt from my bag."

"How about you wear the t-shirt before you go chat?"

"What's the rush? It's not like the t-shirt is going to run away."

It wasn't, but if Fatih kept this up, I was about to lose my mind!

"Fatih! Will you please just put it on?"

Fatih patted my shoulder soothingly. "Who's going to walk all the way to my bag to get it? I suddenly feel lazy."

Sighing with exasperation, I stalked off to where Fatih usually sat in class. Reaching his desk, I unzipped his sports bag and pulled out the t-shirt. Returning to him, I thrust the grey shirt into his hands. "Will you wear it, or should I dress you myself?"

As he took the t-shirt from me and slipped it on, a smile tugged at his lips. "You're even more beautiful when you're angry."

"Nonetheless, I'd advise you not to anger me too much, Fatih. I have a heavy hand."

Fatih smoothed down his t-shirt after putting it on. "Our girls in the Black Sea region are like that too. I'm used to it."

"Now that you're dressed, go ahead and chat with Alya, mountain-head."

"I'm not going to."

"Why not?" I asked, surprised.

"I never intended to. I just wanted to rile you up a bit."

I stuck my tongue out at him. "Oh, what hilarious jokes!" I smacked his shoulder firmly.

The next day, after school...

As the ordinary school day drew to a close, it was time to head home. I sat at the very back of the school bus. Apart from Alya, who had arrived just after me, the bus was still empty. We would leave once the other students arrived.

Suddenly, I heard shouting outside. The sounds came from the old mansion about 30-40 meters away from our school. According to the rumors, the mansion had been condemned for being structurally unsafe, and a demolition order had been issued, but for reasons I didn't know—likely bureaucratic—the demolition had been delayed for over a year.

As I listened closely, I realized the voice I heard was Derin's. It sounded like she was arguing with some men.

"Alya?" I asked anxiously. "Isn't that Derin?"

Alya, sitting just behind the driver's seat, turned her head toward the window. "Yeah, it's probably Derin. She's been going to that old mansion for the past few days to hunt rats or something. Snake business, you know. Typical stuff."

As the echoes of distress filled the air, I rose from my seat, my steps already guiding me toward the door of the shuttle. "It sounds like she might be in trouble," I murmured, gesturing to Alya. "Come on, let's go check."

Without turning, Alya waved her hand dismissively, her voice dripping with indifference. "You're talking about a giant anaconda, Ece. Derin can handle herself. Just relax."

But worry gnawed at me. "I'll go take a look anyway." With that, I stepped off the shuttle, breaking into a run toward the old mansion.

Ah, Alya. For someone who claimed to be one of Derin's closest friends, she seemed remarkably unconcerned. Her heart didn't seem to stir half as much as mine did for our friend.

The mansion loomed before me, its iron gate slightly ajar, rusting in neglect. And there, on the creaking wooden porch, I saw her—Derin, lying on the ground, one hand bracing herself against the floor, the other clutching her naked body in a desperate attempt at modesty. She must have shed her clothes when she transformed. Blood seemed to trickle from her head, her features pale with weakness. Yet, despite her frailty, she hissed at two disheveled figures standing nearby—rough men with the unmistakable stench of vagrancy clinging to their tattered clothes.

"Get lost!" Derin snarled through gritted teeth, her body trembling with exertion as she tried to push herself upright. But even her supporting arm trembled, as if it might give way at any moment.

One of the men, tall and lanky, nudged his partner. "This girl's one of those freaks from that special school, right? She had to be, to turn from a snake back to human."

The shorter, stockier man with a cap grinned wickedly. "Oh, I think you're right. She's quite the beauty too. What do you say, snake girl? Want me to take you home and keep you as my pet?"

Without thinking, I charged toward them, shouting, "Leave her alone!"

The taller one sneered, unfazed by my presence. "Well, well, looks like snake girl's friend has joined the party. Guess that means double the fun for us."

I drew myself up, feigning ferocity. "You'd better be ready for the most painful date of your lives," I spat. "Because unlike my snake friend, I don't just bite—I shred. My special power? I turn into a lion."

A lie, of course. But a bold one.

"A lion?" The taller one's face faltered, the uncertainty creeping into his voice.

"Is she serious?" muttered the shorter man, his beady eyes narrowing.

"How the hell should I know?"

I dropped to all fours, mimicking the stance of a lion about to pounce. "You have three seconds to run, or you'll regret it. When I shift, I can't go back, and I never stop hunting my prey until it's torn to pieces. This is your last chance. I'll start counting now."

"Three..."

"Two..."

The stocky man cursed under his breath. Before I could utter "one," the pair turned and bolted, not daring to look back.

A victorious smirk curled my lips. "Meow," I purred after them, playfully swatting the air like a cat. That was about as close to a lion as I could get. It was a miracle they had fallen for it.

Dusting off my knees and hands, I rose to my feet, watching their retreat with satisfaction.

With the threat gone, I rushed to Derin's side. She was still weak, her face a mixture of relief and pain. Blood glistened on her forehead.

"Isn't lying a sin, spiderling?" she whispered, barely audible. Her voice was weak, her breath shallow. I gently lifted her, wrapping my arm around her to help her sit upright.

"I may have lied about turning into a lion, but in Islam, lying is permitted in times of war," I said with a slight grin. "There's even a hadith about it: 'War is deceit.' And I'd say this situation was a battle, wouldn't you? Two girls against two men? And one girl was even wounded. I'd say we came out of that war victorious with a small bit of trickery. Besides, Islam also allows lying to reconcile people, or to smooth things over between a husband and wife."

Derin's lips curved into a faint, mischievous smile. "Well, without that lie, I think those men would've played the part of a husband and wife with us anyway. They weren't exactly here for tea and cookies."

I laughed, a lightness returning to my chest. "If I'm going to play house, I'd at least like a cottage with pink shutters, not some decrepit old mansion," I teased, glancing at the crumbling walls of the once-grand house. My gaze then shifted back to Derin, noticing the blood again. "You're hurt. Are you alright?"

CHAPTER 24

"I'm fine, don't worry," Derin muttered, her voice quiet but firm.

In the vast garden of the manor, beneath the boughs of an ancient tree, her discarded clothes lay in a heap. I moved towards them, gathering the scattered garments and handing them back to her. As she began dressing, my eyes briefly traced her form. Bruises and scratches marred her belly and one leg—faint, yet unmistakable. Those two thugs must have been responsible for this.

"What happened?" I asked, the sorrow in my voice betraying my concern. "Did those boys hurt you?"

Once fully clothed, Derin straightened herself and sank into a chair on the veranda. I joined her, sitting at her side as she began her story. "Sometimes, after school, I'd sneak over to this manor. I'd turn into a snake and hunt mice or other small prey," she explained, leaning her head on my shoulder. "Today, I transformed like usual, but those two jerks appeared in the garden. I tried to ignore them, just focused on my hunt. But they followed me, started throwing rocks. I must've taken too many hits... I lost strength and reverted back into human form before I knew it. That's when you came."

I wrapped an arm around her, comforting her. "You really shouldn't do this," I said softly, my voice laced with a plea. "This place has been abandoned for so long, it's become a hideout for thugs and drifters. It's not safe to hunt here alone. If you must, at least bring Kerem with you. Don't go by yourself."

Derin exhaled in frustration, her breath heavy with the weight of resignation. "Kerem used to come with me when I went hunting. But..."

"But what?"

"Never mind, spider girl," she said with a sly grin, her hand resting on my knee, fingers gently stroking. "I don't want to burden you with my relationship problems."

"Burden me?" I gasped in mock disbelief. "Sweetheart, I spent half of last summer watching morning talk shows, listening to strangers pour out their relationship dramas. If anything, hearing about your love life might be fun for me. If I had some sunflower seeds, I'd be cracking them open while I listened."

A pink smile crept across Derin's lips. "Alright, if you insist. But I can't promise you sunflower seeds. Kerem and I were fine, but for the past week, I feel like he's been pulling away from me. I can't put my finger on it, but something's changed between us. Can you believe he left early on my birthday? And without even telling me!"

My jaw nearly hit the floor. "How could he? What time did Kerem leave?"

Derin looked up, her hazel eyes narrowing in thought. "I don't remember the exact time, but my friends told me that right after you said goodbye and left with Fatih, Kerem slipped out, too. In a real hurry, apparently."

"Hmmm..." A shadow passed over me. Could it be? No, it couldn't be. The man in the overcoat I had seen from the restaurant window while dining with Fatih—the masked man I suspected of cursing Fatih's lovers—he had followed us. Was Kerem's sudden departure at the party more than just a coincidence? Could it be that Kerem was the one trailing us that night?

"You've drifted off, Ece," Derin's voice broke my thoughts. "What are you thinking about?"

I shrugged. "Nothing."

"Come on, something's bothering you," she pressed.

I dropped my arm from around her and leaned forward, resting my hands on my thighs. "It's nothing, Derin. Just a silly thought."

"You trust me enough to let me spill my guts. You can tell me what's on your mind, too. Whatever it is. Let me crack some sunflower seeds for a change," she teased, wrapping an arm around my waist.

I bit my lip, smiling slightly. "Derin," I began, taking a deep breath. "Do you know if there's been any tension or rivalry between Kerem and Fatih?"

Derin ran her fingers absentmindedly through her hair. "Not that I know of," she replied. "They're both on the swim team. There's some friendly competition between them, sure, but nothing serious. Fatih's generally better in the pool, but it's just light rivalry. In fact, tomorrow after school, they're supposed to meet at the indoor pool for a race. The guys made a bet, apparently. We could go watch, if you'd like."

"Why not," I murmured softly. "We could."

Derin's arm still circled my waist as her hand absently stroked my side. "Why are you asking about them?" she questioned, her voice curious yet gentle.

"Well... after Fatih and I left your party, we stopped at a restaurant on the way home. While we were eating, I noticed a man outside the window. With my telepathic powers, I realized he was the one who cursed Fatih's past lovers, causing their deaths."

"No way!"

"Exactly," I continued, my voice low. "And I think he might've been at your party, too. I believe he followed us from your house to the restaurant. Otherwise, how could he have found us? And now... well, when you said Kerem left right after we did, in such a hurry, it made me wonder..."

"Are you suggesting Kerem could be the one cursing Fatih's lovers?" Derin asked, her brow furrowed.

"I don't want to accuse him of anything. But these little details—him leaving right after us, the strain in your relationship starting the same week I joined your class—it all seems too coincidental. I mean, the rivalry on the swim team isn't strong enough to drive someone to curse his opponent's lovers, but..."

Derin sighed, pulling her hand away and resting her elbows on her knees, her head sinking into her palms. "I've known Kerem for so long," she said, shaking her head. "He wouldn't hurt a fly. But still," she added, turning her face towards me, "I'll keep an eye on him. Don't worry."

"Thanks, Derin. I'll keep considering all possibilities. Instead of focusing on Kerem, I'll try talking to everyone in our class. Either by conversation or using my telepathy, I'll find out who's behind this. Kerem doesn't seem like the right fit."

Derin nodded thoughtfully. "If you start noticing any bad luck coming your way, let me know, Ece," she said, her voice soft with concern. "I don't want you to become a victim of this curse."

I waved my hand dismissively. "Don't worry about me, girl. Did you forget? I can turn into a lion. I'll protect myself."

Derin burst out laughing. "You're something else, Ece."

Her lips, I noticed, were stained with blood. Likely from the mouse she had devoured in her snake form. She looked like something out of those Twilight movies—like a vampire girl plucked straight from the silver screen.

"You've got blood on your lips, Bella Swan," I teased, referencing the film as I pointed to the reddest spot with my finger.

"Thanks, Edward." Derin pulled out a tissue and gently dabbed at the spot I indicated. "Probably mouse blood."

"Try wiping a bit more to the side," I instructed.

Derin, like some dainty Spanish countess, elegantly dabbed her lips.

I smiled. "Girl, your mouth's practically painted in blood. Dainty little dabs won't do the trick." I pulled a wet wipe from my pocket and began scrubbing her lips. "You've got to press hard, like a mom cleaning her kid's face. Not like a Victoria's Secret model afraid of smudging her lipstick."

To be fair, she did have that model-like beauty. As I wiped her lips, she suddenly opened her mouth and bit my hand.

"Ah!" I shot her a mock glare. Thankfully, she hadn't drawn blood. This mischievous snake girl had bitten me twice now. "Control those teeth, girl!"

"What? Can't a girl crave a little dessert after her meal?"

Apparently, I was the dessert she craved. "Now that your lips are clean, we should deal with that cut on your forehead. Let me take you to the school's infirmary, Derin."

"The nurse is probably long gone by now. Don't bother."

"Who needs the nurse? I know what I'm doing. I'll take care of you."

"Alright, fine," Derin sighed as she stood up. I followed suit. "Before we go, though, want me to catch you a mouse, Ece?"

"Thanks, but I just ate."

"I'll catch one for you to take home. You can have it later," she insisted.

"It wouldn't taste good cold. Thanks anyway," I said, linking my arm with hers and steering her towards the school.

"Microwave it for thirty seconds—it'll warm right up."

"Derin, if you keep this joke going, you're about to find out what I last ate. You're going to make me puke!"

"You don't know what you're missing," she laughed, pinching my cheek affectionately as we walked.

"I'm serious. Cut the jokes!"

"Alright, alright. I'm done. Thanks, Ece. I don't know who I'd tease if it weren't for you."

"Oh, you don't know the half of it..."

CHAPTER 25

M inutes later...

Upon reaching the school infirmary with Derin, it fell upon me to tend to her wounds, as the nurse had already left for the day.

"Don't worry, Derin. I have a bit of knowledge when it comes to medical matters."

"Isn't there a saying, Ece, about a little knowledge being dangerous? They say half a doctor, kills the patient."

"I'm not half a doctor, don't worry," I said with a cough, adding quietly, "Maybe a quarter of one."

Whispering "Bismillah," I donned gloves and carefully applied antiseptic to her forehead with a piece of gauze.

"It's not deep enough for stitches," I announced. "It'll heal in three or four days, inshallah."

"Good to know."

I then gently lifted her shirt to inspect the bruise blooming on her side. "Hirudoid cream," I murmured. "It'll help the bruising fade faster. I use it myself sometimes—clumsiness, you know... I think I have half a tube in my bag. I'll put some on for you. Just promise not to bite me when I do."

"Relax, Ece. I'm the non-venomous type of snake."

"Just make sure you don't swallow me whole in the process..."

"I'll do my best."

My eyes widened. "So there's a chance that could actually happen?"

Derin laughed. "I'm kidding! Just go ahead and apply the cream."

I found the cream in my bag and began to massage it into her side. Her leg only had a minor scrape, so I left it as it was.

"I'll give you the rest of the cream, Derin. Apply it twice a day for the next few days. Does that sound good?"

She took the tube from me with a nod. "Sure thing, Doctor."

"One day, inshallah... I've been thinking about med school, honestly."

"Ah, too bad!" Derin exclaimed.

"Why?"

"If you were a vet, I could come to you every time I got hurt."

I chuckled. "You should talk to Kerem about keeping you out of harm's way next time."

"I'll do more than talk. I'll bite his ear off if I have to."

Wednesday, 5:20 p.m.

The long-awaited moment had arrived. Soon, Fatih and Kerem would be locked in a swimming race, and I had been invited by Derin to watch.

After the last class, we had gathered at the indoor pool. Apart from Derin, Kerem, Fatih, and me, the pool was empty. While Derin and I still wore our school uniforms—white shirts and skirts—the boys were already in their swimsuits, preparing for the race.

Though the pool wasn't as large as an Olympic one, it was significantly bigger than the one at Derin's place. It was wide enough to comfortably accommodate five or six swimmers racing side by side.

When we arrived, Kerem switched on the lights and ventilation, which had been turned off. We then walked over to the pool's edge.

The boys donned their swimming goggles and began warming up, stretching their perfectly sculpted bodies. Or, at least, from my perspective, Fatih seemed to be flaunting his flawless, triangular physique right in front of my eyes.

"Guess the defeated rooster wants another round, huh, Kerem?" Fatih said, smugly adjusting his swimsuit.

"Don't get too full of yourself just because you've won our last 1,683 races, Fatih," Kerem replied with a playful grin. "Mark today in your memory, because all you'll be seeing in the water today is my back."

Derin moved closer to Kerem, playfully adding, "Love, make sure I'm the only one seeing your back from now on! You've been neglecting me lately. Is there another girl who's caught your eye, hmm?"

"Never, my love. You're the only one for me."

"I'm not so sure..." Derin said with narrowed eyes. "I'll be watching you closely, Kerem." She made a playful 'watching you' gesture with her fingers.

"My love, my eyes can't see anything other than you."

"And what's that supposed to mean?" Derin playfully bit Kerem's arm. "Are you saying I'm too big, that my backside is blocking your entire field of vision?"

"No, baby. It's just perfectly... hand-sized."

Fatih interrupted, "Can we stop the butt-talk and start the race already, Kerem? Or are you stalling because you're afraid of losing again?"

"Fine. Let's do this."

Kerem's carefree demeanor and untroubled spirit made me less suspicious of him being the curse's culprit. Yet, people could surprise you, even after decades of marriage. So, I remained on guard.

"Where's my good luck kiss, Derin?" Kerem asked.

Without hesitation, Derin threw herself at him, kissing him with such fervor that, with that kind of morale boost, Kerem would likely break any chains that held him back and win the race easily.

"We'll continue this later," Derin said with a teasing look.

There would be more? "That's doping, Derin," I protested. "Totally unfair."

"Don't call it doping. Call it... an incentive."

"Ece," Fatih whispered, coming closer. "Can I get a good luck kiss too?"

I pretended not to understand. "Derin only kisses her boyfriend, not you."

"I meant you."

Fatih closed the distance between us, standing so close that I could feel the warmth of his breath. His hand found my waist as his thumb gently brushed my cheek, his fingers threading through my hair. It wasn't fair; he was making it nearly impossible to refuse him.

I planted a quick peck on his cheek.

"That's it? If I lose, it'll be your fault, Ece."

"Oh, so you want a kiss on the lips?"

"I've been wanting that since the day I first saw you."

"You've waited a long time."

"I have," Fatih murmured. "But some things are worth waiting for."

When his lips touched the corner of mine, for the first time, I felt the rhythm of my own heartbeat. My eyes fluttered closed.

"Kissing before marriage is a sin," I whispered as I slowly opened my eyes, taking in the blue of his, as endless as the sea.

"But I've kissed you before."

"That time I wasn't prepared. And doing it again doesn't make it any less wrong," I said. "It's still a sin." My lips, however, betrayed me, parting ever so slightly, revealing that a part of me wanted him to kiss me again. "You can't."

Looking into my eyes, Fatih spoke softly, "Ece, you may make up for missed prayers, but what about me? There's no making up for the days I've spent without kissing you. I'll burn in the fire of longing. Is there truly no chance?"

He was using religion and romance at once, and I was helpless against such a combination. "You can kiss me on one condition: if you promise to pray at least one unit of prayer every day," I said. "Let's say Maghrib. If you vow to pray three rak'ahs of Maghrib every evening, then my lips will be yours."

"Deal."

"Really?" I asked in disbelief.

"Yes. That way, I'll be closer to you—and to God."

"I like how you think," I said, bringing my lips to his. Our lips sealed together, and I felt as if a black petal fell from the rose blooming within me, its blossom opening.

Fatih's hand moved from my waist to my back, pulling me closer as his other hand held my face. Our bodies pressed against one another as our lips anchored together. But my sense of modesty couldn't allow it to continue. Yes, I loved him. But I loved Allah and my integrity more.

"Fatih..."

"Yes?"

"I... I don't think I can do this. I know we had an agreement, but..."

Fatih pulled back slightly. "Whenever you're ready. Don't rush. But until then, I'll keep my promise."

"Thank you for understanding."

"Fatih," Kerem interrupted, "did you give up on the swim race and decide to compete in a kissing contest instead? If that's the case, you can't win."

"Why not?" Fatih asked.

Because of my modesty, perhaps.

"Derin and I have been together longer. We know each other better. Like things that turn us on..."

"Or know better what doesn't turn us on," Derin added with a dreamy look. "What kills the mood."

"Whose side are you on?" Kerem asked.

"Don't worry, love. I won't mention your weird and boring fantasies." She winked. "Oops! Did I just say that?"

It seemed I wasn't the only one Derin teased. She was an equal-opportunity tormentor.

Kerem sighed, covering his face with his hand. "Alright, I guess you've already won this flirtation contest, Fatih."

"Glad you realized it."

Embarrassed by the conversation, I took tiny steps away from Fatih and began inspecting the pool's ceiling as though I had noticed something. I must have looked like a painter analyzing a ceiling before starting his work.

Truthfully, kissing before marriage was a sin, but it seemed I had fallen victim to my own desires. Maybe that's why I had made Fatih promise to pray daily. I hoped that, as the one who led him to prayer, I could gain some merit. Or by any chance it would serve to veil, even erase, the sin that had arisen from the kiss. Moreover,

I was certain that, having started Fatih on the path of just one daily prayer, I could gradually and gently guide him toward two, then three, four, and finally, the full five prayers a day.

Yet, I must admit, what I had done -the kiss- did not sit well with me. To resort to such means in order to cover up one sin—this was far from ideal. Perhaps it would have been better not to have committed the sin in the first place. But I would seek refuge in Allah's mercy. I prayed that He would open a blessed door for me. At least I had managed to halt my descent into further error, for I had refused that second kiss.

CHAPTER 26

The race between Fatih and Kerem had unfolded amidst the cheering of us girls, and once again, Fatih had claimed victory. Emerging from the water, he dried himself with a towel before walking toward me.

"Congratulations," I said as Fatih drew nearer. "It was a fine race."

He approached the spot where I stood. Perhaps I was still under the spell of our earlier kiss, for I stood there, fidgeting like a schoolgirl experiencing her first blush of love. My hands were clasped behind my back, and I swayed my body gently from side to side, absently nibbling on my lip.

Fatih, his soaked chestnut hair falling over his eyes, wrapped an arm around me. "That good luck kiss worked wonders, my Ece."

"You're getting me all wet!" I protested, trying to pull away, but his strong arm held me firmly. He cradled me close, running his wet fingers delicately through my hair. They say love makes you soaked to the skin—well, in this moment, it wasn't even a metaphor.

As he held me, he took a step forward, pressing closer. Unconsciously, I stepped back. He took another step, and I, once again, retreated. One more step, and another, until I felt the cool edge of the pool beneath my heels.

I turned my head slightly, casting a glance behind me at the water. "Fatih?" I murmured, my voice laced with apprehension. "You're not planning to do what I think, are you?"

"No."

I turned to face him again, locking eyes with his. "How can you be so sure you know what I'm thinking?"

"Because I know you... as always."

"Arrogant Laz boy! You can't know what I'm thinking. But I can read your mind—telepathy, remember?"

Fatih grinned mischievously. "Then go ahead, read my thoughts."

The moment I delved into his mind, my eyes widened. "No, no! You're going to throw me into the pool!"

Before I could escape, Fatih's arm slipped beneath my waist, lifting me effortlessly. I screamed all the way down as he tossed me into the water, the cold splash enveloping me. Seconds later, he jumped in after me, laughing.

After flailing for a moment, I managed to grasp the pool's edge, pushing my wet hair back from my face. "You're terrible!" I scolded, shivering slightly. "The water is freezing, and now my school uniform is drenched."

Fatih gestured toward my clothes. "Well, they're no longer black."

"What?" I asked, glancing down at my soaked uniform. "You're right! My skirt's back to gray, and my shirt... it's pink again!"

I suppose I was no longer the black rose.

"How do you think that happened?" Fatih asked, curiosity piqued.

"Sinem and I had a theory," I replied. "For my clothes to stay from turning black, I'd have to let go of those gloomy feelings, maybe experience some romance. And after kissing you... well, maybe that did the trick. For now, at least."

Fatih swam closer, his voice dropping to a teasing tone. "Shall we try for a little more, just to be sure?"

"If we go any further, my pink shirt might start flashing like a disco ball! Let's not overdo it."

Just then, a shriek pierced the air, and I caught sight of something soaring above me. Was it a bird? A plane? No—it was Super Derin!

Derin flew over my head and landed with a splash. Kerem, having taken inspiration from Fatih, had thrown her into the pool, and then, like a true partner in crime, he jumped in right after her, joining us.

Seconds later, I let out a cry, wincing in pain. There couldn't be a shark in this pool, so the bite just below my knee could only be one thing.

Derin emerged from beneath the water's surface.

"Derin!" I yelped, glaring at her. "Is there nowhere I can be safe from you? This is the third time you've bitten me!"

"Eventually, you'll lose count, Ece," Derin replied, brushing her wet hair from her face and giving me a playful pinch on the cheek. "You'll get used to it."

I rubbed my sore leg. "Why couldn't I have found a friend who turns into a cute kitten? I would've settled for a grumpy Persian cat, but no—you had to be an anaconda, didn't you? Sigh..."

Kerem swam over to Derin, and the two lovebirds started splashing and teasing each other in the water. Meanwhile, Fatih was watching me closely.

"Why are you staring at me like that, Fatih?" I asked.

"I'm taking a mental photograph of you, babe. Later, when I'm home, I'll sketch your portrait from memory."

Hmm... I rather liked the sound of that—babe. Having never dated anyone before, I wasn't sure when it was appropriate to use such romantic terms. Since Fatih had said it first, I figured it was fair game for me too.

But could I call him my love? It felt like the right word to describe the fluttering, effervescent feeling inside me, but it might be too early for such a grand declaration.

Calling him babe would feel like I was copying.

My Laz prince or my horon dancer? Not quite romantic enough.

Lovydovy? Too much like a cliché from İzmir.

Husbandito? Maybe someday...

Honey, my sweet, my nectar? Too much like a shopkeeper.

Darling or sweetheart? Yes, those would do for now. So, I took a deep breath and gave it a try.

"Sweetheart, if you're taking my mental photo, I should at least strike a pose."

I held onto the pool's edge with one hand and plunged my other hand into my hair, tousling it dramatically. Tilting my head this way and that, I tested different expressions.

"Hold that pose."

I froze. "Should I wait until I hear the click?"

"Don't move," Fatih warned.

Without moving, I blinked twice in acknowledgment.

"There," Fatih said with a nod of approval. "You're locked in my memory forever."

"Or at least until you get Alzheimer's."

"Do you always have to kill the romance, babe?"

"Guess it's just my nature. But for some reason, you haven't run away yet. For now, anyway."

"You know I'm in construction, love. I don't leave projects unfinished, especially the long-term ones. I'm patient, and I take my time."

"Alright, Architect Sinan, but I'm freezing here. I'd better get out of the water before your project catches a cold."

"As you wish."

I grabbed the pool's ladder, climbing out with slow, deliberate steps. My skirt and shirt clung to me, dripping wet. I twisted my hair, squeezing out as much water as I could.

"I hope you've got a spare set of clothes, Fatih. Achoo! Because I can't go home like this."

"Don't worry, darling. There's a change of clothes in my bag in the locker room."

"Well, then I'll just go—"

Before I could finish my sentence, I slipped and fell, landing hard on my back. I groaned in pain.

"Are you alright?" Fatih called, rushing out of the pool toward me.

Eyes squeezed shut, I lay there, wincing. "I hope so."

Seeing my futile attempts to stand, Fatih reached out to assist me, lifting me to my feet with a tenderness that belied the fear I could see etched into his features. Never before had I seen him so alarmed. His eyes, wide with dread, seemed to scan me for hidden injuries, and the way his jaw clenched—tight enough to shatter his teeth—spoke volumes of his internal turmoil.

Reading the distress that flooded his thoughts, I attempted to soothe him. "Do not worry yourself, my love. Contrary to the dark imaginings running through your mind, I don't believe this was some kind of curse. I am merely a clumsy girl, betrayed by the slippery floor, her wet shoes, and a poolside edge too treacherous for her own good. Nothing more."

Fatih gave a silent nod, the motion wooden and mechanical, yet his unease remained palpable, clinging to the air between us. His lips remained sealed, for what else could one expect from a man who had already lost two lovers to the jaws of an ominous curse? Silence was his only refuge.

"I'll borrow your towel and spare clothes," I said, glancing around, my voice a light attempt to break the oppressive atmosphere. "Where did you say the changing rooms were?"

Still frozen in shock, Fatih said nothing. It was then that Kerem emerged from the pool, shaking the water from his hair. "I'll take her to the changing room, Fatih," he said, his tone steady as he motioned for me to follow.

As we walked, Kerem's voice, calm but with a hint of reproach, cut through the stillness. "You'll have to excuse Fatih's... blue screen of death. You know his history."

"I understand," I replied quietly.

Upon reaching the men's changing room, Kerem flipped on the lights, revealing a room scattered with their belongings—backpacks strewn across benches, and clothes left carelessly in piles. With a gesture, Kerem indicated Fatih's bag. "You can use his clothes if they fit, or mine, if you prefer."

"Thank you."

With a sigh, heavy with unspoken words, Kerem finally spoke what had clearly been on his mind. "So, you've decided to ignore my warnings about the curse and go ahead with Fatih. Today's... intimate moment between the two of you confirms as much."

Meeting his gaze, I gave a small nod. "I am not the kind of girl who lets fear of curses dictate her life."

"Well, don't say I didn't warn you," he muttered, shaking his head. "If strange things start happening, let me or Derin know. We'd like to help in any way we can."

"I can handle myself," I said firmly, my voice steady. "Instead of worrying about me, you should focus on Derin. Be there for her. She says you've been neglecting her, especially in the past week."

Kerem's expression tightened, a shadow crossing his face. "Did Derin tell you that?"

"She did."

Kerem turned away, his gaze becoming distant as he sank into thought.

"On Derin's birthday," I pressed on, "you left early. Just after us, in fact. And you didn't even tell her. She was understandably hurt."

Kerem paced slowly across the room, hands on his hips, clearly uncomfortable with the turn of the conversation. "It's better if you don't pry into private matters."

"Where did you go that night?" I asked, my tone sharpening as I leaned into my telepathic abilities, probing his mind. Yet, to my surprise, I found nothing—no trace of the memory I sought. It was as if the answer had been wiped clean from his consciousness, leaving behind only an unsettling void. Normally, even if he resisted speaking, his thoughts would betray him. But not this time.

Kerem stopped, staring blankly at the wall. "I said it's none of your business."

"If you don't tell me, I'll let Derin know how you came on to me at the party," I said, my voice cold with the threat. "You know she'll believe me, given how strained things have been between you two since I arrived."

"Are you threatening me, Ece?"

"Yes."

Kerem considered this for a moment, then slowly walked to the bench by the wall and sat down, his posture tense. He motioned for me to sit beside him, and after a moment's hesitation, I did.

"I can't tell you," he said, his voice barely above a whisper.

"Why not?"

"Because I don't know where I went after the party."

His words rang with sincerity as I delved deeper into his mind. For once, he wasn't lying. He truly didn't know. Or perhaps he had found a way to conceal the truth even from me, to hide behind a wall I couldn't breach.

"What do you mean?" I asked, baffled. "Were you drunk? Is that why you can't remember where you went after leaving Derin's house?"

Kerem shook his head slowly, his expression troubled. "No. I wasn't drunk. I'm sure of that."

"Then why can't you remember?"

"If I knew, I'd tell you. This has happened to me several times in the past week. I lose control, as if my mind slips away from me. Hours later, I come to, only to find myself in a completely different place. If I'm at school, I might wake up in the streets. If I'm at a party, I'll open my eyes back home. And in between those points, I have no memory of what I've done."

This was beyond strange. Could Kerem truly be innocent in all this? Or was he simply spinning lies, carefully constructing a defense that even my telepathy couldn't penetrate? Was he the one behind the curse, acting without his own knowledge, or perhaps willfully hiding his actions?

"I want to help you," I said, my eyes locking onto his, searching for any hint of deception.

"How?" he asked, a note of weariness in his voice.

"I could stay close to you for a few days. That way, if you lose control again, I'll be there to observe what happens. We can document everything you do while you're in this... altered state. And maybe we'll find a way to stop it."

Kerem nodded slowly, though his gaze remained distant. "Perhaps... it could work."

If Kerem was truly innocent, this was my way of helping him. But if he was the one casting the curse—if he was Fatih's enemy in disguise—then I was willingly walking into the den of a ravenous wolf. Yet, no matter the risk, I had to see this through.

For myself. For Fatih. For the poor girls who had already lost their lives. And perhaps, even for Kerem and Derin. If I could solve this mystery, maybe I could mend their fraying relationship too.

CHAPTER 27

A t 8:50 p.m. on a Thursday...

On one of those days when my uncle and his family were once again away, Fatih had come over after school. We spent some time studying in my room. Although it seemed to me that Fatih's focus was more on me than the English lesson I was trying to explain, I hoped he had retained a few bits of knowledge. Or rather, I'd be satisfied if he hadn't completely forgotten what he already knew.

Dressed in my long black leggings and a casual t-shirt, I sat beside him on my bed, as we worked through vocabulary words together.

"Could you repeat those two words again, Ece?" he asked, his tone gentle but playful. "Satisfaction and amateur."

"Satisfaction and amateur."

"Once more. Slowly, love."

"S-a-t-i-s-f-a-c-t-i-o-n. A-m-a-t-e-u-r," I murmured. "Why are you so fixated on these two words, Fatih? Are you trying to perfect your pronunciation?"

"No, no. You just say them so sensually. That's why."

As I playfully bit my lip, I closed the book. "Well, now that you've officially derailed the lesson, it's time for a break. Come on, let's get up, you little troublemaker. It's time for evening prayer."

"Me too?" Fatih asked with feigned innocence.

I grabbed his arm, urging him to stand. "Yes. Especially you."

"Oh, come on..."

"Remember the deal we made at the pool? If you kissed me, you'd pray. Though I ended up backing out of the kiss, you did promise you'd still keep your word until I was ready. Funny how you were in no rush to hold back when it came to the kiss, but when it's about prayer, suddenly you're full of excuses."

"A promise is a promise," Fatih said, but then added, "Though I might be a bit rusty when it comes to ablution. Maybe you could remind me, love."

When we got to the bathroom, Fatih pulled off his socks.

"Start by saying 'Bismillah,' and it's like you've cleansed your entire body in reward," I explained. "Then, wash those Yeti-sized hands of yours three times."

Fatih followed my instructions.

"Next, take water into your mouth three times, then into your nose three times. After that, you've got to wet that thick head of yours."

"Thick-headed and with Yeti hands... If you were an imam, you'd break a lot of hearts with that sharp tongue, Ece," Fatih chuckled, continuing with his ablution.

Step by step, I guided him through. By the time we got to the end, I said, "Finally, you'll wash your hooves three times."

Fatih grinned, doing as I instructed. After he finished, he dried off, and we returned to my room. I briefly explained the evening prayer, and soon after, Fatih performed it.

"Now that you've prayed, I'd say I've won the bet," I declared with satisfaction.

"What bet?" Fatih asked, confused.

"We made a bet, remember? That within a week, I'd get you to start praying once a day. How quickly you forget!"

"Oh, right! You're right... looks like I lost that one. Hmm... How about another bet, Ece?"

"Ah, a sore loser, I see. Very well, what kind of bet are we talking about this time?"

Fatih's smile turned sly. "Within three weeks, you'll sleep with me."

I laughed. "You'll never win that bet, darling. I don't commit fornication, with Allah's permission, of course."

"If you're so confident, why not take the bet, Ece?"

I sat down on my bed. "You'll lose, sweetheart, I'm telling you. I'd never have a relationship outside of marriage. Again, with Allah's permission. But if you're that eager to lose, sure, I'll accept the bet."

"Deal then," Fatih said, a glint in his eye.

"I'm going to go perform ablution and pray myself now," I said, getting up. But just as I took two steps, something strange happened. My right foot, as if it had a mind of its own, decided to take an odd, disjointed turn, causing my leg to awkwardly twist. Before I knew it, I was on the floor.

I was startled. I hadn't tripped on anything, nor had I misstepped. This had never happened to me before.

"Are you okay, Ece?" Fatih asked, his voice tense with worry.

"I-I'm fine," I stammered in disbelief. I wanted to stand, but strangely, I couldn't regain control of my foot just yet.

My clumsy state only seemed to heighten Fatih's concern. Shaking his head, he helped me up and guided me back to the bed, his grip steady but anxious.

"I need to leave, love," he said, his voice suddenly cold and distant.

"Huh? What?"

"I need to go," he repeated.

"Now? Where to? You could stay a bit longer if you want."

"I'll see you tomorrow," Fatih said, leaning down to plant a quick, almost mechanical kiss on my cheek before walking hurriedly to the door.

For someone who usually couldn't keep his hands off me, his kiss felt unusually cold and distant, like it was forced. Either our neighbor Şevval's flowerpots had fallen on his head, or he was spooked by what had just happened, thinking it was some sort of curse. I couldn't think of any other explanation for his sudden strange behavior and abrupt departure.

"I'd walk you out, but my foot's fallen asleep," I called after him, though what I was feeling didn't quite seem like numbness.

"Don't worry, love. Take care of yourself."

I listened to the sound of his footsteps fade, followed by the creaking of the front door and a harsh slam as he left.

As Fatih exited the house, I felt a pang of sadness. Sure, I could understand if he thought I was cursed, but would someone really flee as if escaping a burning building? Even if the curse had finally settled on me—hypothetically speaking—wasn't this the exact time he shouldn't have left me alone and defenseless? Perhaps the little genius had something more pressing than me on his mind.

Minutes later, I regained control of my rebellious foot. I could rotate my ankle where I sat. After some warm-up stretches, I stood up and took a few cautious steps.

It had passed! I could walk again. Whether this had been a curse or some kind of temporary paralysis, I wasn't sure, but I didn't like it one bit.

At 10:00 a.m. on Friday...

When the bell signaling the end of the first lesson rang, I exhaled heavily. Fatih hadn't come to school today, and he wasn't answering his phone either. After seeing him rush out of my house the night before, my worry had only grown.

Oddly, Alya and a few other students who usually sat behind me weren't in class either. Had everyone agreed to ditch school today?

Scanning the room, I spotted Kerem lounging in his usual spot in the middle rows. His long hair was tossed back, his shirt slightly unbuttoned, and he twirled a pencil idly between his fingers. I approached him.

"What's up, Kerem?"

"All good, Ece. How about you?"

"Alhamdulillah... Actually, if you've got a moment, can we talk?"

"Can't you see how busy I am? I've got to twirl this pencil 254 more times," he teased with a playful grin.

I smiled, making a quick grab for the pencil, but Kerem was faster, snatching it out of reach. "Come, sit down," he said, pulling out the chair next to him in a gentlemanly gesture.

"You know, Kerem, maybe you should get a tasbih instead of a pencil. That way, while you're twirling, you can also make dhikr and earn some reward."

With a slow and deliberate gesture, Kerem pursed his lips, letting out a contemplative hum. "Hmmm," he began. "You're not wrong, truly. Yet, in this school, I would undoubtedly draw too much attention. After all... the majority of our fellow students don't seem particularly warm towards Islam."

I nodded, acknowledging the truth of his words. "Yes, that much is true. However, you don't really need a prayer bead. To avoid drawing attention, you could just spin your pen as you always do, and with every silent revolution, whisper 'Allah' within yourself. In doing so, each utterance would earn you tenfold rewards, in-sha'Allah. And in Ramadan? Imagine those rewards multiplied by a thousand! It's a grand opportunity. I've noticed you often spinning your pen during breaks. Just thought it might be a fruitful chance."

Kerem tilted his head thoughtfully, his eyes narrowing slightly. "You may be right. I could give that a try."

"But, that's not why I really wanted to talk to you," I interjected, leaning slightly forward, the air between us growing heavier with a more somber note. "Something strange happened to me yesterday."

"What happened?" Kerem's playful expression fell into one of serious concern. He leaned in, the distance between us closing, his eyes fixed intently on mine.

I recounted the bizarre events of the previous day — the inexplicable movement of my leg, acting of its own accord, the way it locked up, and then, how Fatih had abruptly left. "Do you think this could be the beginning of the curse?"

Kerem's gaze darkened as he lowered his head, considering my words. "I wish I could say no," he murmured gravely, "but Eda's curse began in much the same way. As for why Fatih left... I can't say for sure. But considering his troubled past, it's possible this situation reopened an old wound, one he's clearly not handling well. That's no excuse for his actions, of course."

"Perhaps," I murmured, my mind elsewhere, lost in the murky waters of doubt.

"Fatih didn't come to school today," Kerem continued, glancing at the empty seat beside mine. "You shouldn't sit there alone, not today, Ece. Grab your things and join me. This way, I can watch over you, should anything happen. Besides, you did say you'd observe me, remember? See what I do during those moments when my mind goes blank."

I nodded slowly, the gravity of his offer pulling me toward acceptance. "Alright," I said, rising from my seat, "I'll move next to you."

As I turned to gather my belongings, I misjudged my step and brushed my leg against the side of the desk. A rusty nail, cruel and jagged, jutted from its side, tearing through my skirt and scratching my leg. I hissed in pain, the sharp sting blossoming across my skin.

Pulling the fabric aside, I inspected the wound. Though not deep, it bled.

"Good thing I had my tetanus shot recently," I muttered, attempting to downplay the injury.

Kerem's eyes reflected a silent worry, as though tetanus was the least of our concerns. His look seemed to say, A vaccine may ward off infection, but it does little against curses. "Maybe we should head to the infirmary," he suggested, his voice laced with quiet concern.

I nodded, agreeing silently.

It wasn't the curse that frightened me — nor the one who might have cast it. In my mind, the background music swelled to the triumphant strains of "Eye of the Tiger." I imagined myself painting black lines under my eyes, warrior-like, preparing for the battle to come.

Lost in my self-motivation, I walked toward the infirmary with an almost ridiculous amount of confidence. Kerem must have noticed because he remarked from behind, "What's with the swagger, Ece?"

I stopped, turning to face him. With an exaggerated flourish, I waved my hand before my face, mimicking the signature gesture of a wrestler like John Cena, as if to say, You can't see me. My newfound confidence seemed to amuse Kerem, for he chuckled and said:

"Ece, I don't know who's behind this curse, but whoever it is — they should be afraid. You look fierce enough to give them a run for their money."

"Sure, they may have drawn first blood," I said, gesturing to my leg, "but when all is said and done, I'll be the one cleaning their blood from the floor. Or better yet, I'll have the janitor clean it while I sit back and enjoy the show."

CHAPTER 28

We walked side by side down the school hallway, heading towards the infirmary.

"By the way, I want to apologize for that day," Kerem said, slowing his pace.

I matched his pace, curious. "What day?"

"For hitting on you at Derin's birthday party. Things were rough between Derin and me at the time—still are, really. And, well, you weren't with Fatih yet. I thought the easiest way to protect you from the curse was to keep you close, instead of letting Fatih get involved. So I ended up hitting on you. Sorry, Ece."

"If it were any guy in your shoes, he'd have done the same. Being beautiful and perfect is such a pain," I teased, flipping my hair in mock arrogance. "But seriously, no hard feelings." I reached out, patting his arm gently in reassurance. "I get it."

"Thanks for understanding."

As I slipped into his mind with my telepathy, I could see Kerem had no intention of making another move now that I was with Fatih. He had too much honor to come between a friend and his girlfriend.

As we approached the infirmary, Kerem added, "And thank you for rejecting me that day. You gave me the time I needed to try to salvage things with Derin. I hope I can manage it."

"I'm sure the two of you will pull through this rough patch. Derin loves you; she won't give up on your relationship easily."

"Hope so..."

Speak of the devil. As we reached the infirmary door, we ran into Derin.

"What's up, you two?" she said, glancing from me to Kerem.

"I scratched my leg a bit," I explained, gesturing to my leg. "Came to the infirmary to get it taken care of."

Derin shrugged indifferently. "What's one scratched leg? Lucky for you, spiders have six legs."

"Eight," I corrected her.

"Well, self-awareness is a beautiful thing," Derin replied, grinning like the Cheshire Cat from Alice in Wonderland. Then, without another word, she wrapped herself around Kerem and started chatting with him.

I rolled my eyes. "Now that I've been subjected to my daily dose of Derin's snark, I can die happy. I'll leave you two lovebirds alone while I go get my bandage sorted."

"Alright, Ece," Kerem called after me.

I stepped into the infirmary and closed the door behind me. I headed over to the corner, where a small medical cart stood. I pulled out a packet of gauze and opened it, tossing the wrapper into the bin. Then, I eyed the large plastic bottle of antiseptic solution sitting on top of the cart. The bottle had a small spout designed to dispense the liquid in a controlled manner.

As I sat down on the examination bed and hiked my skirt up to my waist, I examined the scratch on my leg. It was ready for treatment. I grabbed the gauze and the antiseptic bottle, tipping the bottle upside down over the gauze to soak it. And that's when it happened...

The bottle's cap, which was unfortunately loose, popped off and fell to the floor, and the antiseptic solution poured out in a torrent, drenching me. My thighs, legs, even my shoes were soaked in the brown liquid.

Damn this curse, damn it all!

Don't lose your temper, Ece. Just play it cool, I told myself. I pressed the gauze into the pool of antiseptic on my clothes and used it to clean the wound. It worked. My scratch was disinfected, and probably any future wounds as well, given how much of that stuff had soaked into me.

Not wanting someone else to suffer the same fate, I bent down to pick up the fallen cap and screw it back onto the bottle.

I got off the bed and crouched down, but when I reached for the cap, I accidentally knocked it further under the bed. Sighing, I dropped to my hands and knees and reached out. At last, I caught it!

Take that, curse! I grabbed the cap triumphantly, but as I stood up, I banged my head against the edge of the bed and groaned in pain. I had celebrated too soon.

The world spun like in a cartoon. I sat back down, rubbing my aching head. Suddenly, something fell on top of me. It was the antiseptic bottle again. After I had knocked it earlier, it had wobbled and lost its balance. And this time, it dumped the rest of its contents over my head.

Brown liquid dripped from my hair onto my face, testing my last nerves. I nearly burst into tears, but I had to stay strong. If I was going to fight this curse, I needed nerves of steel. Besides, I had once thought about dyeing my hair brown—I just hadn't planned on doing it this way.

Maybe this was karma for dumping water on Fatih's head. I was drenched, though in a much worse way.

Kerem must have heard me hit my head, because he burst into the infirmary. "Ece!" he exclaimed in shock. "What happened to you?"

"You remember Stephen King's Carrie? The book where they dump paint on the girl's head at a party? I look like her, don't I?"

"Yeah, you do. But how did this happen?" Kerem came over and started wiping my face with one hand, while gently dabbing my cheek with the other. His efforts were futile, given the state I was in.

"What happened? Well, I bandaged myself."

"Bandaged?"

"Yes, bandaged," I repeated, shrugging. "Not a fan of my work?"

"Ece... If I ever get hurt, just leave me alone, alright? Let me die. Please, don't bandage me."

"Your loss."

Kerem took my hand and led me out of the infirmary. Derin was gone by then. She must have left.

"I'll take you to my place," Kerem said. "You can wash up, and if I start doing something out of line, you can keep an eye on me."

"Alright, Kerem."

Twenty minutes later...

We arrived at Kerem's place in his car. Apparently, he lived alone. As we entered his top-floor apartment, I kicked off my shoes, still dripping antiseptic, and he led me straight to the bathroom. He handed me a fresh towel and some clothes.

"They're Derin's," he said, passing the clothes to me. "She must've left them here the last time she stayed over. You can wear them after you shower. They should fit."

"Thanks."

I took the clothes from him and inspected them: a pair of charcoal-gray athletic shorts with white stripes and a matching crop top.

A bit short for my taste, but I couldn't be picky as a guest. Oh well.

After a warm, soapy shower and a thorough drying, I put on the clothes and dried my hair with a blow dryer. I stepped out of the bathroom and found Kerem sitting in the living room, watching a documentary on mountain climbing. He handed me one of the lemon iced teas from the coffee table, and I opened it to take a sip.

I tugged at the hem of the shorts, trying to stretch them out. No luck. Today would just have to be one of those days. Kerem, meanwhile, was dressed in gray sweatpants and a white t-shirt.

I decided to get straight to the point. "Kerem, how are things between you and Fatih? I mean, you don't have any bad feelings toward each other, do you?"

Kerem turned to face me, eyes wide. "Bad feelings? He's like a brother to me. I'd die for him if he asked."

"God forbid."

Using my telepathy, I probed his mind and confirmed his sincerity. Kerem had no reason to curse Fatih.

"You must have some kind of special ability, seeing as you're in our class," I said. "Mind if I ask what it is?"

"Instead of telling you, why don't I show you?" Kerem replied.

"Alright."

Kerem stood and left the room. I waited. When he returned, he sat beside me again, holding a deck of cards in one hand and a pair of dice in the other.

"Take the dice and roll them, Ece," he said flatly.

I took the dice from him, shook them in my hand, and tossed them onto the couch. One of the dice fell off and rolled onto the carpet, while the other landed between my legs. I spread my knees and found it.

"Guess that doesn't count. Let me try again," I said, gathering the dice. I rolled them again. "Three and two."

Kerem smiled. "My turn." He shook the dice and rolled them. Both showed six. He picked them up and rolled again. Another six and six. By the third time, my jaw dropped.

"You're ridiculously lucky, Kerem!"

Kerem held up a finger as if to say "just wait." Then, he asked me to draw a card from the deck. I drew the five of hearts and showed it to him.

"Now my turn." Kerem shuffled the deck and started drawing cards one after another, laying them on the couch.

King of hearts. King of spades. King of clubs. King of diamonds.

Then four queens.

And four jacks.

I had never seen such luck. This couldn't be coincidence. Clearly, his power was extraordinary. Kerem was a walking four-leaf clover! Or maybe five, if that's even possible...

CHAPTER 29

"So, your power is to be... lucky?" I marveled, my voice a mix of disbelief and awe. "And not just any luck—absurd, exaggerated luck. I bet if the skies darkened and the wind began to howl, before a single raindrop even kissed the ground, an umbrella would descend from the heavens just for you. You wouldn't even get wet. No, I take that back! Not just an umbrella. Barbara Palvin herself would land a mere 15-20 meters away in a private helicopter, stride over to you, and hold the umbrella above your head. And of course, dear Mr. Lucky, you'd stay bone dry."

Kerem smiled, the corners of his lips curling with amusement. "Yeah, I suppose you could say I'm lucky," he said, leaning back in his seat beside me. "I mean, I wouldn't have someone as wonderful as Derin for a girlfriend otherwise."

"Well, she's lucky too. You two suit each other, more so than Barbara ever would." I thought for a moment, then added, "But now that you're practically an angel of luck, couldn't you have used that power to save those two girls from the curse? I mean, shouldn't your luck be able to counterbalance it?"

"You think I haven't thought of that, Ece? I tried. But the curse was stronger than my luck."

"I don't know..." I muttered, deep in thought. "Maybe if you stayed close enough to the girl, your luck could keep anything bad from happening to her."

Kerem slung his arm around me, his smile a bittersweet curve. "If that were the case, you wouldn't have sliced your leg on the desk just by standing next to me earlier. And in the infirmary, disaster followed you around even though I was just a few steps away."

"Hmm, you're right..." I sighed, exasperated. "I'm just trying to find a way out of this mess, but I can't. If only we knew what this curse was, who cast it."

Kerem gently stroked my shoulder, his hand resting behind me. "I have a few theories," he said, his voice thoughtful. "Here's the first: I'm an incredibly lucky person, right? What if the universe, in an attempt to balance itself, radiates bad luck—this curse—around me as a counterweight?"

I shook my head firmly. "The universe isn't a sentient being, Kerem. It doesn't think, it doesn't will, and it holds no power. That power belongs to Allah alone, and I don't believe He would punish others because of your luck. Allah opens doors, gives chances even to His most rebellious servants. He wouldn't inflict such swift and merciless destruction on the innocent because of you."

Kerem nodded, conceding to my point. "You're right. Which brings me to my second theory: What if someone has found a way to reverse my luck, turning it into misfortune? After all, we are surrounded by students with extraordinary powers. Couldn't someone absorb my luck and twist it, turning it into a curse?"

I paused, the wildness of the idea settling into my mind. Could it be? It was an outlandish theory, but not impossible. "I don't know... But if someone could do that, and if they've targeted

Fatih's girlfriends with it, then whoever is doing this must hate him. Who could it be, do you think?"

Kerem fell silent in thought. "I can't think of anyone right now."

We spent the day in conversation, my eyes ever watchful of Kerem, wondering if he would lose control and do something he wouldn't remember. But he never did. When night fell, I decided to stay and keep an eye on him.

Kerem, ever the gentleman, offered me his room, while he himself would sleep on the couch in the living room. As the clock approached 11 p.m. and Kerem retired, I found myself in his luxurious yet disheveled room, closing the door behind me.

Exhausted, I collapsed onto the bed and fell into a deep sleep almost immediately.

When Kerem's voice reached my ears from outside the room, my eyes fluttered open. It was still dark; dawn had not yet broken. Groggily, I reached for my phone on the nightstand and checked the time. It was only one in the morning.

Who was Kerem speaking to? My question was swiftly answered as Derin's voice followed. My eyes widened.

Derin was here—at Kerem's house!

Their relationship was already strained, and Derin was suspicious of him. If she found me here, she would think Kerem was cheating on her, and as sure as the sun rises, she would transform into a deadly anaconda and devour me whole! No, no—I was far too young to become snake dung.

I sat up in bed, straining to listen to their conversation.

"Welcome, baby," Kerem said. "I didn't know you were coming. What a lovely surprise. How are you, my love?" His voice was louder than normal, as if warning me to find somewhere to hide.

"I'm good, darling," Derin replied. "I missed you, so I came."

"You're taking me by the hand—where are you taking me, Derin?" Kerem asked, again loudly, as though urging me to escape. "To my bedroom, I guess."

"Yes. We're going to play a little cops and robbers, sweetheart. I've been a very, very bad girl, and you, as the cop, are going to catch me and... punish me."

As her next few sentences delved into scandalous, explicit detail, my face twisted in discomfort. Ah, my poor ears! So, this was the infamous "ear adultery" I'd heard about. Derin described her fantasy with such seductive flair that I half-expected to become pregnant just from listening!

But that wasn't the real problem. No, my issue was where to hide, as Kerem had just warned me that they were headed to this very room.

The wardrobe? Maybe. That could work. Grabbing my phone, I tiptoed to the wardrobe and opened it. Was there enough space to squeeze in?

Oh, Kerem... His wardrobe was more like a chaotic storage unit! He'd stuffed anything and everything inside, leaving no room for me. I understood the mess, but why on earth were there fire extinguishers and ski poles in there?

Wait a minute. I got it! The fire extinguisher was to put out Derin's flames. And if Kerem grew too tired in bed, Derin could poke him with the ski poles, urging him on with a "Come on, keep going!"

As footsteps approached, I scanned the room in panic, searching for a hiding place. Finding none, I crawled under the bed, the last resort.

Moments later, the door opened. From my vantage point under the bed, I could see the feet of Kerem and Derin as they entered.

Without wasting a second, Derin's skirt dropped to the floor. I watched as her shirt and then her undergarments followed, forming a pile not far from where I lay. Her red, lacy panties were undeniably sexy. But to be honest, they were so tiny they didn't seem designed to cover anything at all.

Soon, they were on the bed. For the next hour, the lovebirds had their fun. And to be honest, I was a little entertained too. I had muted my phone and spent the time under the bed taking an Arabic lesson on Duolingo.

Eventually, they both seemed to fall asleep. Or so I thought. But when Kerem slipped out of bed and began dressing, I realized that wasn't the case. He donned his pants and shirt and left the room, heading toward the front door.

Quietly, I crawled out from under the bed and stood up. I was about to follow Kerem when he grabbed his keys and slipped out of the house.

Where was Kerem going in the middle of the night? Wait a minute... Was this it? Had the moment arrived? Kerem might have lost control, acting unconsciously, and I needed to follow him if I wanted to uncover the mystery of the curse.

But just as I was about to leave, Derin's voice came from the bed:

"Come back to bed, baby. I want to cuddle," she mumbled, her voice drowsy, her eyes still closed. She was in that liminal space between sleep and wakefulness.

If I tried to follow Kerem now, Derin would wake up when she realized he wasn't there, see me, and turn me into her next meal. I wasn't afraid of meeting my Creator, but tonight wasn't the night.

Kerem was already gone, though, and obviously couldn't respond to her request. That left me to play his role. My only solution was to climb into bed, pretend to be him, and let her cuddle me.

And, of course, I prayed—earnestly—that she wouldn't notice the difference. It was a solid prayer, too, because the resemblance between Kerem and me was about as strong as the likeness between Kylie Jenner's pre- and post-surgery faces. We were worlds apart.

It could hardly be said that Kylie's transformation was as different as mine from Kerem's, of course. The woman had undergone a metamorphosis so complete that it was as though her very essence had been rebuilt, akin to urban renewal where decrepit buildings rise anew—smaller, sleeker, and far more beautiful than before.

As I crept into bed beside the starkly naked Derin, I steeled myself, tensing every muscle in my abdomen and arms, trying with all my might to mimic the solidity of Kerem's form. I flexed so hard, I thought I might burst from the strain, every fiber coiled in the hopes that she wouldn't detect the impostor lying beside her.

When I turned my back to her, Derin's arm slid around my waist. I froze, heart thundering, but to my immense relief, she didn't swallow me whole. It seemed she hadn't realized that I wasn't Kerem after all.

Moments later, her arm withdrew, allowing me to exhale. I cautiously shifted to lie on my back, the tension beginning to ebb away.

"Goodnight, darling," Derin murmured, her sleepy voice softened by a lingering kiss she blew into the air. Within minutes, she was fast asleep.

Had I committed a great sin this night? I wondered. The closeness between women, according to our faith, was forbidden. There was a hadith that explicitly condemned one woman sharing a bed with another, without necessity or legitimate excuse. But surely, the imminent threat of being devoured by a monstrous, jealous anaconda of a woman provided just such a justification. I prayed silently, hoping Allah would forgive my transgression.

For tonight, the thrill had been more than enough, far more than I could handle. After this ordeal, I figured I could go without watching horror films for at least a month. When I was certain Derin was deep in slumber, I gently slipped out of the bed.

I rummaged through my bag, pulling out some money and tucking it into the pocket of my shorts. My clothes, still tainted by antiseptic, I sealed in a plastic bag. Grabbing that and my school bag, I quietly slipped out of Kerem's house into the night.

CHAPTER 30

At three in the deep night...

Having finally shaken off Derin, I could at last return home. Once I'd left Kerem's place, I hailed a cab, and after a short ride, I arrived at my street. I asked the driver to stop at the corner, paid the fare, and stepped out of the car. As the cab pulled away into the distance, I began the walk toward my building.

But as I neared the apartment complex, the scene that greeted me slowed my steps until I came to a complete halt. Just outside the garden gate, someone stood, head tilted upward, staring fixedly at my building. Upon closer inspection, I realized it was Kerem. His lips moved as if in a silent chant, his eyes trained on the building in eerie focus.

What could Kerem possibly be muttering to himself? Had he come all the way here to utter words that would bring a curse upon me? It certainly appeared that way. Yet, something within me resisted the notion that he was doing this deliberately. For reasons I couldn't explain, I still wanted to believe in his innocence.

Slipping into telepathic mode, I plunged headfirst into Kerem's mind. But the moment I entered, I found myself drowning in a sea of icy, chilling hatred. Normally, Kerem harbored fondness for Fatih, but now his mind brimmed with rage, seething with an intensity that took my breath away. He was here, as I had feared, to direct the curse at me, the dark force hanging over me like a blade poised to strike.

In short, Kerem wanted me dead. Whether conscious of it or not, that was the undeniable truth.

Suddenly, a man's voice, thick and slurred, jolted me from behind.

"Look at this beauty," he crooned, his tone sleazy. "Are you a genie come from my beer bottle, or are you a fairy?"

I whirled around, my gaze landing on the source. A man in his fifties, grey-haired, with a beer bottle clutched in one hand, leered at me. His distended belly strained against the fabric of his thin, gray shirt, evidence of a lifetime spent in the losing battle with alcohol. But still, repentance was possible, even until the final breath. I prayed that Allah might guide him, freeing him from the grip of this grave sin.

"I'm neither a genie, a fairy, nor an Irish leprechaun," I retorted.

"Ah, but you must be a tooth fairy then. Why don't you come to my place, beautiful fairy?" He drew nearer.

"I'd advise against coming any closer, because this tooth fairy is liable to punch you hard enough to knock out that gold tooth of yours. I'm more of a back-alley, rough-around-the-edges kind of fairy, you see."

"You misunderstand," the man slurred, swaying on his feet, barely able to stay upright as he leaned against a nearby car for support. "I just wanted to sit and chat with you for a while."

"And may I ask what your name is?"

"Rıza. And yours?"

"My name is Ece. But Mr. Rıza, I am not the type of girl who goes to a stranger's house at three in the morning for a chat."

"We could meet tomorrow, then," he suggested. "In the daylight."

I sighed. Just when I'd caught Kerem in the act of casting his curse, this walking beer barrel had to make a move on me. His breath wasn't merely unpleasant anymore; it had moved past that stage. It now carried a stench that felt alive, a reek that seemed to breathe on its own.

"I'm afraid I'm busy tomorrow as well. I've got a six-year-old girl whose tooth I need to collect, Mr. Rıza. I'm sorry."

Rıza took a step closer, edging toward me. "Are you a student, Ece?"

Was this man even aware that he was more than thirty years older than me? Or had alcohol so fried his brain cells that the age gap escaped his notice entirely? Allah had forbidden alcohol for good reason.

Alright, but how on earth was I supposed to escape this guy?

Wait a minute! A plan formed in my mind. Considering his love for drink and the empty bottle in his hand, perhaps I could get rid of him by offering him money to buy more beer. I had a bit of cash in my pocket. I'd give him some, suggest he head to the liquor store, and pray that he took the bait.

Giving him money to fuel his vice was sinful, I knew, but I'd do it to save myself. Otherwise, this man was bound to turn sinister. I prayed that Allah would forgive me.

With this thought, I reached into my pocket, preparing to hand him some cash. "I have a suggestion, Mr. Rıza. Here, why don't you take this and go enjoy yourself?"

But as my fingers brushed against something inside Derin's shorts, I realized with horror that what I'd pulled out wasn't cash at all—it was a condom, still wrapped. Of course, it had to be Derin who'd left this behind.

"You're giving me this to enjoy myself, huh?" Rıza grinned, his eyes lighting up with twisted glee. "A condom, eh? You move fast, Ece. Alright, if it's sex you want, let's use this and have some fun."

"No, no, you've misunderstood me!" I protested, but Rıza lunged at me before I could explain further. "Wait, I was going to give you money, really."

"I don't ask money for this, gorgeous. It is pleasure for me."

"Rıza, no!" I cried, panic rising as his hands groped at me. With the curse still hanging over me, the situation felt more dire than ever. But then, as if summoned by fate, Kerem appeared out of nowhere and shoved Rıza off me. In a flurry of curses, Kerem dealt Rıza a vicious beating, enough to send the man running for his life.

I was safe.

"Are you alright, Ece?" Kerem asked, his voice full of concern. "What happened? How did I even get here? I remember nothing."

"I-I'm fine," I stammered, my heart pounding wildly from everything that had just transpired. "I think you had another blackout, Kerem. You left your house in the middle of the night and came here, to my place. And I'm afraid you were saying the words to activate the curse."

"I was?" Kerem's face fell, shame and disappointment washing over him.

I nodded, sorrowful. "Yes."

Kerem lowered his head, his voice thick with remorse. "I don't know what to say, Ece. None of this is in my control."

"I know, Kerem. Don't worry. I won't let this go. I'll dig deeper into it, because something just doesn't feel right."

"Then stay close to me until we figure this out, Ece. If you can stop me from saying the curse, maybe the spell will break."

"Perhaps," I agreed. "But it might be better if Derin keeps an eye on you. Being around you seems to attract trouble for me."

"Why?" he asked.

I recounted how I'd had no choice but to share a bed with Derin that night, and how terrified I'd been that she might wake up and find me there.

"Alright, then," Kerem said, his voice steady. "Let Derin watch over me. And you can focus on the others in the class. There might be someone else involved in this."

Friday morning, just before the first lesson...

With the weight of my backpack pressing into my shoulders, I followed the path of the school corridor, heading towards my classroom. But just then, Alya appeared in front of me.

"Do you have a few minutes?" she asked, her gaze fixed on me.

Surprised, I blinked. We weren't exactly close, so her addressing me was unexpected. "Me? Sure, I have some time."

Alya hesitated. Her expression, devoid of its usual brightness, told me whatever she had to say wasn't going to be good news. "Perhaps we could head down to the cafeteria to talk? Does that work for you, Ece?" she suggested.

"Alright, let's do that."

As we walked side by side down the hallway, reaching the stairs, we began our descent. Alya, with her full lips, her face as smooth as porcelain without a single blemish, and her hair tied in a silken bun, shone like a statue carved by a master sculptor. She resembled those striking Russian girls one might see in films, a living embodiment of cold beauty.

Unable to resist, I finally asked, "Hey... Alya, is there any Russian heritage in your family? You remind me so much of Russians. Don't take it the wrong way, it's a compliment. You look like you could be from the Balkans or Russia."

"My mother's Russian, and my father's Turkish," she replied. "It was love at first sight for them. My father fell in love with my mother, and she fell in love with Turkey."

"Hmm, how lovely."

By the time we reached the cafeteria, we found a quiet corner and sat across from each other at an empty table.

"Ece..." Alya began, her voice dropping to a near whisper. "There's something I need to tell you... Yesterday..."

As she hesitated, clearly struggling to get to the point, I pressed her. "Well? What happened yesterday?"

"Yesterday... Fatih asked me out."

"Fatih?"

"Yes, Fatih."

"My Fatih?"

"Your Fatih."

"He asked you?"

"Yes, me."

"To date?"

"Yes, Ece, date. Must you make me repeat every word?"

My jaw nearly hit the table. So that's what Fatih had been up to! The man who'd switched off his phone, skipped class, had been busy wooing another girl since yesterday! How could he have done such a thing? I'd let him into my heart despite the curse, despite the risk to my life, and here he was, off enjoying himself without a care in the world?

"And what did you say to him?" I asked, feeling my muscles tense.

If she told me she'd accepted, I was going to flip this table and tear her silky blonde hair from her head, forever erasing her resemblance to Russians. Allah willing, the Black Sea wouldn't become a Russian lake under my watch!

"I turned him down, of course, Ece. I knew you two were together. I'm not the kind of girl who'd step in between another couple. It's a matter of principle."

"Well, obviously," I said, my fury cooling just slightly.

"Besides, with all the rumors about that curse, do you really think I'd choose him as a boyfriend? No offense, but I'm not that foolish."

"Offense slightly taken, Alya."

"Anyway, I just thought you should know that he made a move on me, Ece. I figured if I were being cheated on, I'd want to know."

"Thank you for telling me, Alya," I said, rising from the table. "Now, if you'll excuse me, I've got an ex-boyfriend to make regret his very existence."

Alya nodded, and I strode away, my footsteps sharp and angry. I was headed for the stairs when, lo and behold, Fatih appeared. Speak of the devil...

Stopping right in front of him, I placed my hands on my hips and glared up at him. "Fatih, my dear Sultan, have you decided to emulate the Ottoman emperors and start a harem? What on earth is this about asking Alya out? What, are you trying to mend diplomatic ties with Russia, you pathetic excuse for a sultan?"

Fatih's cold, empty gaze met mine. "We had a good run, Ece, but it's over."

"Oh no, it's not over yet." I slapped him, hard, across his cheek. Then the other cheek. "Now it's over."

I was just about to turn and storm away when something bizarre happened. Fatih began to shrink before my very eyes. No, not metaphorically, as in he lost stature in my eyes—although that, too, was true given his recent behavior—but physically. He was shrinking, his body reducing in size.

Within seconds, Fatih had transformed into an eight- or nine-year-old girl, slender, with chestnut hair, dimples, and hazel eyes. A familiar little girl. Fatih had morphed once again into Ceren, the same girl he'd turned into just a week ago after our shopping trip.

Despite my anger toward Fatih, and despite the fact that technically, Ceren and Fatih were the same person, seeing those innocent eyes gazing up at me made my older sisterly instincts kick in. I couldn't just leave her there, frightened and confused. The poor thing had no idea how she'd ended up here and looked at me with wide, anxious eyes.

Fatih's clothes hung off her small frame, the oversized fabric swallowing her up like a pile of cloth. Thankfully, I'd thought ahead and stashed some of my old childhood clothes in my locker for just such an occasion.

Squatting down to Ceren's level, I murmured softly, "Don't worry, Ceren, I'm here."

Without warning, Ceren flung herself at me, wrapping her arms around my neck in a tight embrace. The force knocked me off balance, and I landed squarely on my rear. "I'm so glad you're here, Ece sister."

"Easy, sweetheart," I said, adjusting my skirt while seated on the floor. "Shall we spend the day together again?"

Ceren loosened her grip on me, pulling back slightly. "I'd love that. What will we do?"

"Well, first, let's get you dressed in the clothes I have in my locker, then maybe we can go grab some ice cream and snacks. After that, we can head to my place and watch that cartoon you like—what was it called again? King Julien, right? We can watch it while we snack. How does that sound? Good plan?"

"Not good. Great!"

"My locker's just down the hall. Let's go and get you changed, love."

As we walked hand in hand toward my locker, Ceren piped up, "Ece abla (sister), all the other girls at school wear pink shirts and grey skirts. But you... you're all in black. Why?"

"Black?" I glanced down at my clothes. Oh no, not again! I'd gone into Black Rose mode once more. After Fatih had kissed me, my colors had returned to normal, but now, having been betrayed, I was clad in black once again.

"Why black, you ask, Ceren? Because I'm a secret warrior, sent to this school on a mission. My task is to protect the principal at all costs. Like Clover, the warrior lemur who protects King Julien."

"You're joking!" Ceren giggled. "Right, Ece abla?"

I stopped and threw a few mock karate moves. "What do you think?"

Ceren laughed again. "Not bad moves, but I still don't believe you."

"Good girl. That's your first lesson from me. Trust no one."

Especially not men.

And especially not ones named Fatih.

Fatih had transformed into Ceren twice now, both times during moments of farewell. It was either a strange coincidence or a sign that this boy had an unhealthy attachment to our partings. Maybe he should've shown the same care when he was busy betraying me, don't you think?

CHapTer 31

Ah, alas! What folly had I succumbed to, daring to kiss a man barely a week since our fateful encounter? Fatih had grown weary of me, dismissing me like one discards a wilted flower.

Yet, in this separation, a curious relief bloomed within my chest. No longer would I be plagued by the sin of sharing a kiss while tethered to another. Perhaps it was a mercy veiled in heartache, a blessing I ought not mourn.

At least I had kept my promise to Ceren. The night we spent together was a parade of snacks and animated shows. Later, I read her a few stories, tucking her into my uncle's bed, where she drifted to sleep without a trace of fear. This time, unlike before, I did not retreat to my room, leaving her alone to fend off the night's shadows. Instead, I stayed beside her, donning a black nightgown—green, truly, but black it turned upon my wearing—its straps clinging to my shoulders and hem grazing my knees.

Yet sleep eluded me. I feared if I let my guard down, Ceren would vanish in the night, morphing into Fatih once again. And I could not bear to share my bed with a man who had betrayed me, however unfaithfully. So, I watched a movie on my phone, determined to stay awake. But, alas, exhaustion is a cruel master, and soon my eyelids fell, and sleep claimed me.

In the fog of night, I vaguely recall the sensation of a kiss upon my forehead, and a blanket being drawn over me. Morning greeted me with a quiet revelation—Fatih lay beside me. As I feared, Ceren had once again shifted into him. He looked like an angel, with hands folded beneath his head, a serene expression gracing his face beneath the thin cover. But appearances deceive. A snake in a prince's disguise, indeed! My mind wandered to the film Sleeping with the Enemy, though this was worse—Sleeping with the Betrayer.

I could have woken him with a splash of ice-cold water, but the thought of committing such a sin at the break of dawn seemed too much. After all, Fatih himself had once spoken true words, though they fell from the mouth of a fool: wasting water was a sin.

Wondering how to fill the time until he woke, I decided to call Sinem, knowing she'd appreciate the irony of Fatih leaving yet another construction project unfinished—me, of course.

I slipped into the living room and shut the door behind me before calling her.

"Hey girl, what's up?" I asked when she finally answered after five rings.

"I'm good, Ece," she replied, but something about her tone struck me as off, strangely quiet, strangely still. "How are you?"

"Ugh, don't even get me started! You won't believe what Fatih did."

"What did he do?" she asked, again with that flat voice. There was no spark of her usual cheer.

"He asked Alya out! Can you believe it? I could just lose my mind!"

There was silence for a few seconds, and then Sinem's muted reply: "Hmmm... Really?"

"But don't worry," I added, "she turned him down. If she hadn't, she'd have felt my wrath. I would've exacted revenge so fierce, the curse hanging over me would tip its hat and say, 'Bravo, Ece! You're more cursed than I could ever be!' I'd rub chili into her lips!—well, something else came to mind, but I held my tongue."

"Oh... really?"

"Sinem, what's going on? You sound... off."

Another pause. Then she spoke, her voice wavering. "I... we..."

"What?"

"Fatih and I are together."

I laughed, thinking she was joking. "That's a good one! Dark humor suits you."

"Yes, but here's the thing—it's not a joke. Fatih and I started dating yesterday."

"What? Has he contracted some acute form of flirtation sickness? Two weeks ago it was me, then Alya, and now you? Sinem, you're next on his sketch list! You know he draws every girl he dates. When he does, tell me—I'll take that drawing, roll it up, and shove it up your... well, let's just say, somewhere uncomfortable!"

"Ece, I—"

"Shut it, Sinem! How could you? You knew I was with him, and yet you went behind my back. Alya had the decency to reject him, but you—my best friend—said yes. You're worse than Alya!"

"Am I your best friend, though?"

"Oh, past tense, dear Sinem—was my best friend."

She began to cry, her voice shaking. "It was Fatih's plan all along."

"What plan? To build a harem of the school's girls? Speak, oh Sultan of Schemes, shall I fetch your prince?"

"Fatih... he wanted to break the curse," she confessed. "He was convinced you were cursed and couldn't bear it. His plan was to date someone else in hopes that the curse would transfer to them."

"What kind of absurd plan is that?" I scoffed. "What, is this curse some city bus? It'll just hop from one stop to the next?"

"He proposed to Alya without telling her, and when she rejected him, he came to me with the truth. He knew I wouldn't agree otherwise."

"You seriously went along with this?"

"Yes," Sinem replied. "I thought maybe I could buy you some time... maybe the curse would latch onto me instead. I don't want you to die, Ece. I don't want you to hate me either. Please, forgive me!"

Her sobs were so pitiful, I could no longer find it in me to be angry with her. "Oh, stop crying, you silly goose. I won't forgive Fatih, but you... I forgive."

"Thank you, thank you, thank you, Ece!"

I rolled my eyes. "You're such a SpongeBob, Sinem, but I love you."

"I love you too, so much."

Hearing a noise outside, I glanced toward the door. "I think Fatih's up. I'll go check on him."

"Wait, Fatih slept over at your place?" Sinem asked, surprised.

"Yep. Just like that. We slept cheek to cheek, heart to heart—totally innocent, right? We've gone past love triangles, Sinem. We're at some mega-star polygon of scandal."

"Well... good luck."

I hung up and stepped into the hallway, making my way to my uncle's bedroom. Fatih had risen and dressed. He stood at the foot of the bed, looking at me.

For a moment, we exchanged nothing but glances, a cold war waged between our eyes. But the weapons lay just behind the door.

"I guess I turned back into Ceren again," Fatih finally said.

I leaned against the doorframe, arms crossed. "Yes, but more than that, you've also become a coward."

"What?"

"I spoke with Sinem. She told me all about your little plan."

Fatih sat on the edge of the bed, covering his face with his hands. "I warned her to keep quiet."

"Fatih, if I feared the curse, if I wasn't ready to die, I would never have been with you. I was prepared to stand by your side through everything—even death. But you... you chose to break my heart to save me. You thought I needed rescuing. But you've only made me realize I never needed you."

He sighed deeply, but I pressed on, refusing to let him speak.

"You don't deserve the name Fatih. The great conqueror who laid down his life for his cause—you could never compare. You broke my heart deliberately, so I would stop wanting you. Congratulations, you've succeeded. Now leave. You know the way out."

Fatih sat in silence for a moment, then stood and walked past me without a word, the door clicking shut behind him.

And so Behlül left...

Just like that. Aşk-ı Memnu, the finale.

A Halid Ziya Uşaklıgil classic.

Monday morning, 8:30.

When I entered the classroom, I didn't head for the desk beside Fatih. I didn't even want to sit near him anymore. I scanned the room and spotted an empty seat next to Sinan, right in front of Derin. That would be my new spot.

As I sat down, my phone buzzed with a message from Kerem:

Kerem: Ece, remember last week when you asked who might be cursing Fatih and his girlfriends?

Me: Yes, I remember.

Kerem: Well, I've been thinking. I didn't have any ideas back then, but now...

Me: Now what?

Kerem: Never mind, Ece. If I mention a name, you'll just jump to conclusions and accuse them of the curse without any proof.

Me: I won't. If I were that hasty, I'd have accused you first, Kerem. After all, you were standing across from my house, muttering curses. But I trust you. So tell me. I won't rush to judgment.

Kerem: All right. I think it could be Sinan. He broke up with his girlfriend Zeynep, and soon after, she started dating Fatih. Sinan believed Fatih had stolen her, that he'd somehow charmed her away. They haven't spoken since.

Ah, how swiftly the tides of thought turned in the depths of my mind as Kerem's words faded into the digital ether of our chat, like the dying embers of a fire once fierce. The specter of Zeynep loomed large in my thoughts—Fatih's oldest lover, even before poor Eda met her tragic fate in the wreckage of twisted metal. A history written in heartbreak and blood.

Me: "Zeynep... She was Fatih's first love, wasn't she? Before Eda, even before the accident that claimed her life?"

Kerem: "Yes, exactly. Zeynep was his first."

The name lingered on my lips, like a bitter aftertaste of lost affection. I mulled over the weight of it, the history they shared, the invisible threads that still bound Zeynep's memory to the present moment. And then Sinan—could he have been the one, silently weaving the threads of this curse that had settled over Fatih's life?

Me: "Hmm... Do you know, Kerem, what Sinan's special ability is? I wonder if it might hold the key to this mystery."

Kerem: "I don't know, and frankly, I doubt anyone else does. Sinan is a solitary soul, keeping to the shadows of his own thoughts. He's never been close to anyone in class, not that I've seen."

Me: "Thank you, Kerem. I'll dig deeper into this. Something feels off, and I intend to uncover the truth."

Kerem: "Anytime. Keep me informed if anything new surfaces."

Me: "I will. Take care."

Kerem: "You too."

With that, our brief but weighty conversation ended, leaving me with a sense of foreboding that clung to me like a thick fog. I glanced sideways at Sinan, sitting mere inches from me, his presence palpable yet distant, as if he existed in a world separate from the rest of us. Could it truly be him, the architect of this curse that wove death into the lives of Fatih's lovers? The thought gnawed at my mind, burrowing deep into my suspicions.

Sinan. The silent one. Always on the outskirts, never fully part of the laughter or the whispered confessions exchanged between friends. His solitude was almost too complete, as though he carried with him the weight of a secret so profound, so terrible, that he dared not let it see the light of day.

Could it be him? The source of all this unseen malice? The puppeteer behind the invisible strings that tugged at the fates of those who dared come close to Fatih?

I resolved, then and there, to uncover the truth. Whatever dark secrets Sinan held, they would soon see the light. And with that revelation, perhaps the curse that loomed over us all would finally be broken.

The first step was clear—I would have to draw closer to him, to peel back the layers of silence that enveloped him like a shroud. Only then, perhaps, would I see the truth.

CHAPTER 32

A h, the whims of fate—how had I found myself back at the beginning once more? This was the very seat I had taken on my first day, beside Sinan. It was here that I had sat before Derin, with her serpentine tongue, shot her sharp jibes at me. Offended, I had moved elsewhere. But now, here I was again.

With fifteen minutes remaining before class commenced, Sinan, sitting beside me, turned to speak.

"I'm sorry for what happened at Derin's birthday party, Ece."

"What happened?"

"When we were dancing, my hand... well, it wandered to your waist. I apologize for that."

"I have forgiven you. If you repent, I hope God forgives you as well."

"Then let it be repentance," Sinan said with a smile.

A voice inside urged me to draw closer to Sinan, to use him as a pawn in my vengeance against Fatih. But I knew well that voice was the devil's own whisper. And one could not heed the devil, nor did such petty games suit me. I would not stoop to flirting with Sinan.

Besides, Sinan, with his long red hair and freckled face, did not appeal to me much. May God forgive me for this thought, as it is not our place to question His creation—but, alas, tastes differ. He simply wasn't my type.

Yet, I could not banish from my mind the schemes Fatih had woven behind my back. Sighing deeply, I exhaled my frustration.

"Are you alright?" Sinan asked, his brow furrowed with concern. "You seem tense, Ece."

I nodded. "I am, a little."

"What happened?"

"Love's forbidden tale," I quipped, trying to lighten the mood. But when Sinan looked at me, confused, I had to explain. "I broke up with my boyfriend."

"If you want, we could step outside for a bit. A walk might clear your mind, Ece," he suggested, his voice soft with sympathy. "You won't absorb anything if you attend class like this."

"Maybe you're right."

Moments later...

We found ourselves outside, strolling side by side along the pavement. The area around the school was rather quiet, as we were far from the city's bustling heart. Passing by an old, empty playground, I sank down onto one of the rusty, weather-beaten swings for a rest.

"That's the gist of it," I said, after recounting the tangled web of my love life. As I spoke, Sinan gave the swing a gentle push, listening intently. "In short, Fatih left me to protect me from some so-called curse. He likely planned to get back together once I was free of it, but I won't have him back. He hurt me too deeply." Grasping the hem of my fluttering skirt, I held it steady as the swing moved.

"I'm sorry to hear that," Sinan murmured. "Heartache... it's a cruel thing."

I had learned from Kerem that Sinan still blamed Fatih for his breakup with Zeynep. This seemed the perfect opportunity to bring it up. "So, you've suffered heartache too, haven't you?" I murmured. "Care to share?"

As Sinan slowly pushed the swing, my gaze drifted to someone standing just outside the park, partially hidden behind a tree. It was Kerem.

It seemed Kerem had followed us from the school. Perhaps he suspected that Sinan might be dangerous, the very murderer we sought, and he was watching over me. Thoughtful of him, truly. During our recent investigation into the curse, Kerem and I had become quite the sleuthing duo.

Sinan, now pushing the swing a bit faster, spoke at last. "Alright, I'll tell you. It was three years ago... Her name was Zeynep, a beauty like no other. She was my first love. We'd been together for a year when, out of the blue, she started acting distant."

"Hm... Are you sure there was no reason?"

"There was a reason, I'm sure of it, Ece."

"And what was that?" I asked.

"Fatih," he said. "It was him."

As the swing flew back and forth faster than before, I murmured, "Are you certain?"

"He has to be the reason. Because there was no other. Just before we broke up, Zeynep and Fatih were inseparable, always talking. And not long after we split, they were together. Fatih stole her from me."

"Could you slow down the swing, Sinan? You're pushing me too fast." I gripped the chains with one hand, my skirt with the other. "And I think you're rushing to conclusions about Fatih too. You're letting your heartbreak cloud your judgment, and you're being too harsh on him."

"It's too late now," Sinan said, his tone turning harsh. He gave the swing such a forceful push that I nearly screamed, convinced I would be thrown off. "Do you know what I regret the most, Ece?"

"What?" I asked, my voice strained. "Stop pushing! I want to get off."

"I regret cursing you for no reason," Sinan said coldly. "If I had known you and Fatih would break up so soon, I never would have had Kerem curse you. You're going to die a pointless death."

Kerem had been right after all. Sinan was the one we had been searching for.

"Did you curse Zeynep and Eda too?" I asked.

"Exactly, my dear."

The swing was flying so high now that I was terrified it would snap. The rusty chains groaned under my weight. Unlike the children the swing was made for, I was no lightweight, and I feared the whole thing might come crashing down at any moment.

"So, you're confessing to your crimes, Sinan? You must know I won't let this go."

"I know," Sinan said, his voice laced with malice. "But it doesn't matter. Do you know what my special power is, Ece?"

"What?"

"Mind control. After everything I've told you, I can simply wipe your memory clean, if I so choose."

"You said Kerem cast the curse. How did you get him to do that?" I asked. "He doesn't have that kind of power. He's a guardian of fortune."

"Ah, but you see, Ece, there's a thin line between fortune and misfortune. Just as Kerem can control luck, he can also control bad luck. I discovered that, and I used it. By controlling his mind, I made him curse Fatih's lovers, ensuring their untimely deaths."

"Couldn't you have killed those girls yourself with your mind control? Why involve Kerem?"

"I used him because this way, everyone would suspect him, and I'd remain safe. Besides, I couldn't bear to get my hands dirty."

"So, you were the one who sent Kerem after us at Derin's party."

"Exactly. I controlled him, made him do my bidding, and then erased his memory afterward. He never even realized he was my puppet."

"How much longer will this go on, Sinan? First Zeynep, then Eda, and now me... How many more lives must be lost to satisfy your vengeance against Fatih?"

"That's none of your concern, Ece."

I had a sinking feeling that this wouldn't end well for me.

"What are you going to do with me, Sinan? Swing me until I'm so scared I soil myself? If that's your plan, you should know, I don't scare easily."

"Oh, you'll be afraid soon enough," Sinan said, his voice chillingly cold. "In a moment, I'll let you off this swing. Then, I'll command you to walk into the street, and when a car comes speeding by, you'll throw yourself in front of it. No one will suspect a thing—they'll all believe you died from the curse. No one will know it was me."

Kerem was still hiding behind the tree. Now was the time to call for help. But just as I opened my mouth to scream, I felt my mind slipping away from me, as though a foreign force had taken control. I couldn't scream. My body no longer obeyed me.

Sinan brought the swing to a stop, helped me down, and with a silent command, I began walking toward the road. I was powerless, my steps moving without my will. This was the end. Sinan was going to have me killed by a speeding car.

They say your life flashes before your eyes when you're about to die. Nonsense. As death loomed near, only one thought consumed me—Fatih. Despite everything, I loved him. I had forgiven him. But I would die without ever telling him.

As Sinan's control led me to step off the sidewalk and into the road, Kerem suddenly bolted toward us, realizing what was happening.

"Sinan!" Kerem shouted. "Let Ece go! You can't do this to her!"

Sinan remained silent, standing by the swings with icy calm, watching me.

A car barreled down the road, and under Sinan's influence, I stepped into its path.

Everything happened so fast.

"Ece!" Kerem cried, as he rushed toward me and threw himself forward, pushing me out of the way.

The screech of brakes filled the air as the car tried to stop...

Two hours later...

"I think Ece is waking up," came a voice, soft and uncertain. It sounded like Sinem.

"Yes," Fatih responded, his voice low, though tinged with relief.

As I slowly blinked my eyes open, Sinem's face came into view. She was seated at the edge of the bed where I lay, holding my hand gently in hers. Fatih stood just beyond, his tall figure cast in the faint light that filtered through the window.

I had no idea where I was, nor could I recall how I had come to be here. We were all still dressed in our school uniforms. The room itself was an expanse of white—from the walls to the furniture to the bed upon which I lay. It felt sterile, cold, like the heart of winter had settled in this place.

Beside my bed, there stood a silent heart monitor, its screen dark. Across the room, a small television hung on the wall, tuned to a news channel, the images flickering softly in the background.

The oxygen masks dangling from the wall, the cheap white slippers on the floor—this had to be a hospital.

"Where am I?" I asked, my voice barely a whisper as my eyes shifted between Sinem and Fatih. "I don't remember anything."

Fatih, his brow furrowed in concern, reached into his pocket and took a step closer to me. "It was a car accident, Ece," he explained, his hand still lingering in his pocket as if searching for something. "It happened about 300 meters from the school. According to witnesses, you suddenly dashed into the road, without looking."

His words explained the stinging scrapes on my knee and elbow, and the dull ache beneath my right rib.

"Kerem was there too," Sinem added, her voice heavy with sadness. "And he..."

She trailed off, leaving me in suspense. "What happened to him?" I asked, my heart quickening with dread.

"He's badly injured," Sinem continued, her voice wavering. "The doctors say his condition is critical. According to the bystanders, when the car was about to hit you, Kerem ran toward you, pushing you out of the way. While you only sustained minor injuries after grazing the side mirror, the car struck him full force. His life is still hanging by a thread."

Fatih had now come to stand beside my bed. With deliberate slowness, he withdrew his hand from his pocket, revealing a tightly clenched fist. His expression was one of deep anxiety, as though he held something in his palm that bore the weight of a terrible secret. You might have thought he had just unearthed a cursed coin from Blackbeard's treasure trove.

CHAPTER 33

I rubbed the slight scrape on my knee with my hand, inspecting it carefully. It wasn't too bad. Thanks to Kerem, I had escaped the accident with only minor injuries.

Fatih's voice broke through the air, soft yet tinged with an unmistakable tension. "I'm jealous of Kerem," he confessed, his cloud-blue eyes locking onto mine. "It should've been me in his place."

"Are you jealous because he's lying in a hospital bed, fighting for his life?" I teased, even though I knew the depths of what he truly meant.

Fatih still clenched his fist tightly, guarding whatever secret lay hidden in his hand.

"No, Ece," he sighed, his voice heavy with the weight of regret. "What I mean is, when the accident happened, I should've been the one by your side, the one saving your life."

"I agree," I muttered under my breath. "But you've been too busy asking every girl in class out on dates, haven't you? I suppose I can't blame you."

"I realize now how foolish I've been, Ece. I'm sorry. I distanced myself from you, thinking I could escape this curse, but if your accident is any sign, the only thing I pushed away was us. We've grown apart, and I won't let that happen again."

"Well, good for you. But don't think I've forgiven you just yet," I said, making sure he understood.

At last, Fatih's hand slowly opened, revealing the object he had been hiding—a ring.

A ring?

It really was! A solitaire diamond, no less!

"Hamsi kafalı?" (Fish head) I whispered in disbelief.

"Pardon, my black rose?"

I looked from the ring to Fatih, wide-eyed. "You're not about to do something incredibly stupid, are you?" I asked, my voice growing louder with panic.

"That depends on how you define stupidity."

Sinem, who had been sitting at the edge of my bed watching us, grinned. I shot her an exasperated look. "Sinem, tell him to stop this nonsense!" I shrieked.

"I won't."

When Fatih dropped to one knee at my bedside, ring in hand, I smacked my forehead. "Oh great, here comes the stupidity! Fatih, did the car hit you instead of me? Stand up already! Where did this pose even come from? And remember, no one kneels before anyone except God."

"Will you marry me, Ece?"

"May I remind you that we're only 18?"

Sinem threw her hands up and cheered. "Hooray! She didn't say no!"

I mimicked her in a mocking tone, "I didn't say yes either, Sinem."

Sinem let out another joyful cry. "But you said 'yet,' which means you'll say yes eventually!"

"You two must be going through a double dose of mad-ness—both of you!" I exclaimed as I climbed out of bed, my bare feet hitting the floor. Where on earth were my shoes?

Fatih remained on one knee, his voice steady. "Ece, no matter the curse, I will stand by your side, even if it costs me my life. But you see, the curse almost claimed you moments ago. As the song goes, death exists, and so does the rose. My black rose, my most beautiful one. I know this is an untimely proposal, but what if I run out of time? The first thing I thought when I heard you were hit by a car and lying in the hospital was this—if we fail, and death comes sooner than we expect, I need to be looking into the eyes of my wife in that final moment. Not my high school love, but my one true spouse, in this life and the next. I have to do this."

Tears welled in my eyes. Yes, it was absurd, but Fatih, with his ever-sweet words, had managed to sell this absurdity so beautifu lly... How could I resist buying into it? And what did I have to lose anyway? In a few days, I'd be six feet under.

"Yes..." I said at last. "My answer is yes."

Sinem squealed in excitement as she leapt onto me, and I winced as my bruised ribs, still tender from the accident, throbbed in pain. "Easy there, girl!" I groaned. "Are you trying to finish the job the car couldn't? Let's not kill the bride-to-be! By the way, you two aren't still dating, are you?" I teased. "I wouldn't want to get in the way."

"Of course not! If it weren't for you, I'd never date Fatih," Sinem retorted with a wink. "What would I do with him anyway?"

"That's a bit harsh, Sinem," Fatih interjected. "Is now really the time to make me look bad? Do you want Ece to reconsider her decision? I'm already walking on thin ice here."

"Alright, I'll stop," Sinem replied, making her way to the door. "Just give me a second. I need to call Mr. Hakkı."

"Hakkı Bey?" I asked, puzzled. "Is he my doctor or something? If so, there's no need to call him. I'm fine. Ready to be discharged, in fact."

"He's not your doctor," Sinem said, opening the door.

"Then who?"

From outside the room, Sinem's voice drifted back. "The imam, Ece."

"The imam?!"

"Yes," Sinem called out. "Fatih called him in case you said yes to his proposal. He's here to officiate the wedding."

"You can't be serious!" I exclaimed, flabbergasted.

"Oh, I'm serious. Sweetie, life is short," Sinem muttered. "Especially for you, given the curse and all. You're not seriously thinking about waiting months with an engagement and all that, are you?"

"Have I had any time to think at all, Sinem? Ten minutes ago, Fatih was my ex. Now, he's about to become my religiously wedded husband. This whiplash is dizzying—either that, or it's my anemia acting up."

Just then, Sinem seemed to invite someone into the room, and moments later, a man entered. He was dressed in a robe, with a skullcap and a long beard—about 30 years old, dark-skinned.

"As-salamu alaykum."

"Wa alaykum as-salam," I replied as I sat back on the bed, smoothing out my skirt. Being in front of the imam in my short school skirt made me feel uneasy, but this was partly Freedom College's fault. And, after the accident, my skirt was a mess—dirty, and torn in one place.

Fatih made a quick phone call: "You can come now, Nurse," he said.

"What are you two plotting behind my back now?" I asked. Sinem and Fatih always had something up their sleeves. "Why is the nurse coming? To give me a special wedding IV? Or are you going to pump me full of medicine like a bride's dowry? Or wait, I know! She's going to hand us a wedding DVD with the hospital's surveillance footage as a keepsake! Is that it?"

"The nurse will be our witness, along with Sinem," Fatih explained. "You know we need two witnesses for a religious ceremony."

"Hmm… that's true. But when it comes to female witnesses, isn't it two women for one man? So two women won't suffice, we'll need another man."

Fatih quickly called the nurse again, requesting that she find a male staff member. The witness issue would be resolved.

Within a minute, the nurse returned, accompanied by a middle-aged man in blue scrubs. Everything was set.

Sinem sat beside me on the bed, her arm looping through mine with a beaming smile that could have fooled anyone into thinking she was the bride herself. In truth, given Fatih's recent habit of proposing to half the school, it was hard to keep track of whom he'd made such offers to. Perhaps Sinem wasn't far off.

Fatih, ever the charming suitor, had claimed the other side of me. He looked striking—his blue shirt clung perfectly to his broad chest, while his tousled hair flirted with his eyes, narrowing those deep blue pools into a gaze that could easily steal anyone's breath.

After a brief introduction between Hakkı Bey, our nurse Neslihan, and the rest, the ceremony commenced.

The imam, with great care, took a slip of paper and began jotting down our names. Following that, the names of our witnesses, then our parents'. After this, he recited a few verses from the Quran, his voice low and reverent.

My gaze wandered toward the window, where a pot of daisies sat on the sill. To my surprise, the flowers swayed in rhythm, as if dancing from side to side. One particularly rebellious bloom seemed to be nodding its head up and down like a rapper lost in his own beat.

"Sinem, this is your doing, isn't it?" I asked, nudging her gently. This was her unique gift.

She grinned. "They wanted to celebrate, so I told them to go ahead and do their thing."

"Tell them to hold off until the ceremony's over," I replied. "We don't want to distract the imam."

With a flick of her eyebrow, Sinem commanded the flowers, and they promptly ceased their performance.

Hakkı Bey cleared his throat then, bringing my attention back. "Ece Hanım," he began, before the imam asked the all-important question: "Do you accept this man as your husband?"

"I do," I replied.

The same question was asked a second time, and again I answered without hesitation. But as the imam posed the question a third time, doubt crept into my mind. Should I back out now? Was this third inquiry meant as a warning, some divine signal for me to reconsider? But no—once again, I affirmed, "Yes." Whatever fate awaited me with this charming Laz boy, I could no longer hold the imam accountable. He'd done his part, three times over!

Fatih's turn came next, and when asked if he accepted me as his wife, he answered "yes" three times with such swiftness, it was as if he feared I might change my mind at any second.

The imam, having fulfilled his duties, declared our union official before Allah and recited the closing prayer. With that, our marriage—spiritual, if not yet legal—was sealed.

After a brief round of congratulations, the imam, our nurse, and the hospital staff departed, leaving Sinem to handle my discharge papers. Now, it was just me and my fresh-from-the-altar husband, alone at last.

Though we had yet to make it official with the state, in the eyes of Allah, we were bound together—and for me, that was the marriage that mattered most. Divine judgment held more weight than any law ever could.

Fatih, gazing at me with adoration, softly whispered, "May I kiss the bride?"

It was sudden, but I smiled. "I'm the bride, right? This all happened so fast... but yes, I suppose you may."

Our lips met in a heated embrace, and I felt his hand—once resting on my knee—creep higher, lifting my skirt as it ventured along my thigh. But I didn't stop him. After all, he was my husband now. My halal.

Our private moment was abruptly interrupted by a knock on the door, which swung open to reveal a man in a white coat, stethoscope slung around his neck. The flush on my cheeks only deepened at the realization that we had been caught.

"Good afternoon," the man introduced himself. "I'm Dr. Tarık."

"Hello, Doctor," Fatih responded, standing quickly. "I'm Fatih."

The doctor looked at me and chuckled. "Our patient here seems more than ready for discharge. I was going to run a few final tests, but it appears your 'partner' has already taken care of them."

I wanted to correct him—husband not partner—but my voice was buried too deep in my embarrassment to surface.

"Yes, Ece's feeling much better," Fatih chimed in. "She's been eager to leave, if that's alright with you."

CHAPTER 34

When Sinem returned to my hospital room after handling my discharge papers, she gave me a once-over. "Ece, you're a mess from the accident. I might have some spare clothes in my gym bag. If you'd like, you can change into them."

"Alright, Sinem. Thanks."

She handed me a spaghetti-strap, powder-pink blouse and a pair of light blue jeans with tears in various places. I took them from her hand and nodded.

"Could you both step out for a moment while I change?" I asked.

As Sinem left the room, Fatih remained standing, smirking at me. "Do I need to step out?" he asked, winking playfully.

"Actually, not anymore." I had to get used to being married, after all. There was no reason for me to be shy in front of my husband.

I set the clothes Sinem lent me, down on the bed.

As Fatih shut and locked the door, I started unbuttoning my skirt. He turned and began watching me from head to toe. As I unzipped my skirt, his flirtatious gaze felt as though it was undressing me on its own.

He stepped closer. The school skirt I had loosened slid down to my feet, pooling around my ankles. His intense blue eyes were locked on me, and as I started unbuttoning my shirt, my fingers clumsily tangled with each other.

Fatih wrapped an arm around my waist, pulling me close. "If we were in a more private place, after seeing you like this, I wouldn't let you dress—I'd strip you even more."

"If the doctor catches us again, he won't politely warn us this time. He'll kick us out for good," I mumbled.

"The door is locked, Ece."

"Which will only make the doctor more suspicious and furious when he can't get in."

Fatih kissed me lightly on the lips and pulled back. "Did I ever tell you how much of a killjoy you are during romantic moments, Ece?"

"Many times. But like a boomerang, you always come back to me."

"I always will."

"Now, if you'll excuse me, I'm going to continue being a killjoy and get dressed," I said, slipping out from his embrace. I quickly began putting on Sinem's clothes. I knew I wouldn't be able to keep this storm of a man at bay for long, so I hurried.

Once fully dressed, I feared I might turn Sinem's clothes black, as I often did when in a bad mood. But nothing happened. The colors stayed the same. Perhaps this marriage with Fatih had lightened my spirit, drawing me out of my dark, thorny rose phase.

However, I wasn't too pleased with the torn jeans Sinem had given me. The rips climbed all the way up, nearly to my underwear, and the blouse left my stomach bare. Yet judging by the satisfied look on Fatih's face, I didn't have much reason to complain.

"The jeans fit you perfectly, Ece," he said, his eyes scanning my waist and beyond.

"Fit a bit too perfectly! They're so tight that my figure is on full display, like a market stall. I could shout, 'Come, choose your melons, folks!'" I tied my school shirt around my waist, covering most of my stomach and backside. "That's better. Otherwise, I wouldn't step foot outside like this."

Fatih pursed his lips and gave me an approving nod. "Lucky me."

"For having a girlfriend with a nice butt?" I teased. "I mean, wife. Habit."

"Both. But also because I have a wife who's modest. Seems like I won't have to tell you what you can or can't wear—you're already quite reserved yourself."

I shrugged. "Of course, I'll dress modestly. A woman who wears revealing clothes and attracts the gaze of men shares in their sin. I wouldn't want that to happen. And besides, can you remember the last time I wore perfume, Fatih?"

After a brief moment of thought, he replied, "No, I can't recall."

"You can't, because I don't wear perfume. At most, I use deodorant. If I wore perfume and a man got aroused by my scent, that sin would also fall on me."

Fatih cut me off. "Let me guess—the man would be guilty, but you'd get an equal share of the sin?"

"Bravo, you're learning," I said, patting his shoulder. "And if a woman speaks in a sweet, flirtatious tone and stirs a man's desires, what happens then, class?"

Fatih raised his hand eagerly. "Teacher, can I answer?"

"Go ahead, my child."

"The girl sins too, teacher."

"'Ten points!" I applauded him.

"Do I win a starry kiss, teacher?"

"Of course, my child."

Fatih pressed his lips to mine. As the kiss lingered longer than expected, I realized that the "star" in "starry kiss" might have a deeper meaning.,,

"I wish to avail myself of your knowledge on a matter of religion. Is homosexuality considered a sin in Islam? I seem to have heard such."

I nodded in quiet affirmation. "Indeed," I began, choosing my words with deliberate precision. "The scholars of the Sunni tradition are in unanimous agreement on this issue. There are nearly a dozen verses in the Qur'an, along with numerous hadiths, that explicitly condemn the act of homosexuality." I paused, emphasizing the distinction. "It is not 'homosexuality' per se, but rather the 'act of homosexuality' that is deemed sinful. A person may experience same-sex attraction, yet so long as they abstain from engaging in homosexual acts and refrain from endorsing or propagating such inclinations, they are not guilty of sin. It is only when these desires manifest in actions that one incurs divine disfavor. Moreover, should an individual, out of reverence for God and fear of His displeasure, consciously choose to avoid such acts, they will be richly rewarded in the hereafter. In Islam, the avoidance of sin is held in far greater esteem in the sight of God than the mere performance of good deeds."

Fatih furrowed his brow as he pondered my words. "I see, but if God created a person as homosexual, would that individual not be compelled to sin, given that it is beyond their control?"

"Not at all, Fatih," I replied with conviction. "Numerous scientific studies have delved into this very subject. The prevailing consensus across these investigations is that there is no single gene that directly causes homosexuality. For instance, a landmark study conducted a few years ago involving a vast sample size of approximately 500,000 individuals, whose entire genomes were meticulously mapped, yielded the same conclusion: there is no so-called 'gay gene.' While certain genetic factors may predispose an individual to a slight inclination towards homosexuality, they are not determinative to the point of compelling one to act upon these inclinations. Researchers have found that sexual orientation is influenced far more by environmental factors—one's upbringing, family dynamics, personal choices, and social surroundings. Thus, scientists have repeatedly demonstrated that God does not create anyone with an inescapable inclination toward homosexual acts."

Fatih, now visibly more at ease, nodded thoughtfully. "That makes sense," he said, a tone of comprehension coloring his voice.

After a brief moment of playful affection, we said our goodbyes to Sinem. When Fatih offered to drive me home, I accepted. We got into his car and set off.

At a red light, my phone rang. It was Aunt Esma. I answered without delay.

"How are you, Auntie?"

"I'm fine, Ece dear, but how are you? The school called and said you'd had an accident. They said you were alright, but I was still worried."

"I'm okay, Auntie, really. Nothing to worry about."

"Good to hear. Where are you now, Ece? Your uncle's out of town, but if you're still at the hospital, I could come pick you up."

"No need, Aunt Esma. I'm with Fatih. He's taking me home."

"Ooo, I see!" Aunt Esma teased.

"Auntie, the phone was on speaker!" I scolded her. "You've embarrassed me!"

"Oops, sorry dear. Well, have a nice and warm time then, you two."

I sighed heavily, my cheeks burning with embarrassment. "Bye, Auntie," I said, hurriedly ending the call.

When I glanced at Fatih, who was behind the wheel, I caught him smirking. I elbowed him. "You hear everything, don't you? Never miss a thing!"

"Now, how am I the guilty one?" he protested.

"Yes, because... Rule number one: Women are always right. Rule number two: When a woman is wrong, refer to rule number one."

Fatih raised an eyebrow in mock disbelief. "Guess I shouldn't expect much from the honeymoon phase, huh?"

"Smart thinking, my Laz love. This isn't some romantic summer fling, it's a Laz love story. And as you know, the forests of the Black Sea are filled with thorny trees and constant rain. Let's get that straight from the start."

"I put my romantic expectations on the highest shelf a long time ago, baby. Whatever comes from you, I'll take it. I never expected a rose without thorns."

"Aww, you're so sweet!" I leaned over and kissed his cheek. Fatih turned his face toward me, stealing the second kiss from my lips.

Moments later...

We arrived at my house. As soon as we stepped inside, Fatih untied the shirt wrapped around my waist and tossed it away. I watched it float down to the floor.

Fatih gazed at me with a mischievous look. Aunt Esma's prediction might just be coming true. At least there was no doctor to interrupt us this time.

"You know, Ece," Fatih whispered seductively in my ear, "if beauty were a crime, you wouldn't get off with just a fine or a few years in prison. Only a life sentence could justify such pure, crystal-clear beauty. And I'd visit you in prison every single day without fail."

"And you would get out on parole, my love," I replied, my heart racing. "You wouldn't need me to visit you." Even at such an intense moment, I managed to kill the romance—surely, I deserved an award.

"You'll see," Fatih growled, lifting me up in his arms.

"Ah!" I squealed.

He carried me down the corridor toward my uncle and aunt's bedroom. It seemed we had reached our final stop.

Aunt Esma usually returned late at night, but on rare occasions, she would come home early. So, the timing wasn't entirely foolproof. But according to the teachings of our Prophet (peace be upon him), if a woman leaves her husband unsatisfied without a valid excuse, she commits a great sin. So, I decided to risk Aunt Esma's low odds of showing up and be with Fatih. Fear Allah, not Esma.

Fatih carried me into the bedroom and walked toward the bed. He was about to toss me onto it when his foot slipped, and instead of throwing me to the middle, I landed near the edge.

I let out a small cry as I landed, hitting my back on the wooden edge of the bed. I groaned in pain, clutching my side.

"I'm so sorry, love," Fatih said worriedly, sitting beside me on the bed and placing his hand on the spot I'd hit. "I don't know what happened. My foot just slipped—it was like I lost control."

It must be because of the curse," I said, biting my lip in pain. "At least it didn't manage to break my back. Or did it?" I tested my theory by lifting my right leg, then my left, and rotating my ankles in slow circles. It seemed I passed the test with flying colors. "I'm not paralyzed!"

Fatih gave me a faint, pitying smile.

I lay there in bed for a while longer. Thankfully, the pain had gradually faded away.

"I'm alright now," I murmured. "We can pick up where we left off if you'd like."

Curse, I will conquer you too!

"Alright. But if your back hurts, let me know, Ece."

An hour later...

I left Fatih in the bedroom and went to the kitchen for a glass of water. Just as I was filling my glass, I heard the front door unlocking. Since my uncle was out of town, it had to be my aunt.

In a panic, I glanced around, desperate to find something to cover my naked body. The only thing in sight was a beige kitchen apron with a strap around the neck and waist. Left with no other choice, I grabbed it and slipped it on. As I fumbled to tie the apron strings around my waist, my aunt walked in. In my rush, I didn't manage to tie it properly, leaving me awkwardly half-covered. I waved to her, trying to act casual despite my state of undress.

"Welcome home, Aunt Esma!" I greeted, trying to cover myself as best I could with my arms.

"Thanks, sweetie. Cooking, are we?" she teased, a mischievous grin lighting up her face as she eyed my poor attempt to cover up with the short kitchen apron. Clearly, she had caught on to the mischief Fatih and I had been up to. "Let me guess the dish. Lentils? Did you pop the lentils into the oven, you lovebirds?"

My cheeks burned with shame as I bit my lip and avoided her gaze. "Um..."

"Ece, darling, that apron isn't covering your backside. You'll catch a cold, or worse, you'll get the runs. Now go back to bed and cover up properly, girl. I'll leave you two alone."

"Okay, Auntie."

Aunt Esma waved and headed for the door. "Take care now, enjoy yourselves."

"See you, Auntie," I mumbled, my face still flushed with embarrassment.

After she left, I returned to the bedroom to find Fatih.

Hearing my aunt's voice must have made him anxious, but now that she was gone, he relaxed and sat on the bed with a relieved sigh. "You lost the bet, Ece," he said with a smirk. "Remember, we had a wager that we'd make love within three weeks."

My eyes widened. "Don't tell me this whole marriage was a scheme to win the bet! You didn't marry me just to get me into bed, did you? That imam wasn't a fake, right?"

"It wasn't a scheme. The imam was real, and so is my loyalty to you. I'm not happy because I won the bet; I'm happy because I won you."

"Good." I made the 'I'm watching you' gesture with my fingers.

Fatih reached out, took my hand in his, and then grasped my other hand as well. When he pulled me back onto the bed, I knew this night was going to be a long one...

CHAPTER 35

O n a Wednesday, in the early hours of the morning...

This whole ordeal was starting to get on my nerves. Not only had I failed to kill Ece in that car accident, but I'd also inadvertently made Kerem aware of everything. Word had it that Kerem, severely wounded, was now battling for his life in the hospital. I couldn't let him recover and expose all I had done.

Kerem had to die...

And yet, I wouldn't bloody my hands in the process. Why should I, when there was a much simpler solution—using Derin, who adored him to the point of madness, as my unwitting executioner?

With that plan in mind, I set to work immediately. I made my way to the hospital and approached the reception desk, asking for Kerem's room number. Armed with the necessary information, I headed up to the third floor. Following the room numbers, I found his door and knocked.

"Come in," Derin's trembling voice called from inside.

I opened the door and stepped in. She was alone with him, keeping vigil at his side. Hands thrust casually into the pockets of my school trousers, I greeted her with a nod. She returned the gesture, her eyes red and swollen from crying, her face haggard from the relentless grief. She looked utterly shattered. Derin sat hunched on a chair beside Kerem's bed, clutching his hand as though it was the last tether holding her to the world.

"Welcome, Sinan," she said between sobs. "Kerem... he's not doing well. They said he's got multiple fractures, organ damage... He's not conscious right now, but I know he must be in so much pain."

I didn't come here for idle chit-chat. There was no time for pleasantries. I moved straight to the point. "Don't worry, Derin," I said, closing the door softly behind me. "Soon, I will end his suffering. Or rather, you will."

Her eyebrows drew together in confusion. Then, with a sudden flash of understanding, her eyes narrowed, and a sinister hiss escaped her clenched teeth. She was preparing to attack. The moment she transformed from human to snake, shedding her clothes and slithering toward me with astonishing speed, I was already prepared.

"Stop!" I commanded, using the full force of my mind control powers.

The serpent froze in place.

"Now, Derin," I continued, "you will return to your human form."

In an instant, the snake's body twisted and warped, morphing back into the slender, trembling girl she was before. She knelt, utterly vulnerable, hands and knees on the ground, gazing at me with a look of helpless dread.

"Stand up and return to Kerem's side," I instructed.

Obedient as a puppet, Derin rose—still unclothed—and walked stiffly back to the bed. She resumed her position, soullessly awaiting my next order.

"Now, you will take that pillow," I said, voice calm and cold, "and smother your beloved. End his pain. Then, replace the pillow where it belongs, get dressed, and forget all that you've done."

The beautiful girl nodded numbly, silently accepting her fate.

My work here was done. As Derin reached for Kerem's pillow, I whistled a carefree tune and sauntered toward the door. I opened it, stepped out, and softly closed it behind me. Leaning casually against the wall, I waited. It wouldn't take long.

Mere seconds later, Derin's anguished scream erupted from the room. "Doctor! Somebody, help! His heart has stopped! Please, help him!"

As I strolled leisurely down the hallway, a middle-aged woman in a pink uniform—likely a nurse—rushed past me, running frantically toward Kerem's room. But by now, it was too late.

With Kerem out of the picture, my focus now shifted to Ece. They say if you want something done right, you have to do it yourself. Since Kerem's curse hadn't claimed her life, the responsibility fell squarely on my shoulders. I had a plan for Ece, too—a plan just as twisted as Kerem's demise. I would have her killed by the hands of her own beloved. Ironically, Fatih would be her undoing.

Wednesday, 8:15 AM...

When I arrived at school, I climbed the stairs to our classroom. Fatih was seated at his usual spot, gazing vacantly out the window. I approached him.

He acknowledged my presence, turning to me with a hollow smile. "How are you, Sinan?"

I've never been much of a talker. "Fine, thanks. You?" I replied curtly as I took a seat beside him—Ece's usual seat. Before he could respond, I leaned in close and whispered my hypnotic commands into his ear:

"You will find Ece, take her to the garden behind the old mansion, and kill her quietly. Dispose of the body. Then, forget everything. Understood?"

Fatih, his eyes glazed and emotionless, nodded in silent agreement.

Satisfied, I glanced out the window, spotting Ece as she arrived at school. "She's here now," I informed him, motioning toward the courtyard. "Go, meet her. Then, do what I've told you."

Fatih stood, his movements mechanical, and left the classroom with the slow, deliberate steps of a mindless puppet.

On a morning where the warmth of the day gently kissed the earth, I arrived at school and began my walk towards the classroom. Our class was on the second floor, and to reach it, I made my way down the long corridor, heading towards the stairs at its end.

One step,

Two steps,

Three steps,

And on the fourth step, as if possessed by some invisible force, my foot moved out of sync with my body, catching on the stair and sending me tumbling to the ground. The sharp pain shot through me, and like a startled kitten, a yelp escaped my lips, echoing down the hallway. I had landed awkwardly, my hands and one knee breaking my fall.

Ah, this curse! It was unmistakable. Once again, it had claimed me. I sat there on the stairs, pulling my aching knee to my chest, gently massaging it when Fatih's cold voice sliced through the air.

"Good morning Ece."

Peeking over my shoulder, I saw him descending the stairs towards me, each step deliberate.

"Good morning to you too, stranger," I replied, my voice laced with sarcasm. "I think you just chilled me to my bones. Could your greeting be any colder, my love?"

Fatih's icy gaze swept over me, taking in my pained expression and the way I tended to my bruised knee. "Did you fall?" His tone was mechanical, devoid of emotion.

"No, I just enjoy sitting on stairs, lifting my knee as a form of exercise now and then." I raised and lowered my knees in a mock warm-up. "Of course I fell, darling! Care to lend me a hand?"

With an abrupt tug, he pulled me to my feet, his grip firm. "Are you okay?"

"Could you be any rougher, love?" I winced as my arm throbbed from his strength. "I'm fine, not that it seems to matter to you. If you weren't a guy, I'd think you were on your period or something. You're acting weird today—your looks, your voice, your moveme nts... Or have you decided that now that you've had your way with me, you no longer need to be polite?"

He linked his arm with mine and led me down the stairs. "Aren't we heading to class?" I asked.

"Let's take a walk and get some fresh air, Ece."

"Alright then," I agreed, looking up at him. "Maybe the fresh air will do you some good."

As we stepped into the schoolyard, arm in arm, I planted a kiss on his cheek. He didn't respond. "What's wrong, sweetheart?" I asked, my curiosity piqued. "Did I upset you without realizing it?"

"No."

"Then perhaps all your ships have sunk in the Black Sea," I joked dryly. When he didn't laugh, I added, "Because, you know, you're from that region and—oh, never mind..." I sighed deeply.

By the time we reached the edge of the yard, we had passed through the school's large gates, continuing our walk among the idle school buses.

To break the silence, I began talking. "Last night, I thought I'd give an old beggar woman money, 10 liras... But when I reached into my bag, I accidentally dropped almost all my money into her lap! In the end, I was left with only the 10 liras I had intended to give her in the first place. No big deal though. I guess it was my curse, but her good fortune. May God accept my charity."

Fatih's cold demeanor persisted, and he remained silent through my ramblings. At the end of our walk, we arrived at that abandoned mansion near the school—the one marked for demolition. It was the same place where Derin would sometimes transform into a snake.

"Here we are," Fatih said as we walked hand in hand through the wrought-iron gate that led into the overgrown garden.

The garden was in disrepair. Without the care of a gardener, the plants and weeds had grown wild, reaching up to our waists. Thorny vines and thick clusters of grass crowded the space.

Fatih continued walking through the tangled plants, and I had no choice but to follow. But with my school skirt, the weeds and brambles brushed against my legs, sometimes even scratching my skin.

"Could we stop for a moment?" I asked. "This garden's practically a forest. I wouldn't be surprised if a fox jumped out at us from the bushes." When Fatih paused, I stopped too. "Shall we head back now?" I suggested. "We've had enough fresh air. Let's not miss class. What do you think?"

Fatih turned to face me, his expression unreadable. "We're going to play a game now."

"What kind of game, darling?"

"You'll run, and I'll try to catch you."

I pursed my lips. "Running through these thorny plants with bare legs? It's painful enough for a normal girl, but with my curse, who knows what will happen to me. I'll probably bleed to death. I'm B Rh (+), by the way, just so you know. I mean, maybe we should skip the chase."

"We won't skip it," Fatih said, his face as expressionless as a wall.

"Really?" I huffed. "What's up with you today? I'm telling you I'll get hurt, and you just brush it off. And how am I supposed to run in this tight skirt? I can barely move my legs. You'll catch me in three seconds."

Fatih's blank eyes met mine. "I'll give you a head start."

"Oh, well, how generous of you!" I blew out an exasperated breath, about to protest when Fatih started counting backward.

"Five..."

"Four..."

"Three..."

Rolling my eyes, I began to move. "Fine, I'm running, darling. Look at me go," I muttered sarcastically, barely picking up speed beyond a casual walk.

"Two..."

"One..."

By the time he reached zero, I had only managed to put about 20 or 30 meters between us.

I continued my half-hearted attempt at running, but glancing over my shoulder, I saw Fatih charging after me, closing the distance with alarming speed.

"I think I'm going to get caught," I giggled nervously.

"I hope you don't."

A few more steps, and he had caught up to me, his hand gripping my arm as he pulled me roughly towards him.

"Now that you've caught me, what do you plan to do, handsome?" I asked, expecting a kiss.

"I'm going to kill you," he said, his words chilling me to the core.

My eyebrows shot up. "Kill me? What do you mean?"

"I mean, I'm going to kill you."

"Fatih, you're scaring me. Could you please start acting normal aga-"

Before I could finish my sentence, he flung me with such force that I stumbled back, slamming into a large tree trunk just a few paces behind me. A groan of pain slipped from my lips.

When my head and chest collided with the tree, my vision blurred. I crumpled to the ground, dazed.

"Fatih?" I called out weakly, barely able to muster a sound. As I lay there, helpless, on the grass, my trembling hand reached up to my throbbing forehead. One knee bent as if trying to help me stand, but it was useless. My eyes fluttered closed, and I felt my strength drain from me.

Suddenly, Fatih crouched over me, straddling my waist as he pressed a hand to my throat. My eyes flew open in terror, and I tried to push his hand away, but he was too strong. His other hand clamped over my lips, ensuring my silence.

Beneath him, I struggled weakly. I couldn't breathe. I tried to scream, but his hand over my mouth silenced me.

I had imagined many ways my curse might claim my life. So many possibilities had crossed my mind. But this? This wasn't one of them. To die in the arms of my first love, my husband—it was supposed to be romantic. But to die by his hands? That was a surprise.

And yet, even as he was about to kill me, I bore him no ill will. I knew this wasn't truly his doing. I was certain of that. No matter what, I wanted him to be my one true love, both in this life and the next. I would go early. And I would wait for him there.

As the last breaths left my body, something strange happened. His grip on my throat loosened. Desperate for air, I gasped, and though I didn't know why, his fingers suddenly lifted from my neck entirely.

Lying on the ground, I coughed, my chest heaving as I gulped down oxygen. My eyes fluttered open slowly. And there she was. Ceren...

Fatih had transformed into Ceren just as he was about to kill me. That's what saved me.

My little heroine, Ceren, sat on my lap, watching me with frightened eyes. I didn't know if Fatih had consciously changed into her to stop himself or if it was pure chance. But with my curse, luck didn't really play a role in things.

Fatih's sister had once told me that he used to control his transformations at will, but he'd lost that ability. Maybe it was returning to him now. Perhaps he was regaining control.

As I lay there, my mind whirling with thoughts, I became certain of one thing. Just like Kerem, Fatih was being controlled by someone else.

Ceren lifted herself from my body and sat beside me on the damp grass. I, too, regained my composure and pushed myself upright, settling next to her. Her small frame seemed to drown in Fatih's shirt, which now hung loosely over her shoulders like a cloak too grand for its bearer.

"I'm glad to see you, Ceren," I rasped, clearing my throat from the remnants of the struggle.

"I missed you too, Ece abla," she replied softly, her voice barely a whisper in the stillness that followed.

As I wrapped an arm around her delicate shoulders, she leaned her head against me, seeking comfort in that simple closeness.

"I always thought I was Clover," I murmured, my words drifting into the air like fragile confessions. "You know, the warrior girl from the cartoon... But it's you, Ceren. You're the real hero. You have no idea what you've done, how you saved me."

Ceren's voice, laden with quiet contemplation, answered, "I guess I kind of knew. Not entirely, but... I remember sensing you were in trouble. I wanted to help, I really did. But it felt like I couldn't."

"Oh, but you did, sweetie. You did more than you can imagine. You defeated a powerful evil," I whispered, drawing her closer. With a tender gesture, I kissed her forehead, my lips brushing against her cool skin like a vow of gratitude. "But the real villain is still out there, Ceren. We need to find them now."

CHAPTER 36

The day after Kerem's funeral, Fatih, Derin, Alya, Sinem, and I had gathered at midday, sitting along the edge of the wall in the schoolyard. They say pain lessens when shared, yet despite our collective presence, the weight of Kerem's loss hung heavy, refusing to lift. His death, particularly for Derin, had shaken us all to the core.

Alya sat beside Derin, gently rubbing her arm in a futile attempt to offer comfort. Derin leaned her head against Alya's shoulder, her body present but her soul seemed far away, lost in the vastness of grief.

I slid down from the wall and stood in front of Derin. "Are you angry with me?" I asked her, my voice tentative, almost pleading.

Without lifting her head, Derin responded, "For what?"

"The day I stepped into the road," I began, my voice catching, "Kerem died trying to save me. His death—it's partly my fault."

Tears welled up in Derin's eyes as she shook her head vigorously. "I don't blame you, Ece. Because stepping into that road wasn't an accident. I'm certain someone forced you to jump. The same person who puppeteered Kerem and Fatih. When I find the one responsible, I'll turn into a snake and devour them without hesitation, just like the rats I hunt behind the mansion."

"Do you remember Kerem's final moments?" I asked, suspicion creeping into my tone.

Derin shook her head, her expression darkening. "No. And that's what hurts the most. I can't even remember the moment my love died. It's all black, a void. I couldn't even say goodbye."

"Isn't that strange, Derin?" I pressed gently. "You were with him every minute. But you don't remember the most crucial moment—his death."

"Of course it's strange, Ece."

"And that makes me think Kerem's death wasn't natural. Someone might have killed him, and made you, the only witness, forget. If it were a natural death, you would've remembered."

"You might be right," Fatih finally chimed in, his voice grim.

I continued, "When you think about it—my leap into the road, Kerem being struck by a car, his death, and Fatih nearly killing me—it all happened within days. The common thread? It all started after Kerem talked to me about the problems between Sinan and Fatih. Everything spiraled after I sat next to Sinan. The closer I got to him, the more trouble followed. That makes Sinan my prime suspect."

"We don't have solid evidence, though," Derin murmured.

"Not yet," I said, feeling the stirrings of a plan. "But I know how we can find it. We just need someone connected to law enforcement."

"My father's the police chief," Alya interjected. "He can help. What's your idea, Ece?"

"My theory is that the killer, the one who manipulated Kerem, forced me into the road and used Fatih to nearly kill me—was at the hospital the day Kerem died. If we can check the hospital's security footage—though I doubt they'd hand it over willingly—we could see if anyone suspicious was there before Kerem's death. Your father might be able to get those tapes for us, Alya."

Derin's face twisted with pain as she squeezed her eyes shut. "Or worse," she whispered, her voice trembling. "What if I killed him? The killer doesn't like getting their hands dirty—they prefer others to do their bidding. Think about what they made Kerem, you, and Fatih do. What if they made me...?"

"Don't even think that, sweetheart," I said, seeing how this thought was crushing her spirit. I knelt in front of her, taking her hands in mine. "We'll find the killer and bring them to justice. I promise you."

Derin bowed her head, and I gently stroked her small hands, offering whatever comfort I could.

Alya pulled out her phone. "Let me call my dad and have him check those security tapes."

"Alright."

About half an hour later, Alya's father sent her a video. It seemed he'd managed to persuade the hospital to hand over the footage. The video showed the corridor outside Kerem's room, close to the time of his death.

What we saw chilled us to the bone. Sinan was captured on camera, knocking on Kerem's door, entering the room, and then, shortly after, exiting with an unsettling calm. He lingered by the door, waiting, and when a nurse rushed into the room following Kerem's death, Sinan sauntered away with a smug look on his face.

But the end of the video tore at my heart. In the final moments, we saw Derin stumble out of the room, her face contorted with grief as she collapsed to her knees, sobbing uncontrollably.

I had seen enough. With firm resolve, I opened WhatsApp and created a new group: Death to Sinan, the Rat. I invited Alya, Derin,

Fatih, and Sinem. The group name was inspired by Derin herself, who had sworn to devour the killer like a rat hunted behind the mansion.

"If anyone's willing to help me kill Sinan, join the group. I won't hold it against anyone if you don't. There's no obligation, the risk is high." I thought of Alya as I said this. We weren't particularly close, and I wouldn't blame her if she chose not to get involved. "So, who's with me?" I asked.

Three people joined immediately, but Alya was silent. I began to worry she wouldn't join us. Just as I was feeling disheartened, a notification lit up the group chat. Alya had joined! Now there were five of us!

Relief washed over me. I looked at Alya with gratitude, giving her a slight nod. She responded in kind with a subtle bow of her head.

Considering my powers weren't especially strong and Fatih struggled to fully control his transformations, Alya's ice abilities might be just what we needed. "Alright then," I said. "We'll use this group to coordinate how we take Sinan down."

They all nodded.

At that moment, I noticed Sinan exiting the cafeteria and heading our way. He tossed a napkin into a nearby trash bin, and Derin, spotting him, jumped down from the wall, ready to charge.

I grabbed her arm before she could move any further. "Not here," I whispered urgently. We couldn't kill him in a public space with so many witnesses around. Even if we succeeded, we'd end up in prison for life. "Leave it to me, Derin. I'll create the opportunity to kill him, somewhere far from prying eyes."

Derin's fiery gaze lingered on Sinan before she turned to me, taking deep breaths to calm herself. "Alright, Ece. I trust you."

As Sinan drew closer, I read his mind, and our suspicions were confirmed. He was thinking about me, wondering, 'Is this girl death-proof? Why won't she die?' I'd show him what death was—he was going to regret ever crossing paths with me.

"I have a plan, guys," I whispered. "I'm going to talk to Sinan in a moment. No one say a word, okay? Let me handle this."

"Alright, if you say so," Sinem said, her voice laced with worry.

Sinan walked up to us, about to leave through the school gate. "Hey, Sinan!" I called after him.

He slowed his pace, turning to face me. "Hey, Ece. What's up?"

"Oh, nothing much," I replied casually. "Cutting class?"

"No important lessons this afternoon, so I'm heading home," he said, pausing a few feet away. He pulled off his sunglasses and wiped them on his shirt before placing them back in his pocket.

I took a step toward him. "Where do you live again?"

"Kadıköy."

I was going to lure him in with an offer he couldn't resist—myself.

"Well, I live around there too Sinan. Could you give me a ride?"

As I read his thoughts, I smiled inwardly. His mind was buzzing with excitement: What luck! If Ece gets in my car, I'll hypnotize her, knock her out, and take her somewhere isolated to finish the job.

"Sure thing, Ece. Come on."

He'd taken the bait. It might have looked like I was walking into a death trap, but the second part of my plan would save me—hopefully.

As we walked, I opened the group chat on WhatsApp and shared my live location. Follow us, I typed before slipping my phone back into my pocket.

If my plan worked, the others would follow Sinan's car to wherever he took me. We'd confront him together and end this. If things went wrong, though, it might be the last anyone saw of me. All I could do was pray.

Sinan and I continued to make small talk as we walked through the school grounds. He unlocked a white Opel parked a little distance away with his key fob. In an unexpected show of courtesy, he opened the passenger door for me. I nodded in thanks and got in. He closed the door and walked around to the driver's side.

As I fastened my seatbelt, a wry smile tugged at the corners of my lips, savoring the irony of it all. I was supposedly strapping in to survive the crash, yet wasn't the real danger sitting right beside me?

We had hit the road... I knew Sinan was planning to hypnotize me, to lull me into sleep. And I hoped that if I stayed awake, I could protect myself, at least somewhat. My only chance was to convince him there was no need to put me under. I racked my brain, and a plan dawned on me.

"Sinan, I didn't sleep at all last night... I'm practically dozing off on my feet right now. Would it be alright if I just leaned my head back and closed my eyes until we get to Kadıköy? Only if you don't mind, of course."

"Make yourself comfortable, Ece," Sinan replied.

"Just wake me when we get close, okay?"

I closed my eyes and rested my head against the seat, praying silently that Sinan wouldn't try to hypnotize me. Here goes nothing...

Seconds trickled by. My mind was still my own. It seemed he was convinced I wasn't looking out the window and that I was indeed falling asleep, so he wouldn't probe into my thoughts. Victory!

I kept my eyes shut the entire drive, not making a sound. For added effect, I even let out the occasional soft snore, just to sell the act. Time passed—how much, I couldn't say, perhaps half an hour—until the car began to jolt over a bumpy, uncomfortable dirt path. We must have been nearing the secluded place Sinan intended to take me. When the car finally slowed and came to a stop, and the engine died with a faint sputter, I knew we had arrived.

I cracked open the eye furthest from Sinan, sneaking a glance out the window for a fleeting second. An expansive stretch of open land met my gaze, trees scattered in the distance. We were utterly alone—no houses, no people... In fact, there wasn't even another road, just the rocky path we'd taken, ending a mere five or ten meters ahead. It was a dead end, quite literally. A small puddle glistened before us.

Yes, this was the perfect place to kill someone. I had successfully led Sinan exactly where I needed him to be. But despite the thrill of success, I couldn't shake a faint shiver of unease. I wasn't one to easily succumb to fear, but when the person beside you could bend your will with a single command, things were far from simple.

A flood of thoughts overwhelmed me. Had my friends been able to track the location I sent to the group? Could we defeat Sinan? Would we lose more than Kerem along the way?

I forced myself to banish the negative thoughts swirling in my head. I had to stay strong. I had to believe in myself and my friends.

I decided to read Sinan's mind.

A gun...

Sinan had a gun in the car!

This was bad...

The gun was in a bag in the trunk, and soon he would retrieve it and use his powers to make me shoot myself.

As I sifted through his thoughts, Sinan opened his door and stepped out of the car. He was headed for the trunk to grab his weapon. My friends would arrive soon, but not soon enough, and if I didn't act, I'd be dead before they got here. I had to buy myself some time.

I blinked my eyes open, and as I glanced around from my seat, I noticed a small knife resting in the cup holder on the center console. It wasn't much, but it was something.

I leaned forward, quietly taking the knife, and with a discreet click, I undid my seatbelt.

Sinan was already at the back of the car, opening the trunk to retrieve his gun. I silently slid into the passenger seat and crouched low, slipping out through the driver's side door he had left ajar. I was going to take my shot at him. I was going to try to kill him.

CHAPTER 37

As I stepped out of the car, I crouched low, walking on my tiptoes toward the back. Had a doctor told me my heart could pound this fiercely, I would have called him a liar. But as I drew near the trunk, I lunged suddenly, darting toward Sinan, my blade flashing through the air. He dodged, swift as ever.

My second strike was no more successful. Once again, he evaded me with an agile motion, but this time, he grabbed my arm, pulling me toward him. The slap he delivered to my face sent me sprawling to the ground. I lay face-down, splayed across the grass. My fingers found my lips, only to return stained with blood.

Pain throbbed in my cheek where his hand had landed, and a relentless ringing echoed in my ear.

"Couldn't you have just died peacefully, Ece?" Sinan sneered, his voice thick with mockery. "Care to explain why not, my dear?"

"You'll pay for killing Kerem, you scum!" I screamed, reaching out from where I lay to grab the knife I'd dropped in the scuffle. But Sinan's boot connected with the blade, sending it skittering away. I tried to push myself up, placing one hand on the ground, but Sinan's foot pressed firmly into my back, forcing me down again with a groan.

"You never know when to quit, do you, Ece?"

From the corner of my eye, I saw the gun he'd retrieved from the trunk. He was going to kill me, I knew it. So, in a bid to stall until my friends arrived, I decided to ramble senselessly.

"I never quit," I said. "You know what Bon Jovi once said?"

He raised an eyebrow. "What?"

"I think it went something like... 'I'm alive, and I'll sleep when I'm dead.' Yeah, something like that. So, I guess I'm living by that. You should give it a try too, Sinan."

"You mean his philosophy?" he asked, amused.

"No," I corrected him. "I mean listening to Bon Jovi. An oldie but a goodie. Timeless songs. Rock music, you know—"

I was interrupted mid-sentence when Sinan suddenly muttered, "You're quite the looker, Ece." My ramblings cut short, I realized he had something far less wholesome on his mind. Was some part of me exposed? I hastily tugged my skirt down, ensuring my legs were covered.

"You know, Ece," Sinan murmured, his tone disturbingly casual, "since Fatih stole my girlfriend from me, how about I steal his? Wouldn't that make things even? Instead of killing you, we could... enjoy the scenery, the birds chirping, just the two of us."

"Could you help me up?" I asked sweetly.

Sinan gripped my hand, pulling me to my feet. I sidled closer to him, playing along with his delusion.

"So that's a yes, huh?" he said, misreading my actions. "Smart girl."

In one swift motion, I spat in his face. "No. My answer is no. Not smart—chaste. I'd rather die than be with you. And besides, I don't like redheads."

He wiped his face with one hand, raising his gun with the other. But instead of aiming at me, he held it out, as if offering it to me. Surely, he was preparing to utter his hypnotic commands, the ones that would have me end my own life.

Just as Sinan opened his mouth to speak, we both heard the rumble of an approaching vehicle. I turned to see Fatih's jeep in the distance, speeding toward us. Thank Bon Jovi for buying me those extra seconds! Rock truly does save lives.

Sinan's eyes locked with mine, cold and intent. "Wait here, Ece," he ordered, his voice dripping with hypnotic power. "I have some guests to greet."

A chilling wave of helplessness washed over me. I felt my mind slipping, as though a blade had pierced my very soul. Nodding weakly, I saw Fatih's jeep pull up, and my four friends emerged from the vehicle.

"Welcome, Fatih," Sinan called out, a sly grin on his face.

"I don't see anything to be welcomed by," Fatih replied, his voice sharp.

"Let's not beat around the bush," Sinan continued. "Let's settle the score, Fatih. You laid your filthy hands on my Zeynep, stole her from me. Now, I'm going to take your girlfriend right in front of you. How does that feel?"

Sinan crept up behind me, wrapping his arms around my frozen body. His touch sent a wave of revulsion through me, but under his control, I could do nothing.

"If you touch her again, I swear I'll beat you so bad your own mother won't recognize you!" Fatih bellowed. "Are you out of your mind? Was all this—these murders—because you thought I stole your girlfriend?"

"It's not a thought, Fatih," Sinan snarled, releasing me in a fit of rage. "It's the truth."

"I never laid a hand on Zeynep," Fatih shouted. "That's all in your twisted head!"

As they argued, I turned inward, seeking refuge in the last haven I had—one I should've sought from the start. My prayers. I began reciting the Surahs of Al-Falaq and An-Naas under my breath. Sinan's power was strong, yes, but it wasn't stronger than God.

"Enough!" Sinan roared, cutting off the argument. Alya, who had been preparing to use her ice powers, froze mid-motion as Sinan's hypnotic words seized control of them all. "None of you will move a muscle," he commanded.

But I... I felt no change within myself. Had Sinan missed me? He was no longer in control of me.

"Fatih and Ece," Sinan continued, "get into the jeep. Fatih, you will drive. Ece, you will sit in the back, without a seatbelt. Then, you'll floor it, driving through this treacherous terrain until you crash and burn. At least, until Ece dies. Understood?"

Fatih nodded, mindlessly following the command, and began walking toward the jeep. I, however, still unaffected, played along. Now wasn't the time to attack. I had to wait for the right moment. So I mimicked Fatih's zombie-like movements, climbing into the back of the jeep.

As we sped away, I knew the danger we were in. There was no road ahead, just wild terrain that tossed and jolted the vehicle. I tried to reason with him. "Stop the car, Fatih!" I shouted from the backseat. But Sinan's grip on him was too strong. "You need to turn into Ceren right now, or we'll crash. Then again, even if you do, how could a little girl drive?"

The jeep surged forward, faster and faster. I realized I would have to take matters into my own hands. Struggling to move, I wedged myself between the front seats, cursing every pizza and mayo I'd ever consumed as I squeezed through the narrow space.

Just as I reached out to press the brake, the jeep hit a bump, launching us off a hill. We crashed hard. Pain shot through my body, and my head slammed against something hard...

The acrid stench of smoke and gasoline filled my lungs as I came to. The first sensations to register were the sharp throb in my left arm and the oppressive weight pinning me in place. Blinking against the haze, I saw that the jeep had flipped, its crumpled shell trapping me inside.

Then I heard his voice. "I'm going to get you out, love!" Fatih called. I turned my head toward the sound, finding him outside the wreck, battered but free. He was tugging at the twisted back door, his hands bloody. But it was no use—it was jammed beyond repair.

Fatih strained, sweat pouring from his brow. But as I coughed weakly, I called out to him, "Get away, Fatih. If the car explodes, I don't want you near it."

He ignored me, redoubling his efforts. "I'll save you," he insisted, his voice tight with emotion.

"You already have," I whispered, my voice barely audible. "In this short time together, you gave me the best moments of my life. We even got married. We'll meet again in the next life, God willing. You've saved me already, Fatih. Now, save yourself."

Fatih's determination only grew stronger, and then—before my eyes—he began to change. His muscles swelled, his frame growing larger by the second. His clothes ripped apart as his body expanded into a hulking, monstrous form. He had transformed—his power fully restored!

With one powerful hand, he ripped the door from its hinges, then bent the mangled metal of the jeep until there was space enough for me to crawl out.

As he effortlessly lifted me from the ground, I found myself cradled in his arms.

Fatih's body had swelled to monstrous proportions, his clothes having torn to shreds in the transformation, leaving him utterly exposed. With a brief pause, he set me down, swiftly tying the remnants of his shredded shirt around his waist to cover his body before picking me up once more.

"We need to get back to our friends," I urged, my voice filled with determination. "We can't just leave them at Sinan's mercy."

Fatih, his voice now as unnaturally deep as his colossal form, replied with grave concern, "That will be dangerous."

"Don't worry, I have a plan."

His eyes narrowed skeptically. "Let's hope this one doesn't fail like your last plan, darling. Sinan nearly wiped us all out."

I jabbed the massive shoulder of Mr. Hulk playfully. "This time it will work. Trust me."

"Alright then."

Without hesitation, still in his hulking form, Fatih sprinted toward the others, carrying me effortlessly in his arms. Despite his enormous size, he moved at a speed far beyond that of any ordinary human. In no time, we had covered a great distance, reaching the area where Sinan's car was parked, reuniting with our companions.

Gently, Fatih set me down. It was then that I spotted Sinan, marching toward us, his breath labored and his expression filled with irritation. "You must have some sort of death wish, girl! But even the luckiest survive only so many jumps... and you're way past your last one. It's time to end this," Sinan declared, his voice dripping with menace. He then commanded, his words laced with hypnotic power, "Everyone, stay exactly where you are. Except you, Ece. You will come to me."

Though my friends stood frozen, I, by the grace of God and the strength of my whispered Felak and Nas prayers, resisted his mental control. He had no control over me. I had earned myself a new title.

The Last Mind Bender.

And soon enough, I would bend Sinan's will to its breaking point.

Feigning obedience, I approached him, standing directly in front of the smug villain.

"Now, Ece," Sinan said with a victorious grin, "you will take my gun."

I took the gun he offered me.

"Now, you will aim it at your head, and end your life, Ece," Sinan concluded, his voice brimming with triumph. "And that, ladies and gentlemen, is the final act. A round of applause for our actors!"

But instead of raising the weapon to myself, I took several steps back, leveling the gun at Sinan. The expression that flickered across his face—a mixture of shock and disbelief—was priceless. He had no idea what had just happened.

"You're going to shoot yourself, Ece!" he barked again, his voice tinged with panic. "Do as I say!"

I shook my head slowly, defiantly. "No, Sinan. You're going to do as I say. You're going to release Derin from your control and set her free. Or I will shoot you."

"How... how are my commands not working on you, Ece?"

"There is someone greater than you, you little vermin. My Almighty God... And He is more than enough for me. I brandished the gun menacingly. "Now, let Derin go. Or else."

Sinan's expression twisted into confusion. "Fine. You can have Derin. But I need to know—why Derin? Why not your beloved Fatih? Or your best friend Sinem? Why Derin, of all people?"

The moment Sinan lifted his hypnosis from Derin, her transformation was instantaneous. She morphed into an anaconda, her snake form shedding her clothes as she slithered with menacing grace toward Sinan. Her coiled body exuded power, and I watched, breathless, as the magnificent creature approached.

"Because," I said with unwavering resolve, "I made her a promise. And I intend to keep it."

Derin lunged at Sinan. I had never imagined a snake's jaws could open so wide. Within moments, she had engulfed him in a series of powerful bites. And when she swallowed him whole, my breath caught in my throat. Relief washed over me like a flood—I had kept my promise to Derin. Sinan was no more.

"And now," I whispered, "the final curtain falls. Applause for the players."

Sinem erupted in cheers, her face alight with joy. "I loved this game, Ece! What a story, what a performance!"

"Thank you, darling." I smiled coyly. "Now, what should I wear when I walk the red carpet on award night?"

"Whatever you wear will be stunning on you!" Sinem squealed, wrapping me in a tight embrace. "I can't believe it—we actually did it! He's really gone!"

"Yes," I replied with a satisfied smirk. "The little rat is dead. Nature's law—snakes eat rats."

I glanced at Derin, half-expecting her to revert to her human form, but she remained a swollen, lethargic snake, basking in the aftermath of her meal. It seemed she wouldn't shift back until she had fully digested her prey. After all, that massive feast might cause some discomfort for my slender friend. As they say—what you devour may come back to haunt you.

Fatih stepped closer, concern etched across his features. "Are you okay, baby?" he asked, noticing how I was holding my bruised left arm.

To reassure him, I swung my arm in a slow circle. "No breaks or sprains, love. Just a little sore from the accident. How's your leg?" I asked, recalling how he'd been bleeding when he saved me.

Fatih glanced down at his leg. "It must have healed when I shifted into XXL mode."

"Glad to hear it," I said with a relieved smile.

Leaning in, Fatih whispered into my ear, his breath sending shivers down my spine. "By the way, I have to say—you looked unbelievably sexy plotting with that gun in your hand, baby. You've really got me worked up today."

I giggled softly. "You've got some strange tastes, love! A cowgirl fantasy? Really? Anyway, I'm going to need you to return to your normal size tonight. If your body parts are as oversized as your form... well, that might be a problem."

EPILOGUE

As the golden sun of Saturday crept higher into the sky, I found myself lounging lazily in my room, stretched out on my bed with a well-worn Stephen King novel in hand. The silence was interrupted by a gentle knock on my door. My eyes lifted from the page, my gaze shifting towards the source of the sound.

"May I come in, my dear?" came the voice of my uncle from behind the door.

"Of course, Uncle."

The door slowly creaked open, revealing my uncle in his familiar gray tracksuit. He approached me with measured steps, his voice soft as he said, "Ece, I believe I made you a promise, if you recall."

"And what was that about, Uncle?" I asked, sitting up from my laid-back position, the yellow-and-white pajamas I wore rustling slightly. I set my book down on the bed, leaving it open where I had stopped reading.

He sat at the foot of my bed, his weight causing the mattress to dip slightly. "I promised that if you managed to adjust to the atmosphere at Freedom College, if you socialized with your peers, then I would transfer you back to the Imam Hatip (Religious

College) you love so much by the middle of the year. And you, my dear, have done your part—you've integrated well, even dating Fatih and adapting to the norms with your behavior and attire. Now, it's my turn to fulfill my side of the agreement."

I smiled politely at my uncle but shook my head. "Uncle, if you're offering to transfer me back to my old school, I must thank you. But I've decided that I want to stay at Freedom College."

His brows furrowed in surprise, and he adjusted his thick glasses with a practiced motion. "Are you sure, dear?" he asked, a hand coming to rest on my shoulder, offering comfort. "I thought you disliked this school. And I keep my promises, you know that. If you wish, I can still arrange for your transfer."

"My decision is final, Uncle. I want to stay here."

In my old school, everyone was devout, and almost every student possessed an impressive level of Islamic knowledge. In such an environment, where could I hope to gain any reward by sharing something someone didn't already know about the faith? But Freedom College... it was different. There were many students here with gaps in their religious understanding, and I could gain so much by offering them little nuggets of knowledge. Just like when I explained the harms of smoking to Fatih, convincing him to give up that reprehensible habit, which bordered on haram. I even managed to get him to start praying! He began with a single rakah a day, but now, mashaAllah, he prays five times daily. Only the other day, we observed a voluntary fast together, breaking our fast in the evening. Though, I must admit, his digestive system didn't appreciate the entire bowl of Russian salad he devoured alone.

Still, staying firm in my faith at Freedom College was no easy task—it was certainly more challenging than it had been in my old school. I had to tread carefully, lest I lose myself while trying to guide others. But over time, I had come to realize the wisdom behind my uncle's decision to send me here. What at first seemed like a curse now revealed itself to be a blessing in disguise. I wouldn't leave Freedom College, not until I convinced Derin to go on Hajj with me, and gave her a sip of Zamzam with my own hands. I knew it was a lofty goal, but I aimed high.

"If you've made up your mind to stay, then so be it, dear," my uncle said as he stood, his movements slow and deliberate. "The offer remains, but I won't press further. Now, enjoy your book." With that, he slipped out of my room, leaving me alone with my thoughts once more.

About an hour later, Fatih would be arriving to pick me up. Today, after a little stroll, we planned to visit a house my uncle was renting out—furnished, but unoccupied. What we would do there as husband and wife... well, you can imagine. And no, we wouldn't be gossiping about our relatives! Nor would we be figuring out how to make it to the end of the month financially. No, it was something far more intimate... what couples do when they're alone in bed, if you catch my drift. Yes, that kind of thing—what we would do, married and all.

When it was almost time for Fatih to arrive, I decided to get dressed. I pulled on a pair of navy blue jeans and a beige short-sleeved shirt. Just as I finished getting ready, the doorbell rang.

"I'll get it!" I called out as I hurried to the door. Oh, how wonderful it was to live without a curse hanging over me! If Sinan were still alive, I would've tripped on my way to the door for sure. But thankfully, his death had lifted the curse from me.

I opened the door and—much to my dismay—there stood Sinan. I rolled my eyes.

"Welcome, Sinan," I said in a mocking tone.

From the living room, my uncle called out, "Sinan? Do I know this friend of yours, Ece?"

"Yes, Uncle, you do. He's an old friend, though he's playing a new role now. It's actually Fatih—he's just pulling one of his pranks. Again..."

"Alright, dear."

"Fatih," I muttered under my breath, "I admit you caught me off guard the first time you did this, but you really need to stop now. I get it, you've recently gained this shape-shifting ability and it's fun for you. But instead of seeing a dead psychopath, I'd prefer to see my boyfriend. Can you please transform back from this... rodent of a man?"

Fatih had been using his new ability to change shape quite frequently these days. And he enjoyed teasing me by shapeshifting into my arch enemy Sinan. Ex enemy lets say...

Sinan grinned, and before my very eyes, his form began to shift. Seconds later, standing before me was a completely different figure: an old singer. Ciguli...

"Fatih!" I said, my lips curling into a smile. "Please, just return to your normal self. Where did Ciguli even come from? I don't want to be your 'Binnaz,' please."

At long last, Fatih shifted back to his real self, and with a sigh of relief, I leaned in, meeting his lips with mine.

"I'll never forget the look on your face the first time I transformed into Sinan," Fatih said with a mischievous grin.

"Well, don't make a habit of it, love. Otherwise, I'll give you a look you'll never forget—the look of a woman who refuses to cuddle with you for two whole weeks."

"Message received," Fatih replied with a laugh. "No more turning into Sinan."

"And no more Ciguli, either."

"Got it."

As I slipped on my shoes, I mused aloud, "By the way, if I could shape-shift, and I offered to turn into your ex, Eda, would you take me up on it?"

"Never!" Fatih said emphatically, cutting me off before I could finish my sentence. "When I married you, I promised to love you in this life and the next. No exceptions, my love."

"Since you answered that so quickly and without hesitation, tonight I'll be just as eager to do whatever you want in bed."

I stood, taking his hand in mine. "See you later, Uncle!"

"Take care, kids."

We stepped out and into the elevator. "I had the strangest, most vivid dream last night," I told Fatih as we descended.

"What was it about?"

"Sinan and Kerem... both of them were alive. It felt so real. And there was a blonde girl with them, talking to them. Her name is on the tip of my tongue, but I can't quite remember. It was something Islamic, I think. Something starting with a 'K.' Oh well..."

"Sounds like a strange dream," Fatih murmured as his eyes lingered on my face. His fingers wove into my hair, and when his lips pressed against mine, his touch sent warm sparks coursing through me.

"Should we play out a Hulk fantasy today?" I teased, my voice playful. "You can transform into your huge form in bed, but try to be gentle."

"Hulk be gentle. Hulk love you."

"Hulk doesn't talk like a caveman, love. What's with that? Haven't you watched any Marvel movies?"

"Hulk angry! You teasing! Green Hulk break bed!" He scooped me up in his arms, and I felt like green hearts were floating above my head...